THE INVESTIGATION *of* ARIEL WARNING

THE INVESTIGATION *of* ARIEL WARNING

A novel by ROBERT KALICH

MACADAM CAGE

MacAdam/Cage
155 Sansome Street, Suite 550
San Francisco, CA 94104
www.MacAdamCage.com

Library of Congress Cataloging-in-Publication Data

Kalich, Robert Allen
The investigation of Ariel Warning : a novel / by Robert Kalich.
p. cm.
ISBN 978-1-59692-372-0 (hardcover)
1. Twin brothers—Fiction. 2. Self-actualization (Psychology)—Fiction. I. Title.
PS3561.A41653I58 2012
813'.54—dc23
2011041725
Printed in the United States of America.
Book and jacket design by Dorothy Carico Smith.
10 9 8 7 6 5 4 3 2 1

For my wife, Brunde, and my son, Knute.

☙❧

I am deeply grateful to my identical twin,
Richard Kalich, for the intellectual assistance
he has given to me in the creation of this book.

CONTENTS

AUTHOR'S NOTE

How do you know when you're meeting a woman who is different? Is it an eyebrow that is slightly off? Cleavage that is overly alluring, a voice that warbles, a sense of danger in your gut? Is it that you have to spend time and listen and watch and discover what it is that makes this person provocative, tragic, dangerous? Or is it the excitement of the woman's mind or lips, or an ankle arching, or the curve of her neck, or something as simple as the way she smiles or doesn't smile, or is it something in you that just knows that something's on, something's off, something's real, something is not real? Or is it that this woman continued to become more unnerving and threatening each day my twin and my friend, Margot Adams, were pushed against her or pulled towards her. Or maybe it was that we were all just ready for something more than the familiar things we were doing every day. Whatever it was, Ariel Warning became part of our life.

PROLOGUE

Experienced glaziers will tell you that
even perfect panes have invisible fissures.

It was set in motion by my twin and I placing an ad in the *New York Times*. "Writer-producers seeking film-writer to work on projects. Possibly assisting with writing as well." The ad definitively specified that we (The Remler Organization) were seeking someone with screenplay writing experience who was familiar with identicals and conjoined twins. These were two of the current projects we were developing. My twin (David Remler) needed an assistant. I (Adam Remler) needed help converting my novel, *Confessions*, into a film treatment and then a screenplay. Who would have expected, though, as they say in the vernacular, that Ariel Warning would show up. After a barrage of e-mails and several interviews, my brother and I were not only intrigued, but both realized without as much as speaking to one another that Warning's "U.C. & P." approach was not only novel, but it worked, won us both over, and distinguished her mightily from the scores of professional writers and academically ultra-qualified applicants. The truth is, there just wasn't anyone else to compare her to. Ariel Warning was the perfect fit.

The initial e-mail:

Thick, corn-colored hair descending to my shoulder blades, lapis eyes, lean with exceptionally long legs, but not proportioned like a fashion model. My breasts are ample, my hips wide. It's obvious I work out and take pride in my appearance.

That's the bait. These are the fish:

I'm twenty-four. I was a finalist for the Windham Award for Distinguished Screenplay Writing. And here's the big fish...I do volunteer work with conjoined twins.

The twins I work with live in the Wagner Projects in East Harlem. I do everything for them, from housekeeping to personal care, as well as a great deal of the recreational therapy they need. My swimming skills come in handy with that. Who would have thought, in New York City, my swimming would be of use. As for working on a conjoined twin script, I'm always taking assiduous notes on both of my guys. When I get home after work I meticulously jot down everything I've observed. Sometimes I work on it till dawn. That's just me.

My twin set up an interview the very next morning. Rather than confirming the interview, we received a second e-mail:

"This is so cool. I know everything about you two guys."

"Like what?" I e-mailed back.

"Like having a twin is more like having yourself than having another sibling. Like you love sports, but you have a serious vice. You gamble on the games. David's vice is reading. And everything he reads he underlines. So do I. Another thing we have in common is that both of us create in longhand. Of course I mainly use a computer, but I love writing longhand. It's much more sensuous."

"How do I write?" I asked.

"You're truly atavistic. You use a typewriter. Another way you two differ is that with David, oratory takes over. While you, Adam, speak in the halting cadences of the regular guy."

One hour later a third e-mail:

"To be honest, guys, the only employment I had since coming to

New York has been as a temp for *Women's Health Magazine*. I hated it, but most of work is keeping your mouth shut and swallowing stuff, isn't it?...I went to the University of Kansas. Its campus is magnificent. There are two Olympic-size swimming pools. I made it my business to swim every day. While in school I majored in film..."

And, then, finally, Ariel Warning appeared for an interview at David's studio-office.

"I was a real cinephile. Test me."

My brother thought for a moment. "PL5-1098."

"Sorry, wrong number, Lancaster and Stanwyck," Ariel instantly answered.

"Who was the director?"

"Anatole Litvak."

"Who wrote the original radio play?"

Ariel Warning squeezed her arm so tight it turned white. "I know film, not radio," she said, her voice quavering. I understood. Many times when I bet on a ballgame, I stopped the circulation in my arms and thighs when the game was on the line. Terror grip.

The way David gazed at Ariel, I knew he was about to mollify her. "You know the name Ariel applied to Jerusalem in the Old Testament. In the bible, Ariel is also the lioness of God."

She recovered her poise.

"I can not only write film scripts, guys. I can even assess the fine print for you in those treacherous ninety-page studio contracts, and I know all about how to promote a film. I can also tell you what kind of film is best suited for today's marketplace, and the best way to sell it. And if you get a housekeeping deal from a major studio, I'm willing to relocate on the West Coast with you."

More questions were raised by my identical. Ariel Warning continued answering them. I was impressed. My twin was impressed.

"When I was at Kansas, I even did a term paper on you and Adam, comparing your novels. My professor balked. She said you two weren't in the literary canon as of yet. But I insisted. I think what hit home was when I told her you were the only twins in literary history that are published novelists. That piqued my professor's interest. Mine, too," Ariel said, smiling. "And I did another paper comparing your twin relationship with other identicals. I brought both papers with me," she said, reaching for her shoulder bag. "They're here somewhere," and before a millisecond had passed, she was rummaging through her bag, expounding on the papers. "The truth is, I didn't want to write a treatise dealing with how identicals share the same unconscious. That they know everything about each other from the time of their birth. Even before. But I believe it is like that. It is with you two, isn't it? I mean the two of you know things about the other half that no one else could possibly know. Yet, still, for your entire lives both of you have felt incomplete. That's true, isn't it?" she asked, peering intently at us.

It was true.

"Listen up, guys. The question my paper poses is: Can twins ever be whole with this kind of lack? Could twins love each other 'unconditionally' while suffering from this ontological insufficiency? This pathological hunger for completion? This incompletion? Could anyone?"

More questions were raised by David. Ariel Warning answered them. And then, another surprise:

"I just finished reading your new novel, *Confessions*. Did Bloom really live in Central Park as a homeless person?"

Let me say this right now, as trite as it sounds. Emily Bloom was the love of my life. When it came to Em I compulsively diverted to whining about losing her every chance I got. How did my identical react? "I don't want to hear you wallowing about Emily. I've had it up to here," he'd yell, raising his hand to his throat.

When this kind of exchange occurred between David and me, Ariel

Warning was munching on a Snickers bar. She shook her head. "If you ask me, if one of you couldn't wait, made in his pants, the other was sure to follow. That's twins!" she said, grinning at both of us.

PART I

VINES AND ROOTS

As soon as I arrived at David's Studio I heard Ariel apologizing to my brother.

"I'm sorry I came late, but it couldn't be helped. I ran into this woman in your lobby. She was having trouble with her twin babies. I had to assist."

"That's Peter Dugan's wife," I said, interrupting.

My identical gave me one of his looks.

He turned to Ariel.

"As I was saying, the predominant reason you've been selected for this position is the volunteer work you are doing with conjoined twins. You see, one of the scripts I've decided to assign you to assist with is on Siamese twins."

On the floor, in a dusty corner, strewn in crumbled piles, were wedding photographs, incidental bounties and other mementos of Thea and David that he had accumulated over the years. I knew my twin—in the middle of the night he had gone on a binge, tossing and turning under the specter of his departed wife. When Ariel noticed him looking at the pile, she hurried over and nudged the entire hoard under the bed.

Since David's wife died—on a horse ranch in the Berkshires, Thea was thrown, sustained a high cervical injury, and died instantaneously—never once did he involve himself in an intimate relationship.

He avoided intimacy, was terrified of intimacy. Until Ariel Warning, my twin was like a watch that had been wound too tight. At times I feared one more twist and the spring would snap. Now he appeared to be loosening up. I was delighted with his choice.

"I couldn't be happier. For me to work with you guys on a conjoined twin project is super cool. As I told you, the only thing I liked about my job for *Women's Health* was that I was near the New York Health and Racquet Club on Fifty-Sixth Street. I loved swimming there and I liked shopping for books at Rizzoli's on Fifty-Seventh Street. You know what Shakespeare said." Ariel's voice rose as she quoted from *The Tempest*: "First to possess his books, for without them he's a sot, as I am."

"The Tempest is being staged at The Public Theater," David innocently mentioned.

"I'd love to go," Ariel responded. "Miranda is one of my all-time favorite characters."

At that moment, in preemptory tones, my twin dismissed me on the spot.

When I started to leave, Ariel said:

"Oh, that's a shame. You know how it is. One without the other is one too few."

Alone! For almost four years David had been alone. Being his twin, I didn't count. Now that was changing. Everything that transpired he reported to me. He had total recall, much the same as I did when it came to recording the vital stats of the two-hundred-plus college basketball teams I gambled on.

After seeing *The Tempest*, Ariel and David went for drinks. My brother remained tentative, as was his nature. He mentioned his diet. He also added that I'd gone off mine, and that I'd stopped working out.

"Since Emily—"

Ariel flinched, chewed on her cheek. "Please, don't use that name. It disturbs me."

David didn't make an issue of it. He immediately referred to Emily as "Bloom," which he had been in the habit of doing anyway. I never liked it when he did this. I felt calling Em "Bloom" was dehumanizing. Emily never seemed to mind.

"Since Bloom left, Adam's diet sucks. As for exercise, without Bloom around, Adam's lost whatever motivation he had."

Ariel frowned. "Can we please talk about something else? Did you know that identical twins have similar fingerprints and blood groups?"

"One fact I do know," my twin announced. "Prenatal and infantile mortality rates in multiples are higher than they are in simple births."

"I'm aware of that," Ariel stammered. She went silent for a long, lingering moment. When she gathered herself, she placed one arm around my brother's shoulder. "I was reading a case study just the other day on identicals. A doctor was looking at them with ultrasound, and they were kissing, no doubt about it. Another time he observed twin fetuses fighting. One slapped the other and the second twin looked shaken. With you and Adam there was intrauterine life. You did fight. You did kiss."

My twin must have taken two large swallows of his drink, because it was here that he stopped choosing his words and simply released them.

"When Thea died, I would only speak with Adam. At four in the morning I would still be sobbing and he would still be consoling me. Without Adam I would never have made it. I would never have taken those first steps outside of my grief. I just couldn't have."

It grew late. David told me he felt something pulling at him he hadn't felt in years. I suspect at that moment he took a deep breath. "Maybe now, Ariel, our twin-glue is sticking to you," he said cautiously.

Ariel exclaimed. "You don't have to be clever. I'm not going anywhere."

"There are a lot of things about me that are shut down," David sputtered.

"Man doth not live by books alone," Ariel responded.

That night Ariel Warning slept over. It was about then that I started thinking maybe this would be the woman for David. Maybe he finally had gotten lucky. Certainly for the first time in a very long time, he seemed to have met a woman who was ostensibly interested, responsive, who pursued him at least as much as he pursued her. Even more.

I was happy for him. No, that's not altogether true. By that time I was already beginning to envy him.

Though I was never alone with Ariel Warning in the weeks that followed, I was with both of them a great deal of the time. David was happy— happier and more content with his life than at any time I had ever seen him since Thea. Perhaps that explains why he was seemingly oblivious to the tempest Ariel was raising, my misery. The more time I spent with them, the more I was falling under her spell. But it wasn't only me. It was Ariel, too. Magically, she made me feel on those occasions that she was as much with me as she was with my twin. That she wanted to know as much about me as any woman I was courting might have wanted as preparation and prerequisite for our becoming lovers. Every time she touched David I could feel her touch. Every time she kissed him I could feel her lips. The way she interlaced her fingers through his, caressed him, stroked his knee. Much, if not all the time, I was aroused.

More and more I was falling in love with Ariel Warning. Or more accurately, I was becoming obsessed with her. Hardly a minute of the day passed when she wasn't in my thoughts.

It was the following day that Ariel Warning entered my life. Inevitably, irrevocably, entered my life.

"I've repeatedly asked David to let me spend some quality time with you," Ariel said affably. Suddenly, she pivoted so that she was facing me directly and away from David. "I can identify with your work at least as much as I do with your brother's," she said. "Take *Confessions.* Wow! You're visceral and cathartic and you never abstract or take off on flights of allegorical fancy. You stick to life's immediacy. David, on the other hand, is contemplative and reflective and he writes like he is. Abstractly. He doesn't deal with real life or real people. You take only from life. Believe me," she said with evident conviction, "I've enjoyed and learned as much from your novels as I have from David's."

"Comparing my novels to my brother's is foolish. Mine are pulp fiction compared to his."

"No, not at all," Ariel protested. "Don't you see it?" she said, her voice rising impatiently. "What one lacks, the other has. It's only by reading both of you, your novels and his, that I can get a whole. To- gether, combined, marrying and merging both of your fictive talents, that would make for a masterpiece. A book round and full. Modern and old-fashioned. What a book that would be," she said excitedly.

I had the distinct impression that Ariel was talking as much about the men behind the books, David and me, as the books themselves. When I said as much, Ariel smiled. A smile that said, if the shoe fits.

She then took David's arm, but continued speaking directly to me.

"My English professor used to tell us to judge a writer by his work and not concern ourselves with his personal life. I've never been able to do that, separate the man from his art." She glanced at David. "Of course, in your brother's opinion, that makes me kind of naïve. Or should I say ordinary." She peeked at me. "That's not how you think, is it?"

It was possible that Ariel was showing off for David, but, yes, it was just as possible that she was sending me double messages. Still it was evident that she was very much enamored of my brother. Her body language: the way she would wrap her arm around his waist. How every now and then she demurely sought his gaze, as if for validation. The way she constantly complimented him, admired him, spoke about him, peppered him with return hugs and kisses. I could tell my brother felt secure. More than secure, he was beaming, proud of the way Ariel commanded center stage.

"Let's go to Blarney Stone for lunch," David said.

"How about Marea," I answered.

David's lips pursed in a grimace.

"Great," Ariel chimed in, looking at me. Wheeling back to David, she admonished, "See what I mean? I love greasy spoons, but Marea, that's great, too. Having it both ways. That's having it all."

After being seated by a haughty maitre'd in a far corner away from the crowd, as David had requested, Ariel tapped me on the shoulder. "I've been thinking about what your edge is. When you gamble your edge is that you're a twin. That means you can take chances, be reckless. Whatever happens you always have your twin to pick up the pieces. Another advantage you have in being a twin is you never get lonely."

"I do. David doesn't."

"When do you get lonely?"

"When the woman I'm in love with leaves."

"Does that happen often?"

"It happened with E."

"That's because she wasn't your twin."

"Does that mean one day you'll be leaving my brother?"

"Why do you say that?" Ariel asked, startled.

"You're not David's twin."

Ariel sat up straight. "I feel like I am. I feel as if the three of us were triplets. And having a twin is the only thing in the world that gives you a guarantee on five sides." A dark cloud came over Ariel's face. A second later, it was gone. "Listen up. This Friday night I'm making dinner for David at my place. Can you join us?"

"I'm sorry. I have to attend a press party with Margot Korman."

Ariel, who had been fondling an empty coffee cup, now gripped it so tightly that her knuckles turned white.

"Who is Margot Korman?" she stammered.

Like so many complex people, Margot Korman could not be deciphered by or slotted into standard formulas. She was more than the sum of her parts. Her pendulum swung from radical feminist to confused feminist. I believed what she wanted in her heart was what I had shared with Emily: sex without combat, sex without control, sex without cajoling, sex without enticement. Whenever she discussed her (ideal) beliefs in the abstract, I became quite specific, referring precisely to what Emily and I had shared: peace, naturalness, tenderness, consideration. "And look at the way you two turned out," Margot would counter.

"Margot's an old friend," I said, glancing at my watch. "In fact, you might get a chance to meet her. She said that if her meeting finished early she'd join us for coffee."

"You're dating this woman?"

Not only was Ariel's voice shaky, but she was holding onto her coffee cup as if it were a life preserver.

"Margot Korman is creepy," my identical barked.

"Whoever I take out, David's going to badmouth," I immediately snapped. "It wouldn't matter if she was Angelina Jolie or Oprah Winfrey."

"Now there's the kind of woman you should be dating," my twin said, pointing to a lanky woman in a pinstripe Donna Karan power-dress standing on the other side of the room with the haughty maitre'd. "How come you never date anyone like that?"

I waved to the tall woman. She waved back and started walking over. When Margot arrived at our table, I introduced her to Ariel.

David's mouth opened wide.

Ariel's mood brightened. "Your brother does this quite often. Doesn't he?"

"What's that?" I asked.

"Put his foot in his mouth." Ariel laughed. "He's just afraid of losing you," she said, rumpling his hair. She turned to me. With her long delicately tapered fingers she brushed down a cowlick, gently stroked my hand. "And so am I," she purred. "Neither one of us wants to lose you."

Margot observed Ariel intently. "I've heard you're working with conjoined twins. I'm glad we're finally getting a chance to meet," she said calmly, taking my hand from Ariel's grasp.

"Where are the twins conjoined?" Margot asked.

Ariel reached for a pen which was clipped to her blouse, grabbed a blank sheet of yellow paper from her bag, and started sketching.

"Bart faces forward and Albert looks backward like this," she said, holding up the yellow sheet. "What I love most about these guys is that they're so well-adjusted. They both insist that they're going to get married and have lots of children. Isn't that neat?"

"That's ludicrous," I blurted out.

Ariel winced. The pained expression on her face made me feel ashamed that I had said what I did. A split second later she picked up the sheet and meticulously tore it into two so that Bart and Albert were separated.

"Now they can!" she said, triumphantly.

Margot and I glanced at each other. Ariel broke the silence.

"When I first met Albert Parker he asked me to feel his head. When I did you know what he said? 'What's taking you so long, Ms. Warning? It's just a head.'"

An awkward silence ensued before Ariel continued, this time going on and on about how much she enjoyed being with David and me. The Twins she called us. How much she loved being with The Twins.

"I can quote from memory from all of the twins' novels, Margot. Here, listen to this. It's Adam's. From *Confessions*. '*I gambled case money. I compromised my heart, my soul, my fingertips. Later on, I was still a civil servant for the city, anonymous, powerless, heavily in debt. I swear I'm going to change. I'm going to make it. Yes. I'm going to be rich. I swear.*'"

Ariel stopped reciting. Took my hand from Margot. A moment later she continued.

"'*And so I became a handicapper. I had more than a few successful seasons. (The key was, college basketball was really a game of 'hidden' information, and the conventional betting line does have flaws. For eight years I was successful, and then the sophisticated computers came along, tightening up the line. My edge began to be taken away. It didn't matter. I was living with Emily Bloom.) None of my winnings nourished me. Only compounding my own ill feelings and divisiveness. That is until—*'" Here Ariel stuttered, "'*—Em…Em…Emily Bloom came along. With Emily I willingly surrendered my very self for another and paradoxically saved myself…*'"

Ariel stopped. "Let me do another. I loathe that one."

Margot raised her eyebrows. Fiddled with her fork. Pressed the tines into the pads of her thumb, looked at David, at me. She kept pressing the fork into her finger, kept waiting for David or me to intervene. My twin didn't. He was hanging on Ariel's every word. I, too, enjoyed listening to her recite. It was flattering. I'm sure Margot didn't. In her face I could see misgivings. Margot squinted at an ornamental branching figure suspended from the ceiling. "The greatest thing about chandeliers is, they disperse light," she said, looking directly at Ariel. Then she added, with a sibilant edge to her thin voice, "Ariel's an interesting name. Of course, so is Warning. Turn Warning around and you know what you have?"

"Monster," Ariel instantly answered. "The term monster itself derives etymologically from a word that signifies 'warning.' A monster, from monere, to admonish, to warn," she said.

"Ariel Monster," Margot enunciated over and over again without as much as a blink. And then, without as much as a smile, she continued her harangue. "Did Adam mention my girl-twin novel to you, Ariel? I especially picked girl twins, especially identicals. As you must know, they're frequently more dependent than either boy/girl or boy twins. Identical girls are most likely to remain very close throughout life, followed by fraternal girls, identical boys, fraternal boys, and boy/girl pairs. This is also the order of their dependence on each other." Margot shrugged. "I assume he hasn't. Neither Adam or David will ever comment on my girl-twin novel. They prefer talking about the book I'm writing." Margot paused to butter a scone. "It's on the history of Siamese twins," she continued, offering an insouciant smile. "With you being as knowledgeable as well as curious as you are, I think it would benefit us to get together. I think we should talk."

David gave me a look. It said: What's this all about? Margot stood up from the table—actually towered over it. She was six-foot-one. "Nature calls," she explained.

"I'll join you," Ariel said, grabbing her bag.

"I told you," my twin said somberly, when they were gone. "Whatever Ariel's reasons, I'm grateful. I can't stop myself from kissing her. I mean it's incredible. I just can't stop myself."

"Are you going to ask her to move in with you?"

"After all these years of living alone, I'm not certain I could live with anyone," he answered.

"You can," I retorted quickly. "And my advice is, do it now! The best time is now. Don't wait. You wait and something can happen."

When Ariel and Margot returned to the table, a stylishly clad young fellow was with them.

"This is Peter Taylor, The Boy Wonder of Hedge Funds," Margot said, introducing Taylor to us.

"I'm going to be living in the city for a while. I've subletted at Fifteen

Central Park West. Alex Rodriguez is my neighbor." Taylor turned towards Ariel Warning with an ingratiating smile. "I have my real estate agent looking for something more substantial in Greenwich," he continued, concentrating on Ariel. "You look familiar. Are you from L.A.? I am. I went to Stanford."

"Stanford," Ariel sputtered. Repeating "Stanford" several times. She chewed on her cheek. "Why do you insist on talking about such things," she said, her voice rising. "None of us are interested. We're not those type of New Yorkers.

"That's for sure," David uttered. "My apartment is rent-stabilized."

Peter Taylor made an effort not to arch his brow.

Ariel unleashed, "You tool. I should introduce you to my friends. They're on welfare. They live in the projects."

When Taylor retreated to his table, Margot, for what seemed to me the first time in ages, actually had a broad grin on her pinched face. "Peter's probably arranging to helicopter to Greenwich right now. Don't you think?" she said, grinning at all of us.

Why couldn't I just be happy for David? I asked myself this over and over again as we left Marea and I watched my identical and Ariel walk off.

In the morning I was still troubled and filled with need such as I hadn't felt in years. I telephoned Margot Korman. "I can't talk now. I have a meeting on my conjoined-twin book scheduled to begin in three minutes. If you're free later, we can catch a movie, have dinner."

Before leaving to meet Margot I took in the last five minutes of a CNN news broadcast. My eyes were riveted on a faded Norwegian woman who for weeks had announced to the press in a disconsolate voice that an unidentified male had kidnapped her young daughter. I peered at the screen as this woman now confessed that it was she who had killed her daughter. Moments later, I hurried out to get to Margot's sunny apartment on Riverside Drive.

Outside Margot's door was a large silver bowl of potpourri, the scent of which I detected as soon as I came off the elevator. When she unhinged three safety latches and opened the door, her diminutive West Highland terrier began sniffing at my ankles.

"Boggie's very macho. He was the leader of his litter. And now he's the same with me. You know a male dog thinks it's his home, not mine. Boggie," she cooed, and the canine leapt into her arms. "It's your house," she cooed to him. "It has your smells." She looked up at me. "Boggie's very into women. He's always trying to hump me. Always!" she said, leading me into her bedroom. Boggie had already jumped onto the bed and was rolling around the king-sized mattress, playing dog-soccer with a flimsy chemise, bras, stockings and other clothing that he had transported from the floor to the bed. Lying in the middle of the un-made bed was Margot's vibrator. Boggie pawed at it, spun it around, carried it off to a dark corner.

I used the bathroom. It, too, was a mess.

One thing about Margot, she was the only woman I knew who didn't apologize for the disorderly state of her home. I could shoot her all the askance looks I could muster to no avail. With Emily, one arched eyebrow and she would flush crimson and apologize profusely. With Margot, indifference.

Margot was on the phone when I exited the toilet, so I went into the den, which wasn't much of an improvement. A thick manuscript, seemingly in progress, was spread in a fanlike shape all over her parquet floor. Magazine articles on feminism and women's psychology, editorial clips on state abortion laws were jumbled together in the making of a papered path leading to her two desktop computers. Three feet from the bay window overlooking the Hudson River was a straw planter holding several columns of medical textbooks as high as the ceiling. As was my lifetime habit, I couldn't keep from perusing the books. By snooping,

I gathered that most of the texts were on Siamese twins and multiple congenital abnormalities. One of the books was by Dr. Margaret Collins Kessler, Chief of Neonatology at the prestigious Boston Medical Center. The text consisted of chapters by medical ethicists, their opinions on conjoined twins and extraordinary cases of corrective surgery and separation.

Margot, who had been talking on the phone to her former husband, joined me in the den. I sat on one side of the room, Margot on the other.

"Last night," Margot said, "This man said he wanted to sleep with me and I said fine. Then, when I didn't feel lonely any more, I changed my mind."

"Just because this guy finds you attractive is no reason to go to bed with him."

Margot sighed. "Adam, it's not because this man thinks I'm beautiful. I grew tired of being beautiful a long time ago. Why do you think I married Coleman and stayed as long as I did? I couldn't take it. All those droopy guys with their lovesick looks. Even when I was in high school." She sighed. "So many men. They didn't know me. They only knew what they projected. Talking about who I really am. I'm an unattractive woman. No, I don't mean that. But I wasn't supposed to be attractive. I was supposed to look like a school marm."

I began speaking of the Norwegian woman, the idea for a novel she had inspired in me. "Everyone lies. People lie to their partners, their lovers, their children, to themselves, especially themselves."

Margot squinted. "Hm. The woman who lied," she mumbled to herself. She crossed her long legs. Adjusted her skirt. "I think you are on to something. Examine the family of man, you'll find lies and betrayals." Margot's mind gathered fuel. "Even amnesia victims lie," she added, accenting her point. "Most of them have a proclivity for inventing horrific fantasies that they insist on communicating as real events. And truly disturbed people, you know, the ones that are completely out of touch, those kind dissimulate without knowing it." Without stopping to blink, she stood up and strode over to a window, gazing out at the polluted Hudson for a protracted length of time before turning her attention back to me. "Of course, the wretched and the mentally ill are not the only ones who cannot handle painful truths."

"That's my point," I said. "All of us lie. In today's world, who has the strength not to?"

More to the point was that at that time I was not merely thinking of my own betrayals of my identical, in deed or in spirit. As long as I can remember, I have always felt lying to my twin was lying to myself. How can I explain it? My thoughts concerning Ariel Warning might be considered loathsome, but my twin connection goes far beyond that. If I'm angry at David, I'm angry at myself. If I'm angry at myself, I'm angry at him. Maybe it's not such a subtle point: not separating the two. As identicals we are conjoined. Genetically. Experientially. Spiritually. When David was disabled by a hip fracture, I hobbled. When he took sick, I became violently ill. When he married Thea, I whispered, "I do." Our mother always emphasized that we were equal partners in every-thing, and that if one of us made it, both would. David believed, "I'm going to make it! And when I do, the two of us will share everything." I remember thinking, if David makes it, I make it. What's the difference who succeeds? I also recall thinking that if he does, well, I don't have to. When David received critical acclaim for his novels, it fed me. It was as much my success as it was his. I also recall thinking, during the years we were growing up: Why can't I be free? Be left alone? Be me? Is he me? Am I him? I'll make it first. I'm better. And, finally, when I made important money via my handicapping: You didn't once even think of giving me a penny!

"Those who avoid taking responsibility are genuflectors," Margot said. "And they congregate at the Church of Self-Deception. I believe in authenticity. Coleman says that's why I'm going to end up alone. I don't want to sound preachy, but we must take responsibility for our own actions."

I stood up. "Margot, we have to hurry if we're going to catch the movie."

After the film we went to a popular café near Lincoln Center. Over dinner I made known some of what was happening. "It's true, Margot. Sometimes I get this feeling that Ariel's pursuing both of us. Take yesterday…"

"Come over here, Ariel," David roared. "I want you to see this."

Ariel trotted onto my rooftop terrace. David opened the door to a pinewood shed I had built for Emily Bloom many years before. We followed him inside. Ariel examined the shed. Took it all in. "This shed is a ghost house," she said. "You should take it down. You must move on."

"It takes courage to move on," David barked.

Ariel took my hand. "There's only one surefire way to get over someone you really love. And that is by finding yourself someone new to love." She smiled at me as if…

"It's obvious that Ariel really likes my brother. But, still, I keep thinking…if I had met her first."

Margot reached for her wine glass, and seconds later for my hand. "There must be something inside you that needs the kind of woman Warning is, something primal," she said.

A conversation I had with Emily Bloom flashed into my head. *Adam, I'm really worried about you. You want to know what I think? I think the reason you liked me as much as you did was because you disliked yourself so much that you needed to like someone. You know, Adam. I was tree moss to you. You know the Indians? They applied moss to get the poison out. You used me the same way. I think now that I'm not there, the poison's coming back.*

I gulped down some wine. "I don't know what's wrong with me. My brother is in love with her."

"Adam, you have to keep working. That's the only answer. You keep dwelling on this woman and you're in for trouble." The waiter appeared and refilled our glasses. When he left, Margot continued. "The worst thing in the world is not to be alone, but to be in bed with your partner and having nothing to say to one another. That's the worst kind of aloneness." She sipped some more wine. "You know what Coleman always said? He said that discourse isn't intercourse. It's better. That's what Coleman and I had: discourse. It was better than all those supposedly great lays I've experienced."

I knew that Margot, once she started pondering like that, could go on forever. I interrupted and told her that to get away from Ariel I was considering leaving the city. My comment snapped Margot out of her funk. She removed her silver-rimmed spectacles. "Face it, she's David's friend, not yours."

"You know what Ariel said the other day?" I retorted. "She's the one teaching David how to make love. He's a slow learner."

For a moment Margot concentrated on chewing her veal. Then she said, matter-of-factly, "When I was married, Coleman and I were both terrible lovers. I hardly ever had an orgasm."

I felt uncomfortable. I'm not sure Margot noticed, but then again, if she did, I suspect, knowing Margot, it was the way she wanted me to feel. At any rate, she ignored my uneasiness and elaborated.

By the time Margot finished I wanted to scream that love didn't need vibrators. We walked back to her place and stood at the door. "We're pals, Adam. We have been for a long time. God, I was the one who pointed Emily out to you that night you met her. Can I ask you a question?"

"Of course."

"Have you ever done it with Ariel?"

Of course not!" I said, indignantly.

"That doesn't mean that there isn't heat between you two. It could just be, as you inferred, that she met your twin brother first." She paused to think. "It could also be something else. It's strange but that afternoon at Marea's when the two of us were in the john…"

"What is it?" I asked anxiously.

"Well, Ariel acted strange. I mean weird strange. I can't put my finger on it and I don't want to say anything judgmental. After all, I hardly know the woman. But that afternoon when she started speaking about those conjoined twins that she's been working with, she couldn't stop. She kept going on and on about them. The Parker twins. I think that was their name. She was so absorbed that it seemed to me as if she were in love with them." Margot peered at me. "And I do mean *them.*"

As I was about to step into the elevator, Margot shouted, "Ariel might be all the things you say, mercurial, beautiful, intelligent, but there's something strange about her. And I don't mean only the Parker twins. It's more than that. The way she was the day at the restaurant. It was as if she were equally involved with the both of you. She certainly was thriving having both of you there," Margot concluded. "Adam, next week, Jason Wyler is throwing a big bash. Want to come?"

"Who?"

"My publisher, Jason Wyler."

I nodded that I would.

"Bring her along. She's intriguing. And remember what I said. Attentiveness and vibrators. You'd be surprised."

When I entered my twin's studio-office he was on the telephone. He waved for me to keep quiet, motioned that I sit down on the sofa next to Ariel. Soon the three of us were immersed in our meeting. The first project we discussed was *Confessions*. I had started the difficult process of adapting my three hundred fifty-eight page novel into a thirty-something page treatment for a screenplay.

"Adam, what I suggest is you study the prologue of your novel. That's where you first meet E. Concentrate on that first meeting along with Part Three where things break down between the two of you. If you can figure out a way to connect them dramatically, not sentimentally, you'll have a solid thematic structure for your screenplay. Now, let's move on to *Pledge*."

"David, can I please get my two cents in?" Ariel said, her voice demanding. "Last night I read Adam's treatment twice. I have a problem with it. The viewer has to wait too long through perfunctory exposition scenes until E. Bloom appears. You should do something about those scenes, Adam."

"Ariel," David interrupted. "Can we please move on to *Pledge*? Here are my suggestions."

Several minutes later, Ariel once again entered the discussion.

"David, I never was enthusiastic about working on *Pledge*. And it doesn't matter how much the two of you changed it. Oh, I know Adam revised it. But, still, it's not that different from what it was. My feeling is whatever you do to it, you're going to end up with the same old thing."

David seemed perplexed. He stopped to think for a moment. "If you don't want to work on *Pledge*, how about this idea I came up with for our conjoined twin project. There's a kind of holocaust going on there, too, and I have what I think is a great concept for a horror movie. I came up with it last night. You were talking about the Parker twins. Well, that set me off. HIV-3. It kills, not only while people are making love, dropping needles, but also when people talk. Now this is how we get conjoined twins into the act."

Ariel's face drained of color. "What do you two know about the holocaust or burnt sacrifices?" she said, not much above a whisper. "Both of you never once had to sacrifice. You guys grew up in a loving middle-class home. Your mother was a doting Jewish mother, your father stern, but fair. You had baseball gloves, oatmeal cookies, books to read. Ask yourselves," she said, her voice rising. "What do people like the Parker twins have? Each and every day of their lives is a holocaust." Turning to address David, she lurched forward. "You're the one who's always using the pretentious phrase 'Self-World relationship.' Think of how that relates to people like the Parker twins. Their world is restricted to Self. They have nothing else. For them the world is solitary. And even if they courageously choose to enter the world," she said bitterly, "their bodies will only be perceived as grotesque. To have the courage to go on like that…" Her speech grew halting. She took several deep breaths to compose herself.

"Here's my idea," she said, fixing her eyes on both of us, and speaking in rapid-fire sentences. "If surgically inseparable Siamese twins who rely on a common heart could be separated. If one has to give up his heart so that the other could live. If only one of them could live through the operation. Which twin?" she whispered. "They share a single heart equally, there is no medical way to distinguish which twin should be saved, which let go. How does one choose which twin?" Ariel nervously rubbed her neck and shoulder. "Think of the implications. How does the family choose? What do they feel? And what about the high priests of our enlightened society? And remember," she said emotionally, still peering at both of us. "These twins, besides sharing a vital organ, can't even look at each other. They're attached at the base of the skull. One looks forward, the other backward. Yes, it's possible for them to perceive mirror images of each other. But what is it they see in the mirror? Distortion," she hissed.

Ariel turned to David. "Didn't you tell me when your own father saw you and Adam through a mirror he could never get you straight? And what about you two? When you look in the mirror, what do you see?"

A thousand times I have thought I was David. David me. Not only when we scrutinized each other in a looking glass, but with photographs, too.

"Which twin lives? Which twin dies? What happens to the twin that lives? That's the holocaust script I want to write," Ariel finished with conviction. David stood up from his director's chair. He approached Ariel cautiously.

"I apologize. Sometimes I get so caught up in my own point of view I don't hear anyone else's. We're junking my conjoined twin script. From now on, you don't collaborate with me or Adam. It's your script."

"Thank you, "Ariel said. Her brow furrowed. "I'm going to place my twins overseas. Their father will be stationed in Italy. In Milan, I think. That's where my girls will be born."

"When will they reach the States?" David asked.

"Oh, soon after birth. The way I'll log the film, they'll leave Milan with their mother and father. They'll rush the infants straight to St. Louis Children's Hospital. They'll confer with the wicked doctor there. He'll examine the twins. Separation surgery will be scheduled. It will be highly technical corrective surgery. All the doctors will have told them by then how unlikely it is that either twin will live. But the malefactor will insist that corrective surgery can be accomplished. 'I can do the creative surgery that's necessary,' he'll insist."

A moment later Ariel gazed over at me. "Adam," she said, her voice once again melodious, soft and beseeching. "If you want, we can still work together on *Confessions*. I have some ideas. What do you say?" she asked, reaching out, taking my hand as well as holding fast to my twin brother's.

"Sometimes when you create a page, if it comes from your unconscious —some otherwise unknowable place—that blank page miraculously might surface pure. Sometimes, when you read what you've written, it's as if it weren't you. You say to yourself: Did I write that? I couldn't have created that. It's too good. That's not me. That's some other writer, some great writer. You stare at the sheet of paper. You read it over and over.

You can't take your eyes off it. You're constantly gaping with amazement at what's there. As if it were going to disappear if you stopped looking."

David sighed. "That's exactly how I feel about Ariel," he said, gazing at her from across the room. We were at Jason Wyler's triplex apartment on Upper Fifth Avenue. David kept his eyes on Ariel. "Ariel has it all," he murmured as he watched her parade around, talking coquettishly with the mature men. Flirting disarmingly with the younger men. Discussing issues. Engaging in literary chit-chat. "Ariel has it all," he repeated huskily, "and I know she cares for me; and yet, as much as I fight against it, part of me is uncomfortable. I feel the kind of tension you must have felt at the end, with Emily, when things were crumbling."

Margot hurried over. Pulled me away. Speaking in urgent tones, she said, "Last night Herb Leno telephoned."

"Who?"

"Herb Leno. I told you about him, remember? We worked on the *Village Voice* together before he hit on the idea of *W.H.* You'd like him. Herb's a real good guy. He was the team manager of one of those UCLA championship basketball teams in the late sixties."

"Margot, Ariel worked as a temp for *Women's Health.*"

"That's what I'm trying to tell you. Herb said he remembered her. She was assigned to him for only one day. And that entire day she glared at him as if she were OJ coming at him with a kitchen knife. Then, at the end of the day, when it was time to head home, Herb asked her what it was about him that made her behave the way she did. She said she didn't know. Now I ask you, is that strange or is that strange?" Margot pulled at the polka-dot tie she was wearing. "I'm sorry. I didn't want to get into this. Especially not here. Forgive me." But a moment later, she continued, "What do you really know about this woman?" I gave Margot a look. "Adam, you're a sucker for beautiful women. Why do you think you're so attracted to her?" she said, pointing to Ariel, before rushing off to speak with Jason Wyler.

Ariel walked over with David.

"The white jade would look fantastic against the dark woods in your study, Adam." She turned to my twin. "And if we sell my film script, David, I'd love to get you a Tiffany lamp like the one in Mr. Wyler's library."

"A Tiffany costs a fortune," my twin responded.

"What would you get for yourself?" I asked. Ariel eyed a printed figure on a near wall. "The Rosemaling," she said. "My mother loved Rosemaling."

"What is Rosemaling?" I asked.

"It's a Norwegian art form," Margot answered, parading over with a distinguished-looking white-thatched gentleman on her arm. "This is Dean Silver. Doctor Silver is a fund raiser for the New York Academy of Medicine Library. He's been helping me with my research."

Dr. Silver tried not to stare at my brother and me. He gawked just the same, an interrogative arch to his bushy white brow. Margot, noticing, chuckled.

"I know how you're feeling, Dean. I've never been able to tell them apart either."

"That's hard to believe," Ariel said. "I've never had any trouble."

Margot took a small pad from her purse and began jotting down some notes.

"What are you doing?" Ariel inquired.

"Oh nothing, just scribbling some notes for my book. I find material everywhere."

"Sometimes when I'm working on a book," I volunteered, "I drop whatever I'm doing. I just have to race home to write down my ideas before I forget how I want to use them. It would drive Emily crazy."

Ariel's eyes narrowed.

David immediately intervened. Don't upset her, he said. He had already asked me to refrain from using Emily's name more than once.

When I asked him why: "All I know is, when Ariel hears it she feels needles inside her belly."

Margot blinked. "Ariel, did you say you like Rosemaling or detested it?"

"Liked!" Ariel responded sharply.

"What she detests is the name Emily."

"It's true," Ariel said. "I'm not really sure why."

Margot wrote down 'Likes Rosemaling; detests use of name Emily,' before proudly announcing that she had become a subscriber as well as a Fellow of the Academy.

Ariel looked at Margot suspiciously. "What made you join the Academy?" she asked.

"The Academy's the greatest place in the world to do medical research," Margot answered.

As Margot stopped to jot down additional notes, I recalled the first year we met. She had been an investigative reporter for *The Village Voice*. She dressed strictly in black; she said it was because she was in mourning over her divorce. It was the winter she wrote an award-winning story on city corruption. She had a reputation for checking facts compulsively. Every story she wrote, and there were hundreds, she fact-checked countless times. Every one of them passed through legal. Of course she took great pride in her accomplishments.

Dr. Silver babbled to David and I. "The Academy receives over 1,400 periodicals and journals a year. Over 14 miles of shelved materials. 690,000 catalogued works. 275,000 catalogued illustrations and portraits…"

As Dr. Silver went on, Margot continued speaking to Ariel: "Since I've gone back to work on my history of Siamese twins book, I've practically lived in the library. The Academy's library has a wealth of material on conjoined twins. If you like, I could get you special permission to reproduce material not owned by the library, the kind of confidential stuff that the public is not allowed to put on microfilm, slides or photo-copies. It's only reproduced for Fellows. One day you should meet me at the Academy. I'm sure you'll find it useful for the conjoined twin script you're working on." Margot pulled at her polka-dot tie. "I'd love to talk to you about your script." She paused for a second before continuing. "Maybe tomorrow or the day after we can meet up in the President's room, under the portrait of Eugene Hillhouse Poole. He was the President of the Academy for fifteen years. You can get a good look at him. He was so good-looking."

Ariel's eyes riveted on the polka-dot tie. "Is he also a friend of yours?" she asked testily.

Margot stammered, "President Poole died in 1949."

Dr. Silver looked blank. So did I

"I don't understand," Ariel went on. "Why do you need to spend so much time at the library?"

"I told you, to work on my book."

Ariel frowned, chewed on her check.Then she gave a brief whistle.

"Adam! Are you blind?" she shouted. "Can't you see what she's doing? She disarms you with all that double talk she does. It's not you she's after. It's my ideas on conjoined twins she wants. I knew it!" she screamed.

A sweating Dr. Silver excused himself and raced off. I grabbed Ariel's arm. "Calm down," I said firmly.

Ariel pulled away from me. "I—I need some water," she said, hurrying off.

David, who had moved on to speak to a German producer, noticed the commotion and quickly walked over. In a moment, he sized up what had happened. "It's my fault, Margot," he said apologetically. "Ariel's been taking this project of ours much too seriously." He shrugged. "You know how it is. She's been working a fourteen-hour day. Tonight she had a splitting headache. I shouldn't have insisted she come." That said, he marched off to find Ariel.

෧෨

Margot drew a deep breath, crossed her long, shapely legs as we sat in her den.

"Something spooked Warning at the Wyler party the other night. And it wasn't me or my book. It's something much deeper." Margot's brow furrowed. "Perhaps it was something unconscious. Some shadow from her past."

I didn't want to think about it right then. "Margot, stop digressing. We were discussing Ariel's script. I thought you were interested."

I wasn't betraying a confidence. David and I had had a meeting. We decided to confide in Margot. She was writing a text on the history of Siamese twins. If anyone could make sure Ariel Warning's facts were in order, overlook the technical stuff, it was her.

"I am interested," Margot said, lifting her notepad from her lap. "So tell me. Did Ariel actually describe the surgeon as a malefactor? She actually used that archaic a word?"

"Yes, and the way she's writing the character, he is an evildoer. The guy's treacherous."

"Malefactor," Margot repeated, jotting down the word on her notepad. She put down her pencil. "Adam, I hope you aren't upset with me, but I'm inspired. I want to do the best book I can."

I gazed at her. I wasn't upset, though I was still a bit disturbed by the way Ariel had acted. What I felt was sort of sad for Margot. It moved me to say something complimentary. "Tonight you look especially beautiful," I said.

"That's so sweet for you to say. But I don't feel beautiful. Next week I turn forty-two," she sighed, "and I'm childless and I'm losing my looks and I'm all alone."

My patience ran thin. "Margot, can we get back to Ariel's script?"

Margot adjusted her eyeglasses. Scrutinized her notes. Removed her glasses. Pondered. Divulged: "If Warning is saying her twins have a single heart, I'd say successful corrective surgery is just about impossible. It wouldn't matter how creative the surgery is. Most doctors would advise against the surgery. They'd say one child would certainly die, probably both."

Margot nibbled on her glasses. "Can you break the scene down step by step?" she asked. I began to describe what takes place in the O.R. "No, before that. When the doctor visits the parents of the twins."

"He swears to them his operation will be successful. 'You must understand,' he tells them, 'this is my procedure. It's new. Experimental. It's never been tried. But I'm certain I can save both of them.'"

Margot started to raise a question. Stopped. Raced to the computer. Sat down in front of the screen. Tapped a few keys on the terminal.

"Malefactor," she jabbered, as she tapped the keys. The computer blinked. Margot squinted. She punched some additional keys. The manmade beast began rumbling, communicating; she moved over to another pandemic monster. Out of her printer spun a bloodied sheet. She quickly tore the printer paper from its mooring. Examined it.

"It's still a jigsaw puzzle," she said, turning her swivel chair to face me.

"Shakespeare didn't need a computer to knock out *The Tempest*," I pointed out.

Margot pounced on me. "Why did you say that?"

"Say what?"

"*The Tempest*. Why did you refer to that particular play?"

"It just came to me," I said defensively. "David took Ariel to see the play. She said her favorite Shakespearian character was Miranda."

"*The Tempest*. How does the story go?" Margot hummed to herself. "It's one of Shakespeare's most beautifully poetic plays." Margot's brow wrinkled. Her face pinched. There was definitely a resemblance to the stereotypical school-marm. "How does the story go?" she repeated as she ruminated. "I miss Coleman. He would know…I got it," she said. "Ariel is the airy spirit. She's the servant of Prospero, the deposed Duke of Milan. By magic he raises a tempest off the island which he inhabits with his daughter, Miranda, and then acts as host to the shipwrecked malefactors." Her brow furrowed. "Malefactors. There's that word again."

"Margot, the one thing I recall from *The Tempest* is Ariel's gender. He's a male."

"Really, I always thought of the character as androgynous," she said, smiling with condescension. "*The Tempest* is a lovely fairy tale, inspiring in its wisdom, distilled by a mature mind. He or she, Ariel would still be the airy spirit. It's the spirit of the play that counts."

Margot lifted her pencil to her mouth, licked it once, then removed it. "Come over here," she ordered.

I walked over to where Margot was camped and stood in back of her chair. She hunched her shoulders, leaned closer to the computer. "Watch this," she said, as she tapped out 'The Tempest' on the keys. 'Prospero's daughter?'

Within seconds the answer fluttered across the screen: MIRANDA.

"Neat, huh?" she said, swiveling around to face me.

"Will you please tell me what you think you're accomplishing?"

"As I said, it's still a jigsaw puzzle, but I think I found an important part of our Ariel puzzle today. It's beginning to make sense."

"What are you talking about? What makes sense?"

Margot whirled around from the screen and explained as much to herself as me, while continuing to scribble on her notepad. "Ariel Warning's favorite character. Miranda. Prospero's daughter. Prospero casts his books into the sea."

When she finished she drew jagged teeth marks around "Miranda." More question marks next to: "Ariel, Delicate Spirit!"

"Will you please tell me what the hell's going on?"

Margot rotated her hips. The chair swiveled. She was once again facing me. "The truth cleverly told is the biggest lie of all," she uttered.

"Shakespeare?"

"Thomas Hardy, Return of the Native," she answered. Margot blinked. "You know me. I love playing with words. It's better than sex as far as I'm concerned."

Margot spun her chair around until she was face to face with the blinking screen. She hummed contentedly as she caressed the keys. "Did you know that prenatal diagnosis of Siamese twins is difficult and was rarely accomplished prior to the advent of sonography? Make sure to tell Warning that. Also, that those that share a single heart with multiple congenital abnormalities do not survive." She paused. "To perform successful corrective surgery would be as impossible for a malefactor as it would be for a saint." She turned and squinted at me. "Make sure Warning's aware of that. It's important."

I looked at the terminal. On the screen sentences again started to flutter.

"I've had enough, Margot. You're too weird for me." I began making my way to the door.

When I reached it, Margot called out, "Adam—Miranda. A vision of young beauty. Ferdinand, his love for Miranda is tender and worshipful. Do you know any two people who fit that description?"

David telephoned early in the morning. "Ariel put in more than seventy hours on her script this week. She's ready." A conference was scheduled on what was named 'The Ariel Project.'

As soon as I arrived, Ariel stared at me. "Your eyes are bloodshot. You must have been up all night."

I had paced the terrace until dawn. I couldn't sleep. The night before, after leaving Margot, I had drifted over to Strawberry Fields. Emily and her husband, Damon Burke, were handing out peanut butter sandwiches to the homeless.

"Hi Adam," Emily chirped. Just hearing Em's voice brought back what was missing in my life.

"I really think you would have a hard time with the way I now am," she said. "Much of the time there is a massage table in the living room, my Mahesh certificate and a picture of Buddha hangs on the wall. Chimes from the ceiling. My idea of happiness. Adam, did you take my advice? Are you dating?"

"Slow down, Em."

"I'm sorry, I'm a bit wired. The baby exhausted me today. But it's okay. Isaac's perfect. Thank you."

"For what?"

"If it weren't for you…you know. Well, I never would have made it. Never."

As I paced my rooftop I thought back to the many times after one of my big wins on a college basketball game when Emily and I would walk over to the Plaza Hotel; how Carmine Denoyer or Andre Bonnhomie or my "best friend Johnny," or some other BM I arranged to collect from would hand me my winning, and how I would click the one hundred dollar notes against my ear and count them quickly, stuff them in my pockets. And then how Emily and I would walk together on the side of the park where the box people camped, and how Emily would chatter about how one day she would concentrate her jewelry business on helping the homeless. One day she wanted to work on a medallion that would hopefully express love and giving, the qualities, as she put it, most necessary to assist the homeless—then she would take from her coat pockets crumpled five-dollar bills, and out of her shopping bag fur-lined gloves, and begin handing them out. Shake hands with the individuals who were sprawled on the benches, or lying soiled, side-by-side, on the cold, dank ground. Crazed-eyed women, stool-stained men, all types of lost souls, but Emily, with her ever sanguine face, would stop to say hello and offer them a hug, a fin and a pair of gloves. "Hi, remember me? I'm Emily. At one time I lived in the park, too."

Strangely enough, the longer I paced the terrace, the less I dwelled on Emily. The more I kept thinking of the day David and I met Ariel Warning: the sunny day they sauntered into the park together; the day David ordered me to leave his office-studio so that he could be alone with her; the first time my identical slept with her. I kept thinking that because of Ariel I was beginning to separate from Emily; because of Ariel, I was getting over…

Also in the dead of night I recalled an evening the three of us were having dinner with my Uncle Leo to celebrate his ninetieth birthday. I kept thinking something had spooked Ariel that night. Some shadow from her past. My uncle had removed his Rolex from his thick wrist, placed it gingerly on the table. "I want one of you guys to have it. Now tell me, nephews. How are we going to decide?"

"Give the watch to David," I said, pushing it in front of Ariel. "Take a look. It's a beaut."

Ariel peered at the glittering timepiece. For a brief moment she began to whistle. Then she dropped her wine glass. It smashed to pieces on the restaurant floor. "What's wrong with me?" she cried out, jumping up from the table. "David, I have to leave," she sputtered, racing toward the exit door.

Was there something missing from Ariel Warning's life. Something lost? Something menacing her that caused these eruptions in behavior? Why these eruptions? Why? I couldn't stop asking myself these questions. What caused Ariel to act the way she did? What was inside her, menacing her, spooking her? What about me? Who was sicker than me?

Ariel scrutinized me from David's director's chair. I was certain, after sending me all those double messages, she'd react possessively, but all she said was, "You were absolutely correct about Margot. She's been a great help to me." The half of me that was hopeful—hopeful for what?—was disappointed.

"Don't look so shocked," she said. "It's not as if Margot took me under her wing or anything like that. But I've learned a great deal from her."

A moment later Ariel caught me ogling her legs.

"Listen up!" she said, grinning. "This is fascinating stuff."

"I will if you talk about your script," I said. "I hear enough gobble-dygook from Margot."

"I'm trying to tell you. The case histories I've been studying have forced me to radically alter my script. My twins no longer share only a common heart. They're also attached at the hip. And they're no longer six weeks old. They're eight years old. They've been examined intermittently since birth at the Pittsburgh Children's Hospital; and all that time the twins' parents have been terrified of an operation. Their terror is well-founded; it's based on stats, little chance for them to survive. One doctor now convinces them differently. He's the new golden boy. Looks like what's-his-name. You know, that great-looking actor from the '30s. Your brother and I watched him last night in that old Bette Davis flick. At least we watched some of the flick." David looked embarrassed. I bit my lower lip.

"Gary Merrill," I guessed.

"Gary Merrill was Davis' real life husband. Real life isn't movie life. Think, Adam. The guy who played Dr. Frederick Steele. He's in love with her."

"George Brent. Dark Passage."

"That's cool," Ariel said.

"It's not cool," David snapped. "George Brent had a kindly face. You're definitely miscasting if you want a Brent type to play the evil doctor."

"That's cool. I'm going to call my evil surgeon Dr. Brent. I want my characters to be arbitrary," she said, scribbling a note to herself. "Now both of you, listen up. The big scene takes place in the examination room. The twins have just turned nine. Since birth the parents have pounded into them that there's not one chance in a million for a successful operation. Now they listen from behind a screen as Dr. Brent talks to their mother."

Ariel looked up from the script. "On and on he goes, never once telling Mrs. Swenson that significant complications may appear with the surviving girl's maturation."

"I'm confused," David said. "Are you certain that you have all your medical facts straight? First you're talking about Siamese twins attached at the pelvis, then at the hip, now you're suggesting they have a common heart. Besides, it sounds to me that if this operation is to have any chance at all, it should be performed at infancy. Not on nine-year-olds." He paused. "With this kind of material you have to be absolutely scrupulous."

"David's correct. It's imperative that the medical facts be precise," I said, despising myself for saying this. As a twin, I hated sounding like my twin.

"I have literary license, don't I?" Ariel shouted, her face turning pallid.

When Ariel calmed down, she apologized.

"I'm sorry, guys, but the point I'm trying to make in this new version is that it's only possible for one twin to survive the operation. The rest of it is…what did you call it, Adam? Gobbledygook?"

"You still have to be sure of your facts," David said kindly.

"Okay, guys, you win. I'll make certain to amend whatever it is that has to be amended. But even more importantly, what do you think?"

I jammed my pen into my mouth to stop myself from saying what

I thought.

"Tell me!" Ariel shouted.

"It's a soap opera," I cried out.

Ariel spun around to face David. "Do you agree with him?"

I knew my identical's answer. Yes, he did.

David spoke calmly. "It definitely will interest a lead actress. And the Brent role could win someone a Golden Globe."

Turning back to me, my identical remained silent: *I'm not the one to destroy her dreams, and I won't let you do it, either,* his lover's eyes told me.

Margot telephoned later that day. "I reread *The Tempest* last night," she said, and commenced pointing out outrageous similarities between Ariel and Ariel. "Now do you see why I'm suspicious? Why I'm almost certain there's a connection between Shakespeare's drama, Ariel Warning and conjoined twins?"

"All I see is that you have a need to occupy that restless mind of yours."

"Adam, remember how flexible and considerate you were with Emily. Try to be that way with me."

I counted to ten. "What is it that makes you suspicious? Give me something tangible."

"I'm not sure yet," Margot answered. "But I think I'm getting closer. I can feel it." She stopped. "One thing I can say that's concrete. That night we were at Jason Wyler's. I corrected Warning when she said we were dating. I emphasized we were just good friends. But then I mentioned that you were dating an exotic dancer. Well, you should have seen Warning's face. Her smile was twofold, carrying with it equal dosages of dark and light." Margot stopped again. "I'd like to study her conjoined twin script. Compare her original draft to her revisions."

When we finished I too recalled how Ariel reacted when I told her I was dating Gabriela Rolon. A tiny blue vein had pulsed in her left temple. She began to whistle. "It's strange," she said. "I assumed you were connected. Not separated." And then in tense tones, "Is it serious? I mean, your dating?"

❧❧

For several days in my twin's studio-office, I noticed Ariel seemed to be inordinately tense. And then, on a morning David was out of the office I unexpectedly dropped in.

"I was vile to your brother," Ariel told me. "I don't know why. I'm sorry for having been so vile to him. He doesn't deserve it. I was just so angry, so confused last night." Ariel shook her head. "'Tempest in my mind doth from my senses take all feelings,'" she quoted from the play. "You know I'm not like that," she said, taking my arm and leading me to my twin's sofa. We sat down. "I feel deeply for David. I feel deeply for you," she said, stroking my hand. "I'm woman enough to tell both of you how I feel." She crossed her legs. Her stockings hissed. "It's true," she whispered.

"What upset me? Last night I asked David to invite you to the theater with us. He refused. I insisted. He kept refusing. He kept telling me that he doesn't need to share me with you. He said he doesn't need anyone but me. Don't misunderstand me. I like your brother feeling the way he does. I love it. But a pattern is developing. A pattern that excludes you."

I kept searching Ariel's face for some buried truth that I was convinced was as much secreted inside her as the stirrings I felt imploding inside myself. Nothing was visible beneath the surface. The only tangible truth I knew for certain was that I loathed the stirrings I felt. I mentioned to Ariel that Gabriela Rolon had left the city. "Oh," she said, her blue eyes rounder and wider.

That night what Margot Adams had said concerning Ariel's initial employment for *Women's Health Magazine* popped into my head. In the morning I telephoned Herb Leno.

"Mr. Remler, Ms. Warning was dismissed because of the way she provoked me. She was transferred from circulation to my office for one afternoon. Any of our other employees would have been delighted. Her behavior was unprovoked, I assure you."

"What exactly was her behavior?"

"The entire afternoon she scowled at me. Actually, she kept staring at my hands. Believe me, Mr. Remler, that woman is strange as well as hostile."

"Did you do or say anything that could have provoked her?"

"Absolutely nothing. The only think I did was offer her some advice."

"Which was?"

"Ms. Warning mentioned she wanted to be a screenplay writer. I told her that she was fortunate. Because of her youth she had plenty of time for marriage and babies. That she should concentrate on her career objectives. Give everything she had to give to her writing. Babies and a husband could wait."

Ariel came running up to me out of breath, wearing one of those faded-flower-print sex-denying Laura Ashley dresses. For that reason she looked all the more disturbingly sexual. A silver crucifix hung around her throat. We were going to the ballet at Lincoln Center. La Bayadere was to begin in a few minutes. David wasn't coming. He was on a jet to Los Angeles. It was the first time that we'd be alone together. All night. I recall the stirring in the pit of my stomach. And then, the internal voice—Are you crazy? She's David's! David's! You're weaned on decency.

You know what's right. You especially know it at the very moment when you're confronted by temptation. But some people think so little of themselves. Are so little. These are the people who give in. It's not an excuse. It's the way people are. Something is missing. Something strong and valuable and whole. Was I that kind of person? I was determined not to do anything to change my role that night. My role as David's twin brother.

As we entered the opera house, Ariel took my arm. I casually removed my arm from her grip. I did it in such a cursory way that it seemed accidental. It wasn't. My whole being ached for her touch.

During the second intermission we climbed the cascading stairs and ended up on the Grand Tier level at the impressive winding bar. Glinting champagne glasses radiated iridescent kaleidoscopic colors across its gleaming top. Each of them was filled to the brim. I looked intently at Ariel. All kinds of distant feelings whirled around inside me. I recall thinking I knew what time meant. I was thoroughly conscious of time. I looked around the opera house.

It seemed like yesterday afternoon that my college girlfriend and I were at the same bar. The last night with Em. Time, for me, it never changed. It was fixed, frozen. Not only in the respect that I was, it seemed, always starting over, but that inside I was still twenty-one. Still needy, hungry, famished…

I gazed at Ariel, who was reaching for a champagne glass. When she saw me gazing at her, she smiled. Taking a sip of the pink bubbly, she looked around. When she was certain that we were out of hearing distance of the other patrons, she whispered, "Can I tell you something?"

"What is it?" I asked.

"I was also a twin."

It was as if I had already expected it. Rather than astonishment or surprise, it was as if my entire nervous system had shut down in preparation for—and with the single purpose of—accommodating itself, myself, to her admission. Nothing Ariel Warning said, or could have said, at that moment about herself could have jarred me out of my stupor. And for that reason I was all the more jarred and moved.

"My twin died of crib death," she said. Pausing, Ariel fidgeted with her hair before continuing. "Roberta died when she was six weeks old. That was my sister's name. Roberta." She stopped playing with her hair, raised her champagne glass to her lips and sipped from it, before deliberately placing the glass back down on the bar top. A moment later, she lifted it again and swallowed the remainder of its contents. Then she helped herself to another glass from the bar, this time drinking it down in one gulp. I tossed two twenty-dollar bills on the bar.

"I remember exactly what happened that night," Ariel said, continuing from where she had left off. "My mother never believed me. She said it was impossible for me to remember that far back. That I only thought I did. But that's not true. I do remember. Roberta died the first time my mother left us alone."

"You mean you were left alone when you were six weeks old?" I asked.

"No, I don't mean that. I mean it was the first time my father and mother went out after we were born. We were left alone with a sitter."

Ariel paused again, looking around. People, still several feet off but inching closer, were standing around chatting gaily. No one was listening to our conversation.

"The sitter kept coming into our room, checking on us every hour. She was obeying her instructions. My mother had told her that Roberta was a quiet baby, that she would sleep through the night. As for me, she told the sitter that I was a crier, needed to be rocked. That I wouldn't stop crying unless I was rocked. And so, naturally, the sitter paid more attention to me. She never even checked on my twin sister." Ariel began sipping her wine again. "I knew something was wrong. I did," she exclaimed, now gulping down the champagne.

It was as if Ariel were telling her story like an old-fashioned story-teller. Separate and apart from who they were. With feeling, yet holding back. Restrained. "Then my father. I mean, he came to the bedroom, but he just stood there at the door. Come to bed, he must have said to my mother, or something like that. I guess my mother just glanced over at my identical's crib and thought she was asleep."

Ariel paused to take several deep breaths. "My mom didn't sense anything was the matter. I, on the other hand, was screaming. Kicking my arms and legs, crying out for attention. Nothing that unusual for me, but I do remember doing that. I knew something was wrong. But when my mom picked me up and began rocking me, I must have been so exhausted from crying and kicking that I fell right off. And then, in the middle of the night, my mother awakened. She couldn't sleep: 'Something's wrong, Chris.' 'What?' my father asked. But my mother didn't know what it was. 'Come on, go back to sleep.' And my mother went back to sleep. What was wrong was that my mom hadn't heard Roberta breathing." Ariel nervously played with her silver crucifix.

"All through the night I didn't hear Roberta's breathing. I know I didn't," she murmured softly, beginning to whistle.

After composing herself, Ariel continued.

"Did you ever hear of Uma Olsen?"

"Wasn't she a poet in the '60s?"

"No. My mother wasn't a poet. She was a watercolorist. Several critics compared her to Andrew Wyeth. They called her a magic realist. My father, too, always said she was more than a simple realist. He liked to quote Wyeth. If you can combine realism and abstraction, you got something terrific, he'd say. My mother won a Winslow Homer Award. That was my mother," she said proudly.

In that moment, flashing through my mind was something I remembered about Uma Olsen, the poet. That she lived with a companion. Another woman, a painter. Obviously I was confusing the poet with Ariel's mother, the painter.

Ariel continued, "From that time on my mother was never herself again. She never painted again. For all intents and purposes her life was over. My father abandoned her less than a year later. He just couldn't handle it, he said. A year later my father died in an automobile accident."

Ariel stepped from the bar area to the Metropolitan's balcony overlooking the entire Lincoln Center complex. Following her to the edge of the balcony, I placed one hand gently on her shoulder. Cascading streams of white water jetted from the fountain in the middle of the promenade area. She focused her attention on the jetting water and remained silent for some time. Then, almost abruptly, she turned to me. "You know what I heard from my mother every day since I was an infant?" She articulated her words slowly, with studied deliberation. "One without the other is one too few."

Ariel rubbed her neck and shoulders before continuing.

"A week before my mother died she made a prodigious effort to paint again. You know what she titled her work? One without the other."

Ariel kept looking earnestly at me. Smiling wanly. When her smile faded, her face took on a wholly different expression. I had seen that look before. On David's face. It was after Thea died. For almost two years he had looked like that.

"Why do you think I understand you and David so well?" she said, twisting her crucifix. "Understand just what it means to be an identical twin. It's because I've always felt the same lack you do. The only difference is, whereas you were marked by the addition of a twin, I was marked by my twin's subtraction from my life. Is it any wonder, then, that I'm so taken with you two? So fascinated by twins? Don't you understand, Adam? Each of us was cursed at birth. Me, for having lost my twin. You and David for having been born identical twins. But the miracle is that now, in finding each other, we've also found our answer. By combining and merging the two of you, partial, rudimentary human beings, separate but unfinished in yourselves; by taking advantage of what the three of us have to give to each other, I'm certain that we can all finally have what's missing in our lives. A sense of well-being and completion."

Ariel uttered the last words in pleading tones that somehow smacked of violence. I tried to follow her but it was as if I didn't comprehend the full implications of what she was saying. And I didn't. But some part of me did. What she was searching for was something that had left an even greater void in her life than Emily Bloom's loss had left in mine. Losing her twin had reduced her being, her essence, by half.

The intermission was almost over. I took her arm. "Come on," I said. "Let's get back to our seats."

When we reached the winding stairs Ariel came to a halt. People scurried by us. "You know," she said, "I was certain you'd be different from David, at least in certain respects. He treats me with kid gloves. As if I were untouchable. He thinks just because I'm almost half his age, have a certain kind of look, graduated from college with honors, that I'm a mummy. I'm not a mummy. I'm curious. There's nothing I wouldn't try. Nothing! And I'm determined to live my entire life on the free side of abandon. To explore everything. Not only as a writer, which David thinks is just fine." These last words were said with an edge to her voice. "But also as a woman." She paused. "In life there just isn't enough time. Especially for a woman."

"Hurry up, Felice, the third act is about to begin," a short, ventricose man wearing an expensive toupee shouted to his wife, who was complaining about a yeast infection, as he rushed by us on the stairs. "It's just like you, Felice. La Bayadere, and you're grumbling about a yeast infection." Several more couples raced by. Soon we were the only people who had not reentered the auditorium. We were by ourselves on the stairs. Ariel seemed oblivious to the music starting up from inside the hall as she looked me straight in the eye. "I'm determined to have both of you. Do you understand what I'm trying to say? I mean you two are polar opposites. David's intellectual, logical, self-contained. You're excessive and undisciplined. If you're hungry in one way, David's famished in another. Together, yes, together, as writers as well as men, you're whole."

"Ariel," I said. "People aren't merely the talent they possess. They're more." I knew my words sounded feeble, but that was all I could come up with.

"Exactly," she answered. "And it's the 'more' I'm interested in." The corner of her mouth had a cruel twist to it.

In just as inadequate a manner as my previous effort, I said, "People aren't books. You can't just edit out the best from them as you can from a page."

"In the case of twins I can," she said defiantly. "I need to be replenished. You and David, together, by having both of you, I'll finally be fulfilled."

"And what does that mean, exactly?" I asked, more afraid to hear her response to my question than not.

"Totality," she answered. "Consummation. I'll have what I've been missing. What was taken away from me so young." She peered at me. "You're not fooling me. You understand what incompleteness is as well as I do. Your entire life you've suffered from this deficiency. You've been Siamese bound to being an identical twin for so long, to being immature and underdeveloped, the other side of your brother's coin for so long. Don't you think it's time you broke away? Rebelled against him? Your bondage. Your fate. Don't you think it's time you grew up, carried through, made good, took responsibility and freed yourself from the ball-and-chain yoke of twinship?"

In Ariel Warning's intense voice I could hear the urgency of her message. The ferocity of her impossible quest. The orchestra had already commenced playing its final stanza; the ballet was fast approaching its end. "Both of you together are a whole person, Adam. I'm not going to end up like my mother. You and your brother together. The two of you. I'll feel complete. I know I will," she said adamantly, "and so will you!"

No matter what I previously thought, or fantasized, or said about myself, or what Margot Korman had conjured up about Ariel, the truth was I was totally unprepared for these admissions. Not so much for what she said, although that, too, but the way she said them. With absolute clarity and conviction. She was utterly convinced that she was right. There was an unquestioning finality in her words and tone. She was categorically unequivocal in the moral correctness of her position. No, I could never have anticipated these proclamations from Ariel Warning. On the contrary, my first response was to be repelled by them.

And yet, by the time we had reached the street, I could already feel something quivering inside of me that was attracted to them. What had she said? It was my chance to become whole. Complete. Freed from the shackles of twinship. How often had I thought those very same thoughts in my most private moments? Now, here, on the corner of Columbus Avenue and Sixty-Fourth Street, I stood trembling, afraid. I was rejecting her words on the basis of…well, instinctively, without logic, or more precisely, some kind of a priori pre-reflective logic. I couldn't utter a word.

Neither did Ariel. She had said all she wanted to say.

It started to rain. I pulled from my shoulder bag one of those dwarfed umbrellas made in Taiwan. As I fumbled with the catch, Ariel jerked the umbrella from my hand and violently smashed it against the curb. "I hate these monstrosities," she said, her face smoldering and vicious. I hailed a cab, almost pushing her into it.

"I'll talk to you," I said. I gave the cab driver her address and a twenty. "Go ahead, cabbie," I said. "Take off." My voice was shaking.

Ariel leaned out of the cab's window. She put her hand softly on my arm. "Your brother has me reading Lawrence Durrell. Do you remember your Durrell? He wrote that this world represents the promise of a unique happiness that we are not well enough equipped to grasp. I'll be home waiting for your call," she said.

That night, in bed, alone, I kept thinking about Ariel Warning, and as I did, I kept seeing my own face looking back at me. Betrayal is a painful thing for anyone, but when it's your identical…I kept hearing David saying, "My heart beats faster when I think of her." I kept hearing Ariel. It was my chance to become whole. Complete. Freed from the shackles of twinship. So much of what I knew in my mind remained hidden in the folds of my soul. As I lay in bed, I became all the more convinced that I was as much attracted to Ariel's evincing words as repelled by them. In retrospect I think I had little choice. I was as much driven to realizing myself, pursuing my own autonomy, as she was impelled to pursue her own.

I reached for the telephone. I dialed her phone number. Hung up. Walked out onto my rooftop. I kept hearing Ariel's explanation of her quest. My quest. "When you love someone, you love them as if they were you. You project onto them all your fantasies and illusions as if they were your twin. But with me you'll have the opportunity to break free from your twin mold. By separating yourself from your twin brother, you'll no longer merely be the other half, but one. Don't you understand? Through me you can finally become yourself."

I continued pacing my rooftop. Whereas with Emily: "Feel guilty? I did for a while, Adam. I don't any longer. We just didn't have the right karma."

With Ariel…Ariel was truly my soul mate. It was nothing less than my soul that was fatally attracted to her. It was my sovereignty as a free and liberated self that she afforded me the opportunity of realizing. My one chance to gain full maturity. To kill my twinship. The biology of my birth. How strange and dangerous and challenging and mysterious and tempting and seductive and ineluctably magnetic was Ariel…and rightfully so. It only seemed logical and correct that she should be all of those things, I continued to muse to myself as I moved back inside. Again, I reached for the telephone. Again I couldn't dial her number. I placed the phone in its cradle. Returned to the rooftop terrace. Paced back and forth. Vowed to myself that I would never call or pursue her. Never. But still, in the pitch black of night, I was not thinking of my twin brother, or even of Emily. I was thinking of Ariel Warning.

☙

At 3:30 AM Ariel called.

"I have a question. Why is it David and you are always quarreling over your gambling? I mean he knows you only won during all those years you handicapped. Why does he deny it?"

"David despised everything about my handicapping. He wrote off my handicapping as a pathology. The dollars I earned were soiled. To this day, Ariel, all I ever hear is, 'Don't gamble! Don't bet! Even if you win, you lose!'"

"Adam, don't you get it? You're saying the same thing I told you earlier. Even with identicals who love each other unconditionally there are increments of separateness. You must act on it. You see that, don't you? Now go back to sleep."

☙

In the morning Margot Korman called.

"Her father drowned in a boating accident? So he's the shipwrecked malefactor," she concluded.

"I didn't say boating accident," I told her.

"Yes, you did. I distinctly heard you."

"If I did, it was a Freudian slip. Ariel's father was killed in an automobile accident."

Margot was driving me mad. She had become obsessed with Ariel Warning. Obsessed with her computer word games, jigsaw puzzles, crosswords and riddles. She kept insisting there was a purpose to her abracadabra. That it was her fun. She continued doing somersaults with her state-of-the-art "thinking" software, each day finding innovative ways to program her bewitching games so that they would make sense out of Ariel's "revelations," as she now labeled them. She approached this as a calling, with the zeal of a convert to a new religion. With an unquestioning belief that there were answers out there. It was a matter of time, she insisted—somewhere in space there was a hellish message to be found in Ariel's messianic revelations. And what was it Margot actually classified as a revelation? It stretched across the vast continent of human nature. The miracle of what most of us simply identify as being human. She questioned Ariel's quirks and foibles, moods and tantrums; she examined outbursts, opinions and declarations; mined Ariel's associations and disassociations, facts and fictions, creations and contradictions; scrutinized her affinity for Shakespeare's drama; the Norwegian art form, Rosemaling; and inquired about her lineage: Uma Olsen was not found on file at Sotheby's Park Bernet. Not an art dealer in the city knew of her. Margot delved further. She ended up with Uma Olsen the poet. I told you as much, I said. When I questioned Ariel about her mother: "I told you. She died." Ariel, as well as

I, left it at that. One gallery owner in Soho said he thought he remembered a watercolorist by the name of Olsen in the '60s. But he couldn't recollect anything more substantial. As for the Winslow Homer Award, not one person that Margot contacted in the art field had heard of it.

Margot added revelation upon revelation to the never-ending pile. Each of these bits and pieces, these so-called "revelations," another piece of the Warning profile, she scrupulously classified as if they were malignant tumors. Tumors that at the time I was convinced were located inside Margot's own mind—admittedly so much like my own.

When I announced that my allegiance was to simple logic, to the fact that a computer could not make two and two into five, Margot announced, "That's why I'm here."

One of our conversations went something like this:

"I know you think I'm possessed. You should catch a glimpse of yourself. The way you drool over and ogle this woman. And you think I'm the quack," she cackled.

When I tried denying this, Margot heaved a huge sigh. "Adam, you were the same with Emily Bloom. It's your nature." And when I continued to protest, "You've grown tiresome today. I'll see you tomorrow."

Each time we were together, Margot kept pumping me for more revelations. Revelations she added one by one to those she had already extracted from her own contact with Ariel.

"Think, Adam, think!" she would implore me, jotting down and underlining just about everything I mentioned from Ariel's lucky number 3 to her family's pet name for her. Caliban. When Margot heard Caliban she hummed, "That figures. Caliban is straight out of *The Tempest*. He's the witch Sycorax's misshapen, monstrous son. Hm. Prospero casts his books in the sea. Caliban attempts to kill Prospero. Hm," she intoned as if the revelation were petrol for her mind. "Is Ariel Caliban? Is David Prospero?" she uttered a second later, more to herself than to me.

The following day Margot informed me, "A real pattern is developing. I'm certain Ariel is trying to tell you, David, maybe herself, something."

"What?" I asked in my soaked-galoshes sort of way.

Margot ignored my sarcasm. "As of today I still haven't a clue what it is, so don't become irksome and ask, but I'm sure these revelations leaking out—and I'm sure that's what they're doing, leaking out—are for a reason. I'm going to keep experimenting. There's a definite correlation somewhere to be found."

I defended Ariel to Margot.

"Did it ever occur to you that Ariel is more than the bloom of youth? That simply put, she's a complex person? As complex as you."

In a confused crevice of my mind I had a suspicion that it might be something as prosaic as jealousy that was driving Margot mad. It seemed unlikely. She did not have a romantic interest in me. Far before Emily, Margot was beginning to redefine our friendship. What made sense was that, for Margot, investigating Ariel Warning was true to her character. She relished the complexity of it all. Every revelation she likened to a poser full of riddles to decipher.

"Adam, please don't distract me. I'm onto something. I've tried sorting these revelations in chronological order, from the first one we discovered—Ariel detesting Emily's name—to whatever; now I'm going to try random tracing, maybe that will tell me something. If nothing makes sense sequentially it's going to be an arduous project. It'll end up trial and error. But I'm certain there's something going on here." She arched an eyebrow. "Dangerously so."

I did not believe in numerology, astrology or in any other magicology, including what I now indicted Margot for worshipping: "computerology." But because she had accented the word "dangerous," I did not call her a quack. I decided to humor her.

"Promise me. Not a word to Ariel."

I was uncomfortable with that. Even more uncomfortable when Margot insisted, "And not a word to your lover."

I was convinced she had said "lover" rather than "brother" to add grist to the mill. I ground my teeth. Kept quiet.

As golden as friendship is, it's not love. With Emily Bloom I never condemned, only justified. My brother said, "That too is wrong." With Margot, once I promised to abide by "not a word to Ariel or your lover," I not only felt uncomfortable, I felt hostile toward her much of the time. Sullen moods and a barrage of churlish insults ensued, finally culminating in Margot not speaking to me.

Nonetheless I answered the phone when she called.

"I thought we weren't talking?"

"We're not. I'm still angry with you. You tell me I'm the All-American neurotic. That your twin brother thinks I have a screw loose. Shouldn't I be? And worse yet, you've allowed this woman to come between us. Even more than Emily Bloom did."

I detected a hint of hurt in her tone. It softened me. I apologized.

"Can we meet for lunch?" Margot responded. "I have something to tell you."

We met at Serafina's. Margot was wearing a tailored black suit and a black lace blouse that was buttoned up to the top. A gleaming black leather briefcase was at her hip. Her black sheer stockings and high heels were the only signs of her restless femininity.

"Notice anything different about me?" she inquired. I shrugged. "My hairdo. You like it?"

Margot had added a wisp of white hair amongst her bangs. Somehow it made her appear ultra-conservative. "It suits you," I said.

A red-faced waiter handed us menus. A sensual-looking Hispanic brought over some ice water. Margot unleashed a coy smile. "Will you please exchange this bread for a loaf that I can bite?" When the busboy left, Margot leaned closer to me. "I'm seeing Kevin O'Connor tonight. His table manners haven't improved one bit, but, still, with Kev I feel the way I would have liked to feel with Coleman. It's the truth." She sipped substantially from her Kir Royale. A frown pinched her face. "Adam, am I going to leave the world lusting after young men?"

Over lunch Margot avoided bringing up Ariel Warning. Instead, she rattled on and on about O'Connor.

"I won't sleep with Kevin tonight. I've learned that if I sleep with him and the sex is great one night, the following night it's terrible. Well, maybe not terrible exactly, but I don't think Kevin can handle two nights in a row."

"Maybe it's that he feels he's getting in too deep," I offered weakly.

"All I know is, as soon as we have one of those perfect evenings, the next time he starts punishing me."

Margot proceeded to go over, orgasm by orgasm, the kinky particulars of her relationship with Kevin O'Connor.

"Isn't this fish delicious?" I asked, trying to divert her.

Finally the chit-chat was exhausted. Margot requested a cigarette from the handsome busboy. "It's against the law," he said.

"Please," she said in a low voice, removing her wire-rims, peering coquettishly at him. "I'll just take one puff," she purred. "I've started smoking," she said, raising the harmless-looking rice paper to her thin lips, inhaling. She peered at me. Her expression changed from gay to grim. "I told you I wanted to talk to you," she said in a reedy voice. A voice suffused with anger. "All this time I've been holding it in. We weren't speaking, you know. You want to know why I'm suspicious of Ariel Warning. Feel this dread. It's because people just don't come out of a vacuum."

I tried saying something. "Listen to me," Margot said in the unwavering voice of the Catholic Church.

"A woman mails your office a résumé. You respond. She knocks on your door. Informs you that she's graduated from the University of Kansas with honors. That her parents are deceased. Intrigues you more by telling you her twin died from SIDS." Margot pushed her repast to the side of the table, squashed her cigarette. The busboy quickly appeared, clearing the table. Poured coffee. She waited for him to leave. "Ask yourself. Why is Warning so impassioned by twins? Why does she revile the name Emily? Why is she writing such a bizarre script? Why does she go berserk at the oddest of times? What makes a twenty-four-year-old woman in the bloom of youth from somewhere in the heartlands act so peculiar?"

"The way you're speaking makes Ariel sound as if she's a character in an Edgar Allen Poe tale," I responded.

Margot removed her spectacles. "Forget her bizarre film script for a moment. What about her fascination with those conjoined twins, The Parkers? Don't you find that a bit Poe-ish? And what about the Valentine's gifts she purchased for your brother and herself. The Glock pistols. Isn't that strange?" She drained her cup of coffee. Carefully put down the cup. The handsome busboy rushed over to refill it. Margot deliberately waited for him to leave. "I asked you to lunch because I wanted to show you something." She opened her briefcase. "I've had a friend of a friend at the University of Kansas check their records," she said, taking from her leather case a manila folder. "In this folder I have a printout of every student that has attended the University in the past ten years." Margot handed me the thick folder. "Earlier I had the opportunity to examine it. You won't find anyone by the name of Warning on the list. Or Olsen. Not one Ariel either. Isn't that strange?"

I couldn't believe that Margot had actually gone this far.

"As far as her alleged mother is concerned, I continued checking even after my investigation into the art world proved futile. There was an American painter by the name of Uma who lived awhile in the red light district of Tokyo. She was a watercolorist as well as a copyist. She studied Utamaro's style and painted over and over again his Mother and Infant."

"Did you speak to Utamaro?"

"Utamaro painted in the eighteenth century, Adam. I also googled the death of Ariel's father, Christopher Warning. I couldn't find a death certificate for him."

"That's impossible. Warning's a common name."

"That's not what I'm saying. Of course I found Christopher Warning. I found 198 of them over the past twenty-five years. But none of them had a wife named Uma. Or a daughter named Ariel."

"You know," she said, blinking. "There are people who can't tell the truth. About anything. Some of them are even classified as borderline psychotics."

Margot chewed on the handle of her glasses. I remained silent. Finally she removed the handle from her mouth. "What we have to do is visit her apartment. I want to look around." I protested. "We have to," Margot insisted. "It's the only way we'll ever solve this mystery."

"I'm not Dick Tracy and this isn't Manhattan Murder Mysteries," I answered.

"And I'm not a second-story woman," Margot said crossly. "But it's the only way we'll find anything out."

"So what if you caught Ariel in a few lies? Everyone lies. It doesn't mean they're dangerous. Maybe she was just embarrassed to tell us about her past. Who knows? Everyone has something in their history that they prefer to hide. As for not attending the University of Kansas, David and I get résumés every day. Whenever we do a random check, we find more than fifty percent are fabricated."

Margot ignored my response. This time she was correct in doing so. I was concerned. My response was a pose, mostly bravado.

"Your brother must have a key to her flat," she said. "Borrow it."

"No!" I shouted.

"Answer these questions," she said. "Has David met any of her friends? Does she even have any? Does she have a roommate? Since that wild night at the ballet when she confessed to you about being a twin, her identical being deceased, all the rest, has she bothered you?"

"What do you mean bothered?"

"You know very well what I mean. Come on to you? Attacked you? Arched her body, giggled at your words, pulled you down, spread her legs, forced you inside her?"

For some reason, maybe it was the wisp of white hair, though that was reaching, Margot looked her age. She seemed more vulnerable. Less in charge. Maybe even somewhat maternal. Though that was reaching even further. In any case I tempered my reaction.

"I have to leave," I said simply.

"Don't leave. There's something else I have to tell you."

Again Margot opened her briefcase. "Here's a list of every revelation I've compiled," she said, removing from the case two sheets of yellow legal lined paper. "They'll be just words to you, but to me each one of these words is a revelation. They mean something. They have a connection. If you examine this list you'll find some of Warning's favorite expressions on it. One of them I'm sure you're acquainted with: 'Listen up.'"

I admitted that I was.

"Good," she said, reaching for her cup, slowly sipping black coffee. When she drained the cup, she continued, "I remembered what you told me about Gabriela Rolon. That she was fired from her topless bar job because of some mysterious woman caller's complaints. I had a gut feeling. I visited that awful place. Spoke to the club's manager. A man named Fusco. He wouldn't speak to me at first. I had to give him a Franklin." It was an expression of mine Margot had fallen in love with. In gambling circles, a Franklin is part of the everyday argot. A Franklin, a one-hundred-dollar bill.

Margot put on her wire-rimmed spectacles. Squinted. "I have what he said right here," she said, shuffling through some papers. She read from one of them. "I was gonna hang up on the broad. I usually don't take complaints like that too serious. But when I told her to stop wastin' my time, she said something that got my attention."

"What was it?" I asked.

"'Listen up,' the broad said. It was the way she said it, lady. 'Listen up!' It gave me the shivers."

When I arrived home I paced my rooftop terrace thinking about Ariel Warning, and in particular Uma Olsen. Lost an infant to crib death, her husband couldn't handle it, deserted. Uma Olsen's life probably hit rock bottom. Hard times are personal. It would have been awkward for Ariel, as I told Margot, to spell out hard times. I thought about Ariel Warning. Why did Ariel lie? In what way did it benefit her? The job? Yes: Without falsifying her résumé, my brother would never have scheduled an interview for her, much less have hired her. And her conduct regarding Gabriela Rolon? That was also simple to justify. I continued pacing. There was a full moon. Everything on the terrace looked lush and beautiful. The large beer barrels around the front housed cherry and ash and a variety of twenty-foot-high pine trees. I used half-barrels for planters for the smaller trees and an assortment of colorful flowering plants. The oak boxes against the picket fences and white guardrails housed either large or small-leafed ivy that grew up and down the brick walls or blossomed interspersed throughout, as well as flushed begonias. Lilac trees added fragrance. Rose bushes, vibrant rhododendrons, and blazing pink and white azalea shrubs bloomed off the entranceway leading from the terrace doors.

I headed for the back of the terrace, the area where Emily's pine-wood shed had been. I had taken it down. Plank by plank. A plank—something that supports or forms a foundation. Emily had been my plank. I walked by a huge rectangular planter with a neglected stone

cairn Emily had erected, tribute to our third winter, a trip, fond memories of the British Isles; another huge planter filled to the brim with
red kalanchoes; another with calamintha. Emily would watch the bees
for hours as they thrived on the calamintha. Alongside the side wall in
large clay pots hibiscus bushes that provided exquisite flowering orange blossoms. I passed Em's favorite chaise lounge, a gash in the fabric,
a rip in the seam, continued walking around the terrace. There were
pellucid shells that allowed for the passage of light, used for smoker's
ashes, as well as two phones resting on diminutive teakwood tables on
the northern end of the rooftop. I reached for a phone to telephone "my
best friend, Johnny," one of my manifold honorable bookmakers. Made
a few bets. And what about my lies, I thought. All I do is lie. David was
on his way to Los Angeles. Before he left: "You're acting weird again. Are
you betting?" I had answered I wasn't. All I did was lie, to my own twin
brother. It was easy for me to explain Ariel's lies. Easy.

From my rooftop I heard the intercom buzzing. I returned to my
apartment and picked up the receiver. In matter-of-fact tones, Justin
Manfredy, the security officer, announced: "A young woman to see you,
Mr. Remler. She says you're expecting her."

I kept thinking, what if David's flight is cancelled. What if he surprises me. When Emily Bloom lived with me, my brother came over
all the time, of course without calling. Sometimes he'd walk straight
into the bedroom and catch us making love. "Emily, what's that big bear
doing on top of you," he'd ask. Emily would look up. They'd gaze at each
other. Violent paroxysms of giggling would follow. He had his own key.

When I opened the door, Ariel hastily stepped inside the doorway.

"I waited for you to call. I couldn't wait any longer." She smiled at
me. "Stop worrying. Even if David changes his plans and does show up,
he won't be able to open the door. I took his key." A split second later
Ariel asked if I had change for a fifty-dollar bill. I didn't but I had two
twenties. She grabbed the bills and pushed in front of me. "Give me five

minutes," she said, racing out the door. Ten minutes later she returned.

"What were the twenties for?" I inquired.

"Down the block there's a teenage couple. They're panhandling on the street. I wanted to give them the twenties. It made me feel a whole lot better," she said, smiling.

"Do you give out twenty dollar bills very often?" I asked.

"Whenever I can afford to," she said. "Besides, the way they were clasping hands reminded me of someone."

"Who?"

"I don't know. But what the heck. It will buy those kids a good dinner. That's what's important, isn't it?"

The ingenuous way Ariel Warning responded made me feel guilty for never having done the same.

She walked out onto the rooftop terrace. Faced the spot where Em's pinewood shed had been. I had filled the area with weeping willows, periwinkles, a wading pool and several dandelion-colored swings. Also a thirteen-and-a-half-foot Roman Arc hammock. I cherished it. It was a birthday gift from Emily. Pigeons camped in the sun on the arc, their droppings blemishing the hammock. Ariel started to lie down in the hammock, but I stopped her.

"Sex with your brother is decent, but whenever I suggest trying a new position he balks. He's inhibited," she said.

A large yellowjacket flew by. It darted from Ariel towards me. I took a swipe at it. Failed. Ariel quietly reached out and caught the buzzing bee in her hand. She cooed to it. "Don't be frightened." She tiptoed over to the edge of the guardrails, opened her palm. Her face turned serene, peaceful, as she watched the bee fly free.

Anton Bruckner's Symphony Number Four, "The Romantic," was playing on my stereo.

"Don't you listen to more modern stuff than that?" she asked when we stepped back inside.

I inserted Andrea Bocelli's "Romanza" into the compact disc player, along with several others, and stepped over to my wet bar. I never drink. Even club soda is unusual for me. But I was still a bit unnerved. I opened a bottle of a select Chardonnay. We sat down in my living room. Finished off several glasses. I wanted to bring up the lies, but I didn't want to change her mood. My first instinct was not to protect my twin.

"David keeps sex in a safe place. I say sex is a wild boar. Needs room to adventure." She paused. "I mean, strictly speaking, your brother may not be a Puritan, but he's hardly an Epicurean either."

Ariel dropped her eyes to look at me. She gave me a baleful smile. The cruel stain was there.

"I just know you're not like that," she said.

"How do you know so much about me?" I asked.

"You keep forgetting I've read all your books and David has told me all about your relationship with Bloom." She grinned. "He says each time you heard Bloom's voice on the telephone, it gave you an erection. Is that true?" Ariel took my hand, peering at me full in the face, as if she were taking measure of me. "I just know you're not like David. More the opposite, I suspect. You're daring, bold, brazen, like your gambling."

"I've stopped gambling," I said.

"You're lying," she said, smirking.

"What makes you say that?"

"Margot told me."

Ariel stood up and carefully placed her wine glass on the coffee table in front of the sofa. Kissing me lightly on the lips, she again took my hand, brushed my genitals.

"Think of me as a friend. An equal. Not a romantic ideal. But something much calmer. More pliant. More healing."

She kept up her soothing words as she guided me to the bedroom.

"Don't look like that," she said. "You're not a guinea pig and I just know you're going to be a fantastic lover."

As soon as we entered the bedroom, Ariel unzipped the very same chaste Laura Ashley dress she wore that night at the ballet, adroitly stepping out of it. She peeled off her panties.

"Think of it this way. As if David, you and I, our whole life we've been swimming against the current."

I protested. She interrupted.

"Don't you understand? It's not that I don't love your brother. I do. But a person can curl up with a good book on a rainy day for only so long. Then one wants to go skydiving, have a little fun. Knowing the two of you affords me that luxury." She walked over to the desk chair where I was sitting. She unbuttoned my shirt. "You have a tiny scar under your right nipple," she said. A strange expression appeared on her face. "Weird about identicals," she said. "There is always something that is different. As identical as they are, if you look hard enough you'll find it." She rubbed her breasts against my chest, then she moved closer and rubbed all of herself against me. Nothing covered her other than the wheat-colored patch between her legs. It was bristly and wet. "You know what?" she said, as casually as if we were innocent lovers. "My first time was with Bobby Cover. He lived in Bird City." I must have made some kind of expression. "I know what you're thinking. All you New Yorkers," she said, shaking her head, continuing to speak about Robert Cover. "It was the best summer I ever had. We were visiting family in Rawlins, down near Middle Beaver Creek. It's a part of Cheyenne, Kansas. Bobby, he'd come over to our place all the time." Ariel's expression changed. "Finally I got him to do it," she said, with a triumphant smirk on her face. She must have read something in my expression. "You're judging me," she laughed. "Stop judging me. I was all of fifteen when that happened. Besides, sex has its own truth. Don't you agree?" She began kissing my fingers. "I want you to understand why I'm doing this. It's not because I don't love your brother."

Even stripped naked, with nothing covering her but her wheat-colored patch, Ariel appeared as chaste as when I first saw her rushing towards me at Lincoln Center. A fresh-faced, youthful woman: lapis eyes, rosy complexioned, flowing yellow hair, perfect skin, buxom, lean, from some place near Middle Beaver Creek in the heartlands. Her visage seemed frozen in some kind of reverie as she again softly whispered her mother's epitaph: "One without the other." Gazing at me, she said, "I want to do it."

"We can't," I mumbled weakly.

Ariel started sucking my fingers. One at a time. Then kneeling down she slowly, deliberately, started unzipping my fly.

At the very core of my identity my twin brother. My unbreakable connection with the world: My twin brother. I had to say no. My identical was able to. Ever since we were children he could always say no. He was always responsible. Not only to me, but to everyone. He was considerate of others to the point of denying himself. I never was.

I stammered. "What about David?"

"I told you," Ariel said. "What I have with David is David's. I'm secure with him. He's predictable. And your brother's affectionate. He's always kissing me. I love that."

Ariel noticed a paperback on the night table next to my bed. She reached over and picked up the book. It was *Legends of the Game*, a basketball book I had written. This one slight sports book made more money than all my twin brother's literary novels combined. Was it any wonder David had turned to Hollywood? Was bitter?

Ariel thumbed through its pages, stopping to examine a profile on one of the game's great legends.

"My grandfather loved basketball," she said, pointing to a photograph of Wilt Chamberlain, the super-giant center who played his college ball at Kansas. "My grandfather insisted that this guy would have been a great player in any era."

Ariel laughed strangely.

"You're more like my grandfather than David is. I admired my grandfather, Adam. He was way ahead of his time. He lived each day to the fullest. At the end, when he didn't have much time left, he called me to his bedside. Don't feel sorry for me, he said. I might not have much longer to go, but I lived seven hundred years in my seventy plus."

Ariel's expression again changed. It radiated unyielding ferocity.

"I'm not that different from my grandfather," she said.

I felt myself giving into the same demons that I long ago exorcised and sated. I knew myself. The more I would explore, the more the explorer I would crave to be. Ariel was pushing buttons, awakening a part of me that had been sealed off and closed down for years. As in my compulsive gambling years I was susceptible to reaching for the infinite, the unreal, defying mortality. Crashing.

"I want to experience everything," she said, as if she needed to justify my silence. She reached up and adjusted the dimmer until the glow was barely perceptible. I stared at her enormous pale breasts. Both coronas starlit with a purple glow. She reached out to me, smiling and bountiful. Taking my hand she steered me to the bed.

"Be right back," she said.

Minutes later, as lithe and supple as an animal, she leaped onto my bed.

Would it have helped to protest? To say I would not be dominated like this? I'm certain I wasn't feeling the way I was out of cowardice. And morality in my way of thinking is growth and change. Aliveness is living with dread. I've lived my entire life with dread. But still, there are boundaries. David was my boundary.

"We can't," I said. "I can't."

Ariel sat up in bed. "Don't worry," she said, "I won't be judging you. Besides, first time is always the worst, you know." She extended her arms as if to take me in. I pushed her away. She returned to me. Again I pushed her away, this time more forcefully. Her eyes bore into mine.

"There are things I will do with you that I dare not do with David. And there are things your twin will give to me that you could never give. You see each of you will bring out a different part of me." She paused. "I know what you're thinking," she whispered softly. "Remember, I, too, was a twin. You're thinking that your twin is a part of you. That David is you. But that's wrong. You're wrong for sentimentalizing twinship just like you were wrong for romanticizing Bloom. There's another part of you. A healthier part. A stronger part. It's fighting inside of you for its own independence. Right now it's tearing you apart. But it really wants to crush, destroy and violate your identical. It wants you to take and possess your own autonomy."

Slowly I approached; I froze.

"Relax," she said. "I promise you David will never know." And then she added, almost as an afterthought, "Besides, I want to get it out of the way now. Before your twin and I marry. Before our committed life begins."

Near the very end with Emily Bloom I had the most intense sex I ever experienced. With Ariel Warning intense sex would only be the beginning.

Ariel was showering when David called from Los Angeles.

"You know, Adam, you were right. Maybe I am becoming more like you. The way you were with Emily. I'm gone less than twenty-four hours and I can't wait to see Ariel. I miss her that much." He paused. "You see it, don't you? How special she is?" My brother with all his brilliance is the most innocent man I know—when it comes to trusting people he loves, that is.

"Yeah. Special. Very special," I droned lifelessly.

"What's the matter? You sound dead?"

"I was up all night."

"With whom?" he snapped. It wasn't suspicion. It was possessiveness.

"I met someone at Joe Allen's," I said haltingly. "She's showering. I was just about to join her." I wasn't amazed by the self-loathing I felt. What amazed me was how facile I was at lying to him.

"I won't interrupt you," he laughed. "It's just that I tried phoning Ariel at her place. She's not answering. And she didn't call me last night. I'm a little worried."

"When are you returning?" I asked.

"I'll be flying back tonight. Keep tomorrow open. We have to talk about *Confessions*. According to Hollywood Pictures, your treatment needs a lot of work. They won't budge until we make changes. And, oh, I'm waiting for a call. We might have a deal for *Pledge*. Focus Features likes it."

"What's it mean?"

"It's a development deal. No guarantee it will ever get greenlighted."

"How much?"

"Enough to keep us going for three months, maybe six."

I cut David off.

"Let me get to the shower."

"Later," my identical said, clicking off.

Before Ariel Warning left I mentioned David had called. "I'll phone him as soon as I get home," she replied. "I love your brother. I wouldn't want him to worry about me." She said this simply, without guile. As the elevator door opened she peered into my eyes. "Program yourself," she said. "Keep telling yourself you're not your brother. You're you!"

"I discovered another lie," Margot announced.

"What is it?

"Robert Cover."

"Who?"

"The boy Ariel said she dated when she was fifteen. I telephoned Bird City, Kansas. Robert Cover is still living there. He wasn't very friendly. In fact, he just about hung up on me. But he did say he never heard of any Ariel Warning. I asked him about her parents. Uma Olsen. Christopher Warning. You name it. This guy said he didn't recall any of them."

"Well, one thing is for sure—unless, of course, there's another Bobby Cover living in Bird City, Kansas."

"What's that?" Margot inquired.

"Ariel certainly did know a Bobby Cover. As you said, people don't just come out of a vacuum."

"There isn't another Robert Cover. I checked. I'm thorough. Hey," Margot laughed. "It sounds to me like you're finally coming around."

Was it as Margot suspected? That Ariel Warning was leaking out bits and pieces, revelations, of some horrific deed from her past? Her way of confessing? Of being discovered? Of communicating something she did not have the courage to directly divulge? Or was it even more subterranean? Some buried truth in her subconscious? Was she expiating buried guilt? Guilt so horrific that it could only come to the surface in bits and pieces, like a monster iceberg beneath the murky gray sea moving on a collision course with some unsuspecting vessel. Were these buried bits and pieces, revelations, on a collision course with David and me?

"Can you fax me your list of revelations? Anything else you have that might be helpful. I want to do some checking."

"Darn it," Margot squealed. "Now that you're really interested, I won't be able to play with you."

"Why not?"

"Tomorrow morning I'm driving to my place in the Berkshires."

"How long will you be gone?"

"As long as it takes. I must get back to work on my book. I've messed up. There are just too many distractions in this city. Not only Kevin. Now Coleman's here."

"In the city?"

"Yes. Didn't I tell you? He's taken a teaching position at NYU. And you're a distraction. And so is Warning. What I have to do is get back the focus I need to write. I'll send you what I have before I leave. I'll even search my computer. I have loads of case histories on file. I'll fax you whatever I think is interesting."

Margot paused.

"Remember how, with Emily, in order for you to see daylight, you had to write *Confessions*. It was only then that you were able to see your relationship with her with any kind of lucidity. Here's something I suggest you do. Start writing down all your impressions of Ariel Warning. And, please, Adam, if you come up with something, let me know."

For three days I couldn't get myself to face my twin. And then, because I felt his suspicions would be aroused by another of my lame excuses, I consented to have dinner at Gulag, a chic downtown bar and grill which attracted a trendy crowd. At the bar, as we waited for Ariel to arrive, David asked, "How much have you done in reworking *Confessions*?"

I anticipated his query and had brought with me an impressive thirty-seven page treatment. "It's all here," I said, handing the treatment to him.

"We'll see what you have when I read it," he said, stuffing the sheets into his shoulder bag, kissing Ariel on the lips as she arrived.

She was wearing a loose-fitting yellow dress which covered her shapely thighs and sculpted legs. A stylish belt around her middle accented the trimness of her waist and large bosom. A sensuous woman with thick, golden hair, arms as graceful as a Bolshoi ballerina's, small hands and delicately tapered fingers as finely chiseled as Michelangelo's right hand on the Bruges Madonna. And her throaty voice, also a weapon at her disposal. As were her full lips, at times expressing petulance, just a hint, other times the inimical, a flicker of heat. And with it all a first-rate incisive mind fused with a singular obsessional purpose. Relentless. Was my twin brother Ariel Warning's match? Was I? Obviously not, but still, how could I be that weak?

"Adam, I haven't seen you in ages," she said gaily. Her youthful face as feckless as a cheerleader. "I guess the last time we saw each other was that night at the ballet. I've missed you."

I peered at her. How could she appear so guileless, speak so engagingly to her lover? Gaze so sinless into his eyes. And then peer with those very same limpid eyes an instant later at his brother, Cain to his Abel. Imperturbable. Could this shiny-faced woman from Cheyenne, Kansas, be that treacherous? Or was it, as she said, that she was actually in love with the two of us? Both David and I. Together and separately. As one.

David kissed Ariel's palm.

"We've decided to live together, Adam. But hopefully by the end of the year I can convince this untoward young lady to marry me." He gazed at Ariel. His trust as unconditional for her as for his twin.

"David," she said, pulling away from his kisses. "I'm not certain when we'll marry. I mean, I need some time." She kissed him softly on the lips. And then again a bit harder. "I told you," she continued, taking in both of us with her eyes. "Let's try to live together for a while on the weekends. Say six months. If you still feel you want me after six months…" She shifted slightly so that she faced me. "The problem is, David's been giving me a hard time about having a family. And the real problem is, and your brother doesn't even know it, that it's because he's a twin." She shifted again so that she faced both of us. "The world doesn't revolve around you two. It's a lesson most children learn. Twins seldom do." She sighed. "I know David will come around. I just have to keep working on him. I do want a family." She smiled at the both of us. "And another thing I want is a church wedding. Can you two blasphemers handle that? You know, it's never too late to open up. Learning about your roots from a place deep inside can help in the healing of your souls."

My twin mumbled some weak protests about his love being un-ending. That she shouldn't be insecure.

"David…" Ariel cajoled.

After dinner we escorted Ariel home. Ariel lived close enough to the heart of Greenwich Village to be able to sit on her front stoop and observe the latest designs in nihilistic haute couture.

Her flat was not much. "If I see one more roach crawl under the door, I'll cry." The toilet was in the hall. "$1,387.33 a month for the privilege of peeing in the hall." Outside her bedroom window was a fire escape. While there, my brother continued to bombard Ariel with his ardent conviction that they should marry at once. Ariel rolled her eyes at me. Then returned her gaze to David.

"Marriage is a giant step. Six months. Please…" she purred. It was the same "please" I had heard her purr during our night together.

When Ariel completed her marginal packing, she stood up and stretched. "Listen up. Let's go and have some pastry," she said. "Down the block there's a Norwegian place. It's not fancy but their pastry is fabulous and I love the wonderful watercolors of Norwegian children they have hanging on their walls." She fixed her eyes on my brother and smiled. "Aren't Norwegian children beautiful?" she said.

After the pastry I rushed home. "Let's dance," I said to my typewriter, crooking my back in front of the keys. If I didn't have the courage to confess to my brother, I could at least do penance at my Smith-Corona. As well as search for Ariel's mousetraps. For me the best way to think is to dance with those keys.

I started dancing.

Revelations, bits and pieces—people did leak out their confessions. I certainly did. Didn't I almost blurt out to David that I was sleeping with Ariel? The way I babbled on about the alleged woman in the shower. Kinky sex. Wasn't I trying to confess? People constantly give off mixed messages. How many of us have the courage to look in the mirror? Hold on to ideals? Take responsibility? Aren't divided? As we take our long journey, isn't it true that more and more of us lose ourselves along the way. Fall into the void. So many times I rationalized my own lies by telling myself that I trumped the truth in my writing, when in truth I'm vomiting from my unconscious. For me, purging is cathartic, not heroic. Exploring one's inner life is therapeutic, not courageous. At best it's a monologic releasing of my own inner poisons. My entire life I've done it. Lied in the real world. Been rewarded for ejaculating [a writer pushes his pen, not because of his skills, but because of an ache, a yearning; a writer writes because of what is missing, not only now, but from the very beginning; it's the empty places he needs to fill, and yet never does] honest intimacies in my fictive one. Words were tools. Writing a way of attending confession. One false/true way of atoning for my Fall. Forget the hurrahs an author may receive. Tomorrow remains tenuous and fickle. A new work, a strikeout, a losing bet, a resolution, can bring on the boos or—to carry the thought to its ultimate conclusion—your worst nightmare. Ariel Warning, I typed out. I started dancing.

It was the middle of the night, and though not well-focused, I felt I was on to something. I kept pounding keys, looking for connections. My mind kept flying. I urged myself to think of Ariel Warning as a character in a novel. In a novel the characters take on their own destinies. They grow, change, follow roads that were never akin to the author's original premise. Surprises and more surprises take place. Craft is essentially a crawling turtle, creation a soaring eagle, winging high. As I pounded digits my mind danced with a startling number of possibilities. Maniacal thoughts jumped in and out of my brain. And then all of a sudden I had the feeling I was getting somewhere. Ariel Warning's truth might be obscured by pain. Why pain? What brought that word to my fingers? Some pain is real. Other pain we inflict on ourselves. I was writing furiously, thinking at the same pace I typed. And then out of nowhere my fingers typed WHAT HAVE I DONE TO DAVID? I stared at the line. I could feel the pain. David's pain. What was inside my heart? My twin's heart I knew. David worried about me all the time. He didn't leave his studio without first calling me. If I left my place without first checking in with him—"Where the hell did you go? Why didn't you call me?"

I needed a respite. I stood up and walked away from the machine. I stood in front of a life-size oil painting of my father, a cantor in an orthodox shul, stepping to the pulpit in a white robe and high hat, tuning fork cupped in his left hand. He used the small steel instrument as a guide to tone his pitch. At that moment I could see my father strike the two prongs of the tuning fork to sound a certain fixed tone, begin to sing, more of a plaintive wail, his praises to the Almighty. And as I continued envisioning my father I could see his Talmudic eyes searching for David and me in the filled rows of seats, spotting us and signaling: Keep your eyes in the prayer book. Pray! Pray!

After a while I calmed down and returned to my Smith-Corona. I forced myself to concentrate on Ariel. Escape with Ariel. And I did conjoin for a page or two, but then David once again infiltrated the page: I betrayed my twin! Terror enveloped me. I felt nauseous. Think! Think about Ariel, I screamed. What is missing in Ariel's heart? What happened to her? What experience did she encounter that caused her to be the way she is? I pounded the keys. Think between the lines. Don't lose her now. What is she trying to communicate? Confess? What does she feel? What is at her center? What is she hiding? Is it something she can't forget? Forgive? Something buried that can't come out? Or is it

Margot Korman and myself that are the crazy ones? Two paranoid New Yorkers made suspicious by supposition and innuendo? No, that's not it. We've discovered too much. What is it Ariel Warning is trying to confess? Think! Think! Confess…Confession…Religion…Something like praying…Is she asking to be forgiven? I kept returning to this idea: Is it something she did? Something she condemns herself for doing? Something similar to betrayal?

Once again I felt terror. I had betrayed David. How could I have done that? Back to Ariel Warning. I screamed Think! She was a twin. Crib death. Guilt…Roberta…Roots…Us…Think between the lines, I muttered. And then the words came, as if they had typed themselves: Does Emily Bloom's story connect in some way to Ariel's? There are similarities. Look for the attachments. Take a step back. Listen to David. See the other with distance. Similarities. Dissimilarities. They're always conjoined. Life is round. Made up of everything. Faith and Reason. Self and World. Comedy. Tragedy. A paradox. Emily might be spiritual. Off the wall spiritual: "…*Douglas, for me, the path to enlightenment is by traveling through India. And when I make my journey to India, my greatest hope is to have my son blessed by a Sri Baba…*"

What if Ariel Warning were the antithesis of Emily? What if to her, us—David and I—twins!—were her roots? Everything? What if Ariel lost her faith. Her us. Not to crib death but to…Think. Think! Just don't write the book. Surrender yourself to it. As you did with *Confessions*. Infinite possibilities exist. It's a long voyage. Where has Ariel been? What happened along the way? What are the unknown factors? What is at her core? Is Ariel like Emily Bloom—but just because of that, the opposite? Was she also terribly damaged from the very beginning? Does it all go back to the very beginning? She lost her us…Focus in…to write a novel you need concentration. Stamina. Don't give in to your exhaustion now.

I'd been at the machine for several hours, was bleary-eyed. It was approaching dawn. I couldn't think straight any longer. Think about

Ariel. Don't be distracted by the need for sleep. I focused on the characters of my banged-up Smith-Corona. The out-of-fashion machine was my anchor. When Emily Bloom left, in the middle of the night, it was all I had.

My mind kept whirling about. Going back and forth. Swinging from David to Ariel, from Ariel back to my identical. As I danced I realized the day of reckoning for David and me was inevitable. It would take no more than a look. One look. Twins, like passionate lovers, exude a chemistry all their own. That's all it would take, I told myself. One look. I felt a chill. Did David and I still have chemistry? A perfect conjoined mesh? Were we still Siamese, like Eng and Chang? Perhaps my identical already knew? Ariel might have confessed. I forced myself to think about Ariel Warning, to stay in focus.

After my spell at the typewriter had run its course, I urinated. Showered. Shaved. Combed my hair. Gulped down half a quart of pineapple juice. A stale croissant. Slowly returned to the real. With my fictive imagination dissolving, I became more and more convinced that a connection existed between Ariel Warning's leaked-out revelations and some deeply buried truth. I was also convinced that I was without a clue as to what to do concerning Ariel and David. Would I have the courage to confess to my twin? Would I continue to see Ariel? I didn't have a clue. But getting away from my own self-loathing, being the bad twin, was necessary for a time. I needed to escape. Put my real life out of my mind. It was easier to think about David and myself tomorrow and to continue my investigation of Ariel Warning today.

I remembered something Ariel had said: I identify with your writing much more than I do with David's. When she said it, she was specifically referring to *Confessions.* The first thing I did was thumb through *Confessions.* Somewhere in the weighty draft, on one of those 350 plus pages, I had written something to do with twins. Shuffling pages, I came upon: "*Adam, in a sense your father gave his whole life to God, singing of his love in his own beautiful, melodious voice. Yet he was blind to his family. It's such a shame for David and you because, as a consequence, he turned you off God." Soon we were discussing Emily returning to school to earn a high school equivalency diploma; going to college; designing jewelry for my Uncle Leo. Soon we were splashing around in the virgin snow on my rooftop terrace. Kissing each other's chapped faces warm, washing them clean with the crunchy cold flakes, laughing a great deal; soon we went inside and in front of the wood-burning fireplace made ardent, sweet love.*

I quickly turned to the final chapter in the book. Six pages from the end, there it was. What I had been searching for.

Emily was as much a part of me as my identical twin. She, like my identical, reminded me of myself all the time. The part that could betray David.

Ariel Warning had betrayed her twin!

I raced to the typewriter. Pounded it out—Ariel betrayed her twin! It wasn't crib death. It was something else. "Listen up"? Gabriela Rolon's firing had been satisfactorily explained. That particular made sense. How many more mysteries, dark secrets, revelations were there to uncover? Ariel Warning was beyond my romantic feelings now, my need, my lust. Not that that still wasn't there—I knew a large chunk of me was still needy. That I could still be triggered by her presence. By her "bloom of youth," as Margot had called it. But for now I was safe in my apartment. I was able to focus.

I tried to imagine something even more insidious. More horrific. Something Ariel did to betray her twin. That morning I began to scrupulously investigate Ariel Warning's childhood.

I dialed Information. Asked for the area code of Bird City. The one thing I was certain of was that in the state of Kansas, its citizens took their basketball seriously. I dialed the number.

"Mr. Cover? Robert Cover?"

"That's me."

"I'm doing a book on Kansas U. basketball," I began, groping to establish a starting point for communication.

"Who is this?" Robert Cover asked.

"I'm Adam Remler. I wrote *Legends of the Game*. Did you ever read it?"

"No sir, can't say I did. But I sure follow Jayhawk basketball." Bingo, I thought. "I have a friend whose uncle played for Ted Owens. He played right alongside of Budd Stallworth."

"You mean the club that Stallworth and Norm Cook spearheaded?"

"Yes, sir. That's correct."

"Bobby, speaking about the Jayhawks. You know how far back I go. All the way to guys like Wayne Hightower and Jo Jo White. Why, in *Legends*, I even did a profile on Clyde Lovelette." Cover started to say something. "Tell me, Bobby," I said, cutting him off. "Down in Rawlins, near Middle Creek, was there anyone you know who might have followed Shakespeare the way we follow our baskets?" I held my breath.

"Sure was. A school teacher. She used to teach here in Bird City. In fact, it was because of her encouragement that my father became an English teacher. He grew to love the Bard, he said, 'cause of that lady."

"What was her name?"

"Don't know her first name. Her surname was Miranda."

"She still live in Bird City?"

"Nope. There was a death in the family. Some kind of tragedy. She moved away."

"When?"

"Let's see. I'm gonna be thirty. Must be a couple of years in back or in front of the time I was born."

"About the death in the family. Know any of the details?"

"I recall my father used to get real upset 'cause people 'round these parts did do some talkin'. You know how people are. They used to do a lot of whisperin' about a homicide."

"Did your father ever tell you where this woman went to live?"

"Nope."

"Can I talk to your father?"

"Nope. He, along with my brother, Lehman, and my mom passed in a fire."

"One more question. Did you ever know an Ariel Warning?"

"Nope. Say, why are you askin' all these questions for, anyways?"

"Bobby, I'm trying to locate this school teacher. You've been real helpful. You know what I'd like to do? Mail you my book. *Legends.*"

"If you do, make sure to autograph it."

I walked over to David's. On the way I mailed *Legends* to Robert Cover. I felt I owed him that much. Once at my twin's I searched his bookshelves. It was inside Toni Morrison's *Beloved* that I found an extra set of keys. Sure enough, one key was tagged A.A. I knew my identical. I was confident the initials stood for Ariel's Apartment.

I quickly dialed the Academy of Medicine. I wanted to make certain of two things: 1) that Ariel was at the library, and 2) if she was there, how long she'd be staying. I said it was an emergency. Was connected with the library. A young male picked up.

"Is there an Ariel Warning in the library?"

"What does she look like?"

I described her.

"You didn't do your girlfriend justice. Hold on. I'll get her for you."

Once he handed the phone over, I asked, "Can we meet for lunch?"

"Sorry, Adam, thanks to Margot, I'm bogged down researching for the remainder of the day. Margot has all her facts mixed up. I just found out that conjoined twins occur once in 50,000 births. Not one in 100,000 as she insisted. Another fact she was wrong on is that not eight, but only six percent of conjoined twins are of the Ischiopagus type."

"Did you hear from David?" I asked.

"Marcia Majors is in town. He's having lunch with her. He's trying to get her interested in *Confessions*. Say, aren't you supposed to be working on the treatment?"

"I can't get my head into the way David sees E.," I answered.

"You better. David says each day you procrastinate, it's costing him credibility with Hollywood Pictures." Ariel paused. "David wants a really tight treatment. And after that, a first-rate screenplay. The last treatment you did wasn't close to what he wanted." Ariel continued talking about what my brother wanted. I asked her to throw out some ideas. "Here's one. Maybe you should change Bloom from an artsy craftsy spiritualist who reads the I Ching, Bhagavad Gita and helps the homeless, to a successful career woman. She can continue to help people. Maybe you can make her a CSW. Remember David's friend Nancy Lee? She's a CSW. She offers the same TLC. Of course, Nancy went into the private sector and is getting paid a lot of money for it. Nothing wrong with that. What I'm trying to tell you is David definitely does not want Bloom to remain a healer. Turn her around. By your doing this, your relationships become more credible, the help she offers comes out of her, not out of some psychic hocus pocus. The way you have her now, she sounds possessed. Give her some inner freedom. Always remember, David does not want Bloom to help people compulsively. He wants her to be helping people because it's the correct thing to do. She isn't a mystic or Mother Teresa. She's just a decent person. See her clearly, Adam. You just don't. If you wan't, I can give you more notes in the morning."

"Ariel, you mentioned you spoke to David. Where is he?"

"I telephoned him at Per Se. The reason it's Per Se is Majors is picking up the bill. Adam, you really sound weird. What's wrong?" I remained silent. "Listen up! I'm glad you called. It took me a while, but I can see what you're saying. You're horny. Maybe I can see you tomorrow. I'm horny, too."

☙❧

I taxied down to Sullivan Street. I wasn't concerned about breaking and entering. If I bumped into one of Ariel Warning's neighbors, they'd assume I was my twin. On the way down I kept thinking of the schoolteacher in Bird City who loved Shakespeare. Her last name was Miranda. As the cab sped down Seventh Avenue, passing Flash Dancers and several other topless bars, Gabriela Rolon flashed into my mind. I forced myself to concentrate on the Bard. What connection did *The Tempest* have in all of this? The schoolteacher Miranda. Prospero host to shipwrecked malefactors. Ariel called the surgeon, Dr. Brent, "malefactor." These things had to mean something. But what? The more I tried linking them, the more it seemed that none of it made sense. Rather than break into Ariel's apartment, I felt I should return home. Get to my Smith-Corona. Start dancing. Maybe then I would be able to sort things out.

"This the building you're lookin' for, Mister?"

I looked out the cab's grimy window.

"I think so," I answered.

Anxious, I rushed up the stoop of the Greenwich Village tenement, feeling relieved that no one was around. I hiked up the squeaking stairs. By the time I reached the top floor I was more than a bit winded. I fumbled with David's Medeco key before it turned in the lock. The plate needed oiling. When I entered the flat the hall closet was ajar. As I opened the door wide, a periwinkle pullover sweater tumbled onto the floor. I examined it. The knit sweater was handmade. I went through the pockets of several pair of jeans. Jammed into many of them were Snickers bar wrappers—Ariel loved them. In one pocket I found a crumbled piece of scrap paper; upon flattening it, I saw a sketch of con-joined twin girls. Written on the scrap—which one lives? Which one dies? A dozen question marks followed. In another blue-jean pocket a tube of lipstick, more Snickers wrappers, three freshly minted one-dollar bills, several shiny pennies. Nothing.

I looked around the room. Slowly approached Ariel's escritoire. The polished wood was jasmine, as soft as rubber. I leaned my hands against the pliant wood, examining the papers on top of the secretary. A batch of bills. Nothing! Gazed at a floor-to-ceiling bookcase, painted blond, in the corner. Walked over: skimmed a dozen or more books. Shakespeare's *Hamlet*, bound in red morocco, was one of them. Is Margot wrong? Is Hamlet the key? I made a mental note to reread the drama. My novel, *Confessions*, was also there. I leafed through the book. Ariel, like David, had the habit of scribbling footnotes in the margins of her books. Underlining significant passages. The following paragraph she had underlined in its entirety:

"…Adam, I've known since I was a little girl in Marathon that there was something wrong with me."

"Em," I said very gently. "Dyslexic children are many times of even higher intelligence than regular children. Many of them excel. With work you can overcome this problem. The first thing, though, is for us to get you a medical screening so that we can determine what kind of learning disability we're going to war against."

"I love you, Adam," Emily said, her face glowing.

I wondered why Ariel had chosen that particular paragraph to underline. The one thing I could think of: It was the first time Em said she loved me. I made another mental note to study these pages when I got home. Use them. I felt they would make good source material for the revised treatment I was writing for my brother.

I turned to the chapter I had frantically sought on Emily. Ariel had scribbled in one of the page margins, *THAT'S ME!*

The telephone started ringing. After two rings Ariel's answering machine picked up. The message was from one of the Parker twins. "Miss Warning, this is Albert Parker. I'm reading your boyfriend's novel. What's this mean? 'Kafka lived in his dream world and saw it as real. We live in the real world and see it as a dream.'"

There were messages from David. One was garbled. I had to re-play it over and over. "You must understand, Ariel. Human behavior is as much defined by self-contradiction as by reason and logic. I accept Adam with all his flaws. I was crazy when Thea died. It was Adam who got me through it. Ariel, if I don't believe in Adam, I don't believe in anything."

Did David know? Did Ariel confess? No. That was impossible. My identical would have confronted me. I was totally convinced of that when I realized that particular message had been left weeks before Ariel and I had slept together. I replayed the entire tape. "Let me ex-plain, Ariel. I was always shy. If I liked someone things only escalated. With Thea, I knew the first time I saw her how I felt. As far back as my freshman year in college. We were in the same psychology class. I would ogle Thea for the entire hour. Then, when I found out she was a regular at the dance lounge, I would go there. Weeks turned to months and I continued to ogle. Thea was a fabulous dancer and I would watch her dance with many other students. One in particular, a fellow who looked like an Indian prince, Kent Drake, was as good a dancer as she was. They would dance together all the time. Never me. It was as if I was nailed to my chair. It wasn't writer's block, it was lover's block I suffered from. I wasn't like that with other women. Just Thea." There was a long pause. "And then, when we were getting ready to graduate, I heard Thea was engaged. Two days later I marched up to her. 'You know, since I was a freshman I've had a giant crush on you.' 'Why is it you never said boo to me? I always liked you, too.' One year later we were married." Another message: "My brother's treatment sucks. I don't want his sentimental effusions on Bloom. I want him to cut all this Virgin Mary crap. He must see her clearly. Get real!" Nothing suspicious. One more message. "Ariel, since Adam's insisting, I decided to take my uncle's Rolex. You know me, I'll just stick it in a desk drawer. The only time I'd put on something that tacky is for a special occasion. Like if you decided to marry me. Want to go over to my uncle's and pick up the watch?" And then another. "David, do you mind if I ask you something? What is it? You and Adam quarrel all the time. I know whatever it is you both move on real quick. But, Adam mentioned more than once that when it comes to E. and his handicapping you two are miles apart. He also said something about a suitcase…When it comes to E., Ariel, I think I made myself quite clear. Adam's still idealizing her. As for his making money by handicapping. He might think he's a big shot and successful. But as I've told you repeatedly, to me it's garbage money. As far as the suitcase. He did bring a trunk full of Franklins over to my apartment when he retired from his so-called profession. I flung the suitcase against the wall. I didn't want that kind of money. To me, it's sickening that a brother of mine thinks it's cool to make money by gambling, involve himself with Dese, Dem and Dose guys. Sleazy women. Not paying taxes."

I walked back to the blond bookcase. Went through more books. One book on the Siamese twins, Eng and Chang. This was an autobiography my mother had recommended to David and me when we were in junior high. The one thing that stayed in my mind—when Chang died, Eng was seized with such convulsions of fright that he was dead within two hours, although his health had previously been fine. The College of Physicians in Philadelphia performed autopsies. Chang had died from a cerebral clot, but they found nothing wrong with Eng.

I walked into the galley kitchen. Six ears of white corn in an earthenware bowl along with a Gulag menu were on top of the sink counter. A roach crawled from under the mini-fridge. I squashed it. Several more. Pinned onto the fridge with alphabet magnets were several photographs of imposing racehorses, along with a couple of take-out menus from neighborhood restaurants. Nothing. On top of the mini-fridge was a bell jar along with one of my identical's books: *The Widower*. I pulled the book from the shelf. Flipped some pages. Read:

> That night as Adam and I sit by her bedside our treasured loving mom quavers in a frightened voice, "I never felt this weak." My brother and I stay over. Adam massages Mom's ice-cold feet. The cantor prays and weeps. At 3:07 AM Mom grasps our hands, Adam's and mine, and with an imploring look on her formerly sweet not yet defeated face asserts, "Remember boys, don't listen to your father. You go to college to learn, not to learn how to make a living." And then at 3:16 AM she whispers, "Be nice to your father." She smiles. "One thing you two boys never had to learn is how to love each other." She smiles again. At 3:18 AM Mom passes.

I stopped reading. Listened. Footsteps were coming from down the hall. I stepped inside the closet. Waited. It turned out to be a neighbor going to the communal toilet. I walked through the narrow corridors of the railroad flat. Rosemalings—the Norwegian art form. I counted at least four on the walls. I remembered that Ariel had mentioned that her mother, Uma Olsen, was a painter. Loved Rosemaling. Were these paintings collected by Uma Olsen? Painted by her? Ariel's inheritance? I stepped into the bedroom. Another splendid Rosemaling. Even more exquisite were three watercolors above her bed. One was titled "Norwegian Pine," its subject fish-eating diving birds that looked like ducks with pointed bills. Later, when I thumbed through my Audubon monograph, I discovered that they were loons, and that some people called these marvelous birds The Great Northern Diver.

Another watercolor was of a tall, wiry woman dressed in a white frock with a high collar. She was wearing a pendant that looked like an heirloom, and a wide-brimmed hat. Its brim was decorated with a nosegay of yellow orchids shaped like a lady's slipper. This artist's initial identified it. "U." I assumed it must be Uma Olsen.

The third watercolor was of flowers that looked like the same kind of pink and yellow orchids I had just seen bunched on the brim of the hat of the lanky woman in the white dress. The title of this painting was "Moccasin Flower."

I looked around the bedroom. A CD was on Ariel's bed. Richard Rodgers, *March of the Siamese Children*. Easily explainable. Ariel was contemplating *Siamese Children* as the movie score for her screenplay once it was greenlighted. Nothing! On an end-table, on printer paper, were dozens of case history summaries on multiple congenital abnormalities in conjoined twins. Also, buried underneath the printer paper, a copy of Ariel's screenplay in progress. She wasn't lying about preferring to write in longhand. I recalled what she had said when we first met: "I like writing in longhand. It feels more sensuous." On a second end-table was a Royal typewriter, circa 1961. On top of the Royal was a small photograph lying face down in gilded frame. I picked up the photograph. It was of Ariel in a graduation gown. The words "Happy Graduation G.G." were written at the bottom of the photograph. G.G.… What did the G's stand for? The best I could come up with was David's affectionate cognomen—Golden Girl.

I continued studying the photograph. It seemed to me as if she was receiving some kind of advanced degree. In the picture the people huddled around her appeared somewhat older than students graduating college. More mature, like graduate students. Ariel looked seventeen.

Another call came in. The answering machine picked up.

"Ariel, are you there? It's Bart Parker. Pick up! I just wanted to tell you last night I got real lucky, twice. Me and Albert went downtown. We began the evening by having dinner at the restaurant you recommended. After that we walked around the Village and ended up in one of those antique junk stores. I found an old 78 of Albert De Costa, Dio Mi Potevi. That's from Otello. I also found a 78 of Gioivani Martinelli-Celeste Aida. It was in the junk store I met this woman, Pia. She went home with Albert and me. I played my entire collection of 78s for her. Tenors are Pia's passion. Kurt Baum. Giamcomo Lauri Volpi. Giacinto Prandelli. Bruno Landi. She likes to make love while listening to the arias. Ariel, you gotta meet Pia. And thanks. It's because of you. You know. You're the one who told me not to lose hope."

I continued searching. In the far corner of the bedroom, next to a tiny window, which provided the only natural light for the entire flat, was a butcher block table. On it another script of hers, this one with handwritten entries on the conjoined twin's project. I read some of it. Each time she mentioned the conjoined twins she used symbols. Hearts, happy faces, things like that. Strange, I thought. Alongside the script was her computer. I wasn't sure how to rev it up, what keys to press. Should I call Margot? Ask her? I mused to myself. Then I remembered that I still hadn't received the information Margot had promised to fax me before leaving for the Berkshires. The list of revelations and the rest of the material. I decided to phone her in West Stockbridge. I didn't want to use Ariel's phone. Besides, it was a good excuse to escape the apartment. All the time I was there I felt as I did when I was gambling case money—or without any money at all to bet. Money I knew when I lost I'd eventually have to beg, borrow or steal to pay off. Whenever you need to win you lose. Count on it.

I telephoned Margot. Before I could get a word out, Margot burst forth:

"It all happened so fast. I was on a tight schedule. I had to catch a Greyhound. But before I left my house I did take inventory. Some of my discs are gone and there's nothing in the computer. I lost my entire database."

"Margot, your apartment was burglarized? And you didn't even call me? How come?"

"Adam, please calm down. I just can't afford to think about it. If

I start to worry about this, I won't have any energy left for my book. When I return to the city we'll talk." I shouted something about her being the nuttiest woman I knew. "Stop upsetting yourself. I wasn't hurt. So what if Ariel pilfered a few discs. It's nothing terrible. I was only playing word games. Having fun. As for my database, I told you, I had my manuscript typed. I can manage."

Margot had said it was Ariel who purloined her discs. Was she assuming? "What makes you so sure it was Ariel? How did she know we were investigating her, anyway?"

"I'm not sure. How can I be? Maybe it wasn't her."

"What about her lies?" I yelled.

"We caught her in a few fibs. Shakespeare and a few fibs." I continued to badger Margot. "Adam, the Bard, Sonnet 44, 'For nimble thought can jump both land and sea.' The Ariel I concocted does not exist. Think about it. What we were looking for was no more than a spirit we hoped would fit neatly into our game. The real Ariel Warning's impossible to concretely connect to our game." Margot exhaled. "Actually, all I was doing was inventing clues. The truth is I was leading you on. No different than a woman does who crosses and uncrosses her legs several times, and then tells you I don't wear stockings. You yourself said you didn't discover anything suspicious."

"Maybe I was wrong. What about those handwritten entries in her script. The symbols. Hearts, flowers, clowns, happy faces. That's strange, isn't it?"

"If it will make you feel any better, I'll speak to my shrink about that. Dr. Porder is an expert on handwriting. But take my advice. Just go home and get some sleep. You'll feel better."

I returned to the flat and headed to where the laptop computer was. Thanks to Margot's instructions I punched the correct keys. Nothing turned up that was of much use. I kept searching, trying all sorts of combinations. As many revealing words as I could remember.

The screen blinked. And then, flashing across the screen: THE MIND OF GUILT IS FULL OF SCORPIONS!

"A neighbor told me she saw David on the street, but I knew it was you," Ariel said, stepping out of the jammed hall closet, walking menacingly toward me. "Your ring left scars. It scratched my jasmine secretary."

As Ariel approached she continued, "When I came upstairs I looked out my window and there you were on your iPhone and heading straight here. Why did you sneak into my place?"

I burst out with the first thing that came to my mind.

"I want you to stay away from my brother. I don't care what you tell him. Just break it off."

"Why?" she asked defiantly.

"Lies!"

"What lies?" she said. "I've never lied to you."

I recalled my Uncle Leo's philosophy: If you do not admit to a lie you always leave doubt.

"You cost Gabriela Rolon her job. You broke into Margot's apartment. Stole her discs. It first dawned on me—a picture of Em was missing—you stole a photograph of Emily from me."

"I told you I detest that name," she said, grimacing, demonstrating a loss of composure for the first time. She moved closer to me. "Adam," she said. "Let's stop fighting. I told you I need you as much as I need David."

"There are other things," I said, about to bring up Robert Cover, Bird City. That he never heard of anyone by the name of Ariel Warning. I stopped myself, not wanting to reveal the extent of my snooping. "What about Margot's discs?" I stammered.

"I swiped the discs," Ariel admitted simply. "I also destroyed her database. All that took was for me to punch a few keys. As for getting into her apartment, you're the one who told me that she kept a spare key in her potpourri bowl. I had a right to," she then added, her voice rising.

"Margot's the crazy one. I discovered what she's been up to. And don't think it was your twin who told me. He's innocent. He doesn't know a thing about this."

"Then how did you know?"

"You told me that, too," Ariel explained. "For some reason, a few weeks ago—probably an oversight—you were talking to Margot on David's speakerphone. I didn't eavesdrop. I'm not a snoop. I was in the corridor. The door was half-open. I couldn't help overhearing the two of you."

Tentative, she placed her hands on my chest. "Let's not fight anymore," she said softly, slowly sliding her hands down my chest.

"Don't!" I said, pushing her hands away.

Her expression instantly changed. "Listen up," she said, taking a deep breath to calm herself. "Your brother's the kindest man I know. I love him. But as I've told you, I also need you to be happy."

I couldn't believe I wanted to make love to her, but I did.

Ariel reached out for my hand. Kissed my palm. I studied her face and form. She looked incredible. Dressed in black leather; jacket, shirt, string tie, pants, boots. Her yellow hair tied back in a tangle only enhanced her sensuality. It was as if she were dressed for a fantasy. My fantasy. My attraction was greater than ever. As she gazed up at me I went full circle, from denial to craving. A rapid pilgrimage to lust. My resolve disappeared like melted snow. Only not that pretty. It was as if I were—which I was—a gambler praying: Just let me win this one bet. After that I will quit. Just this one, God…I swear!

For a lingering moment I tried holding onto the feeble entreaties buzzing around in my head. I mumbled something incoherent about consent.

"Consent? Consent from whom?" she intoned loudly. "Consent doesn't matter."

My brain rebelled. It does matter, it said. David does matter. Both of us remained silent.

The body does not lie. I followed Ariel Warning as she headed to the bedroom. She took my hand. "You're kinky," she said. "You love taking photos of nude women. And David told me with Gabriela Rolon you were into ménage a trios. Now in my opinion that's a little too much, but I'm not like that brother of yours. He's plain old-fashioned," she said, with a hint of irritation in her voice.

"I thought that was what turned you on. Us being opposites."

"It does," she said. "But sometimes it just irks me that I can't find more of you in him."

"Maybe if you look you'll find more of David in me," I retorted.

Ariel pondered my comment. "You're correct," she said, stretching her arms to the ceiling while gazing fondly at me. "That's why I love David." Placing her arms around my shoulders, she hummed content-edly. "That's what's so great. Having the both of you affords me the luxury of having it all."

Ariel hopped out of bed. "I really have been considering marrying your identical," she said.

"What about me? Where do I fit into these domestic plans?"

"You don't," she answered. "What we share together has nothing to do with hearth and home. To share with you anything more than wonderful lovemaking would not only spoil what we have, it would endanger David. And David is the one person who must be protected at all costs. Of the three of us, he is the one both of us need the most."

The telephone rang. Ariel picked up on the first ring.

A split second later she covered the mouthpiece. "It's David." I could barely make out my twin's voice. Then I saw Ariel flinch. I leaned closer. Listened harder.

"I'm worried about Adam. Something's bothering him. I can always tell. It's either Bloom or he's gambling again. Gambling more heavily than I think. I know he lies to me. He's always lied to me. But that's my brother." David hesitated. "Don't mention this to Adam, Ariel. I don't want to place any extra pressure on him. It's hard enough to write without thinking you have to, but I need *Confessions*. Remember, not a word to Adam. You tell him I have financial problems and the first thing he'll do is really start gambling again. Anyway, it's my problem, not yours. I'll work something out."

I left Ariel's flat, and as I reached the street I telephoned Emily Bloom. I didn't know where the conversation would lead, but I did know I desperately needed to talk to someone I could trust.

"That's horrible," Emily exclaimed. And the next thing I heard was Emily sobbing. "Your brother loves you. How could you?" When Em composed herself, she said, "Tomorrow morning, if you need me to, I can come uptown. I'll bring the baby with me. We can have lunch together and talk. But…please don't drain me by going into our past. I'm exhausted and I have to keep my strength up. Promise me you won't start going crazy with how much I mean to you. How much you need me." I promised. But minutes later, even before we had finished talking, I told Em not to visit. I knew myself. The moment I saw her I'd break down and babble on and on about how much I needed her.

The following morning I visited David. He was on the phone with Ariel. When they finished talking he remained silent. My brother, unlike me, thought before he spoke. If anything, his problem was he thought too much. All at once his face looked troubled. "What's the matter?" I sputtered.

"It's strange," he said, "but sometimes Ariel makes me feel like an interloper. As if I were intruding on her and her lover. I know it isn't true, but that's the feeling I get."

I drew a deep breath. "Ariel's not exactly your everyday woman," I said, this one time making every effort to choose my words carefully.

"I know," he answered. "She's so unpredictable. But the volatility is what makes her so enlivening. I never know what she's going to do or think next."

"She's dangerous," I said. The words leapt out of me despite myself.

"Yes, she is," David said, attempting to defuse my comment by making reference to Jean Genet's *Saints and Sinners.*

"This isn't literature. She might disappoint you."

David breathed deeply. "I know Ariel told you about her twin sister's crib death. I know that's why you've been behaving so weird. The ramifications. But I think I'm as capable as anyone could be of understanding the dynamics of her childhood. How much pain she must have suffered because of it. I also think I'm capable of giving her the space and the freedom she needs. So you see, when all is said and done, I think I'm the right person for her." A phone call came in. It was Marcia Majors about *Confessions.* When David continued, his eyes bored into mine. "You know better than anyone. I have so much inside me that I haven't communicated. So much learning and buried feeling. I think Ariel recognizes that and wants to share it."

And love, too, I wanted to say.

"Enough talking," David said. "Go home. Get to work on *Confessions.* Right now it's the most viable project we have. And please, for the zillionth time, listen to me. Study my notes and go over my tapes and stay with the prologue and Part Three. If you just do those four things you'll prepare a decent treatment and pull out a good screenplay. Now go home. Get to work."

A strong-faced homeless man squatting at the entrance to my building shouted to me, "Hey you! Whatever happened to your girlfriend? Tell her I miss her hot soup." His gangrened feet were covered by strips of filthy cloth. "Tell her I also miss her clean bandages."

I returned to my apartment. Not only to listen to David's tapes and read *Confessions* because of what he had said, but also, in the back of my mind, because I thought maybe I'd find some insight into the flaws in my own character. Through my life with Emily Bloom I would find parallels to my relationship with Ariel Warning. The first thing I did was to read the Prologue.

One night at a local brasserie I had been sitting with my twin brother and another writer, Margot Korman. Actually Margot is much more than that. She's just about my best friend. Suddenly Margot pointed to the bar.

"Look over there. They're letting the homeless in."

David looked over. "A street person."

Alone at the bar was a sad-faced, emaciated young woman in a drab olive dress shaped like a knapsack. The dress draped her like a folded umbrella collapsed over a maypole. She looked like a holocaust victim. Maybe ninety pounds. Scrawny. I mean a rail; dark rings under her languid eyes, stigmata that turned her skin pasty as chalk; hair stringy and choppy. I walked over, asked about the bracelet she was wearing. It had a tiny red AIDS ribbon on it. "I won't take it off till the battle is won," she said. Within minutes Emily Bloom was wiping tears from her eyes, sobbing to me.

"I can't do it."

"What can't you do?" I asked.

"I'm a waitress. I was laid off. My boss told me to take over the cash register. I'm not good at adding and subtracting. I'm much better at waitressing."

I remember the way Emily Bloom said "much better" sounded feisty. I liked that. I invited Emily to join the three of us for dinner. Margot and David soon decided to join other friends. When we were by ourselves Emily and I continued talking, for hours.

"All indications were I was between four and six weeks old when my parents spotted me. The day was July 4th, so I figured July 4th was the right birthday for me. You know, Independence Day. How many kids get a chance to choose their own birthday?"

Emily had been abandoned soon after birth. The authorities told Victor and Claire Bloom that the Canadian territory where they had found Emily between Lake Superior and Kirkland Lake was notorious for drug trafficking. She was probably birthed by a drug person who just kept going, they said. Addicted to heroin. The Blooms, who lived in nearby Marathon, decided to adopt her anyway. "After my father died, my mother began drinking, had affairs, and then she met a man who moved us from Canada to New York City, but he started abusing me." I hesitated, not feeling I should inquire. "He didn't demand I touch him, Adam, he just rubbed himself against my body until he had an orgasm," Emily said, her voice a matter-of-fact, lifeless drone. "I took it for a long time, but I had a plan. I saved up my allowance and at fourteen I ran off. I hung out on the streets for a long while, worked a few odd jobs, but was always let go, and then I drifted over to Central Park. That's where Tommy Signorelle found me. In the park. It was one in the morning and I was under a Gingko tree cryin'. All I had was my blue bag," she said, pointing to her duffel bag. "We've been like married ever since."

Emily and I closed the brasserie down. I walked her to Lexington Avenue. Hailed a cab. Kissed her on the cheek and said goodnight, thinking I'd never see her again. At three-thirty in the morning my telephone rang.

"Adam, Tommy and I had a bad fight. I told him all about you. He got jealous and beat me up. He's drinking vodka and he's using—heroin. I'm afraid."

"Give me your address."

As Emily and I raced down the stairs from Signorelle's flat I could hear him shouting, "You might think you got some virgin there. But you don't. She's had two abortions during the time she shacked up with me. Neither one of them were mine." Signorelle kept screaming at us the whole time we were leapfrogging down the stairs.

In the taxi on the way to my apartment, Emily turned to me. "I can explain about those men, Adam."

I placed my hand over her mouth. "No need."

"But I want to!" she said, removing my hand from her mouth. As Em began to explain I kissed her on the mouth. Each time she tried to explain, I gently kissed her again. Soon Emily started laughing. Placing my hand in her lap she gazed at me. Her face turned serious as she said, "When I was a little girl, seven or eight, I wanted to be liked by the boys, so you know what I did? I was the girl behind closed doors, in the elevator, on the stairwell, in the basement. You know the one. The one who would lift her dress and let the boys peep. It helped me make friends with them. I needed friends. I was no one." I kissed Em and held her tight. Her face buoyed up. "You know who I always envied as a little girl, Adam? Shoemakers. They're wonderful. And boy did they know it. Every cobbler in my neighborhood made sure that everyone could see them working from their shop windows. They took pride in their work. I never felt like that but someday…"

"You will," I said.

I pushed away *Confessions*, listened to David's first tape. Inserted the second.

"It's imperative you try to see Emily Bloom for what she is. She's an open wound, damn it. An empty bucket that you can never fill. And now, finally, you realize it. You stand up in this scene and tell her so. Tell her that her copout spirituality isn't healing, it's harming your relationship. Destroying everything."

I shut off the cassette player. I tore up my treatment—the one David hated. I started over again. I flipped through *Confessions*. Stopped at a page in the novel where I was speaking to Margot. *"Nostalgia de la boue,"* she hissed. I was familiar with the expression. In French it means nostalgia for the gutter…

I began rewriting. I worked through the evening. At two AM I went to bed. At six I woke. Took a shower, had some O.J., gobbled up several oatmeal cookies and returned to my working table. I continued like that for the entire week. I kept reading from *Confessions*, taking notes. Reconceptualizing. Trying out new scenes. Crossing them out. Beginning again. I continued reading from *Confessions*. Part Three of the novel: It Was Not Always Perfect. David had strongly suggested I read it in its entirety.

"Adam, the last thing I would ever want to do is cause you pain. When I think of your pain I shudder." Emily moved out. I couldn't let go.

"I can't handle the pressure you place on me. Damon is a happy person. He's so much easier to be with. He's fun. We do fun things to-gether. We comb each other's hair with our fingers. We play football with his friends in the park together, we go to concerts, together, we like the same kind of music, we go clubbing together. You never once went clubbing with me, Adam. It's not an illusion. He does want to share his life with me. And his family loves me. I never had a real family. It's a whole new experience for me, all of it."

I couldn't let go.

"I know you love me. It's not the problem. At night I would lock myself in the bathroom, agonize over what was missing. Some nights I would masturbate while you were reading a book or watching a game or writing. Why is it that you didn't become aware that something was very wrong?"

I couldn't let go.

"You have to move on. Be strong. You are strong in so many ways. If it weren't for you I would never have survived. Now you have to be strong for yourself."

I couldn't. A telephone call. A letter. A not so chance meeting.

"I upset Damon as much as I do you. He is also a very good person. He loves me, too. But I've become numb with him, too. I can't go on hurting people, Adam. I have to stop. I'm scared and I feel nothing. My body and the rest of me are so far apart."

One month later:

"What I want, Adam, is to not need Damon or you. I want to feel strong and independent. Not to be dependent on any man. I have to take

time to get to know who I am. I'm so in touch with what you and Damon want that I lose what I want. Why is it, Adam, that the less I want of men and the more I try to distance myself from them, the more men need of me? The closer they try to get?"

Several months passed.

"I wasn't feeling good with our relationship. I felt I was being accused. I felt cornered. I didn't feel as if I, as an individual, was being seen. I kept hearing about your feelings and your needs in the same way I now keep hearing about Damon's needs, and I've got to deal with my needs. Emily is important! And I have the right to do that, and I wasn't. I'm searching for what the answer is. Not to just run away from you, but to move closer, because I feel a desperate need to stay away from you and…um…that's all I can say right now. That is what I'm feeling. What you feel…That's… That's your truth. I've got to deal with mine. I can't look the other way. I've done that too much of my life—looked away from what I'm really feeling. Adam, take care of yourself. Okay?"

I flipped to the book's final chapter. The day Emily returned.

"I thought about what our life would be like if we were married. I'd run my jewelry business and that would be a full-time job. And you would work on your books. We'd go to the movies together, and the theater when we had the time. We'd take walks and talk. You'd read your creations to me and recommend books for me to read and we'd talk about them, as well as everything else. We'd travel, too. It would be a nice life. I think we could be happy." Emily's brow furrowed. *"I've made up my mind. Let's go down to City Hall today and get married. I'm ready now. Let's jump right in. No, make it day after tomorrow. That'll give us time to get the blood tests."*

We decided to go to Palm Court in the Plaza Hotel for tiramisu and talk.

"You are my best friend, Adam, but it's hard for me to remember the rest. I don't know what it is," she said anxiously. *"I'm not in touch with those feelings any longer."* She looked up at me. *"But we'll get them back.*

Won't we?"

As soon as we returned to the apartment we sat down on the leather sofa. Em crossed her arms over her chest. "I know how much I love you. I'll be a good wife. I'll always respect you, do anything you want me to. But do you think I'll ever feel as I did? In those ways I want to be with you, too."

I gazed at Em, knowing I had lost her. I started to say something, then stopped, feeling depleted, knowing what I had set out to say was the only inevitable answer.

"Em, in a few days we're supposed to be going down to City Hall."

"I know that. I'm ready. This time I won't run away."

I sat there silently gazing at Em's face. Finally I said, "You know, Em, I no longer have those romantic notions about us. I'm not holding onto them any longer."

Emily's face brightened. "I knew you would outgrow them. You're an intelligent man. You're brilliant. I learned so much from you. So much of what I am, I owe to you. I knew you would let go of them sometime."

Momentarily I choked. I couldn't speak. Finally I said, "You're very special to me, Emily. I want you to be happy." Then I fumbled again as I searched for the right words. When I recovered, I said, "I want you to find the most you can out of life. You know that." Emily stared at me. Perplexed. I felt like grabbing her. Never letting go. I gulped down hard. We gazed at each other. Words weren't necessary. Our understanding without words was as complete as mine was with David.

"Adam, I love you."

"I know you do," I said, beginning to cry.

Emily lifted herself from the sofa, kneeled down in front of me. "Adam," she said, looking up at me. "If it were ten years, even fifteen, I'd stay with you. I can sacrifice ten or fifteen years. But you're not that old. You're going to live another forty years. I can't sacrifice forty years. Can I?"

Emily calmly walked to the guest closet and took out her night bag. Her jacket. She quickly moved through the foyer. I groped to say something. I *couldn't.*

"*Adam,*" *Em said, wiping a tear from her eye. Then she straightened her shoulders and took several more hesitant steps toward the door. She turned.* "*I don't know. Maybe it's because I don't think I've finished my relationship with Damon. I mean you just appeared and I felt compelled to come back to you. You have some kind of magical hold over me. Maybe if I resolved my feelings for Damon.*"

"*You will, Emily. And I'll wear a tux at the wedding.*"

"*You'll always be in my heart, Adam. Always.*"

"*And you in mine.*"

I tried to gather myself together one more time. I took hold of her shoulders. "*I love you, Em. God, I never loved anyone like I love you.*"

"*Adam, I wanted to give you what you want. I still do. I just can't.*" *Emily paused, and then her whole face seemed to light up.* "*When I have a baby I'm going to give it so much love. The kind I felt I missed out on until you came along. I will teach it all about spirituality and feeling thankful. I just know it will be a special child. I can feel it even now.*" *She paused again.* "*I feel great thankfulness that because of your love I am now ca-pable of giving life to another person. It is something I will never forget.*" *I wiped a tear from her cheek.* "*When I have a child, my child will know you as soon as he's ready to. That I promise you, Adam Remler.*"

I opened the front door and stepped out into the hallway. I took Em's hand, half-pulled her through the door. She began to sob softly.

"*Emily,*" *I whispered,* "*you know I can't take it when you cry.*"

My father wiped the feces from my mother's backside when she was dying. He wept salty tears as he cried out, "*My life is over without your mother.*" *My father passed away soon after. I understood my father. I wasn't my father. Though I did cry salty tears.*

"*Make a muscle, Emily.*"

She looked up.

"*Come on, let me feel your muscle.*"

Slowly Emily made a muscle.

"Now let me feel the other arm." She did. "Just as I thought. Your wings are strong now. So fly, Emily Bloom. Fly!"

A gentle half smile crossed her face.

"My Adam," she chirped. "My Adam." She extended her hand and touched my face. "Goodbye Adam," she said. "You're the best." She stepped inside the boxcar and flew out of my life, on her own, forever.

I handed both the treatment and the screenplay to David. He flipped the screenplay to Ariel, who was sitting in his director's chair. "I want a written report tomorrow morning." I hadn't spoken to or seen Ariel Warning since our last meeting. It shocked me seeing her now. When I finish frenzied writing, coming back to reality is jarring. The actual world takes a while to get into focus. I scrutinized Ariel. It was if I had forgotten she was real. She had become unreal; didn't exist. While I read from my novel and sculpted the screenplay scenes, Emily Bloom had once again become my entire reality. Everyone else, non-existent. Ariel glanced at me. She appeared quite calm.

"You came in at nine pages," David said, sounding pleased as he examined the wafer-thin treatment. He turned to page one. "Confessions," he muttered, commencing to read aloud various scenes I had outlined. Grimacing, he stopped. Barked out, "Here's something to correct. People no longer get married at City Hall. They have to go to 141 Worth Street. And for your information you no longer need a blood test. Thank Ariel for that tidbit. She called the marriage bureau just the other day." While David was reading I nervously paced the room, finally settling in a desk chair opposite where Ariel Warning was seated. In deference to Ariel he made one accommodation. Each time he read Emily's name he said "E."

Within minutes he turned to Ariel. "You don't have to bother reading the screenplay." He wheeled to me. "Writing should get the best out of you, not the least. The way you see E. is kitsch. You think this is writing?" he yelled. "It's not writing. You don't have the courage to write. What you're doing is masturbating. It feels good. Like E. felt good. It's what you do with everything." He glanced over at Ariel. When he returned to face me he was glowering. It instantly crossed my mind: he knew! "I'll call in another writer or write it myself," he said.

Ariel gazed at me quizzically.

"E. really said that?"

"Said what?"

"'I'm scared and I feel nothing. My mind and body and the rest of me are so far apart.' What a strange thing to say."

The telephone was ringing. It was Margot.

"I spoke to Dr. Porder. It looks like those symbols are definitely another revelation. He said all criminologists look for such things. Symbols like the ones you described—hearts, happy faces, clowns—are very common. They're used by people who are trying to deny something horrific that probably happened in their lives."

I tried getting a good night's sleep. I ended up tossing and turning ceaselessly I kept hearing Bobby Cover's "homicide," Margot Korman's "dangerous," inside my head. I picked up a novel in which the author posed: Are hurtful events better forgotten or remembered? Can people truly invent themselves, or do they lose something essential in trying to shed their past? At six AM I splashed my face with cold water, scrubbed with black soap as rough as pumice, the two words still circling like raptors in my head. At times we can detach, escape into a forgetful state. I could not.

The cupboard was opened. I could not shake Ariel Warning. Was that what I was doing? Escaping? Once again I was on the go—determined to find the trail of blood, running from guilt, rather than owning up, facing my twin, confronting my own cyclopean culpability.

☙

For days I kept obsessing, certain there was some horrific secret Ariel Warning was hiding in her cupboard.

After being away from Ariel's grasp for a month, I once again felt equilibrium returning. Felt capable of examining with vigor and a modicum of distance the list of revelations at my disposal. All that week I scrutinized Margot's list: the different labels, keys, codes, and connecting tissues I felt gave a trace of meaning to the subject I was exploring. Each day I hurried to my Smith-Corona, aligned my body with the machine. Remember, I told myself—Ariel Warning is not only codes and words. She exists in today's problematic world. Her character, as much as any of the characters in my novels, can no longer be clearly defined. People are not what they seem to be. A state of flux exists. The terms keep changing. The sand keeps shifting beneath our feet. We vanish in the flux of ambiguity.

On one of those days, to further accent my awareness, I made reference to my own particular case: creating in silence and seclusion, profiting. Gambling, tension and dread, losing. My twin screaming, "Adam, you're such a coward. That's why you gamble. You're afraid to take your shots in the real world."

I typed onto a clean sheet of paper: PEOPLE WEAR MASKS.

In all probability Ariel Warning chose to escape a difficult road. What happened on her journey? What went wrong? What was it she had to flee? What was her crucifixion? I came up with nothing. I scanned my revelations, pen in hand for note-taking. Drew a blank. Not knowing what else to do, I tried to find new primal clues in the accumulated revelations. Two hours later I had exhausted my search. Again at a loss as to where to turn, I reread the page in *Confessions* where Ariel had scribbled in the margin: THAT'S ME!

Emily Bloom was my conjoined twin that cannot be separated. She was as much a part of me as my twin. She, like my identical, reminded me of myself all the time. That part that could betray David…

☜☞

"What would you do if your twin died?" the psychiatrist had asked me when I went for help.

"That's like asking me what I'd do if I died," I said.

"That's the problem," he said.

David came over.

"You've been acting strange for a long time. What is it? What's going on?"

For a split second I was going to tell David the truth. Then I panicked, diverting the conversation.

"I've been thinking about Ariel and Emily. How similar they are. They even have a similar look."

"That's not true at all. Emily has a seraphic gaze. Ariel has an intelligent look. Ariel has highly developed critical faculties. Emily's cloudy."

"Has Ariel ever discussed Emily with you?"

"I told you Ariel and Emily have little in common. Ariel isn't hung up on the spirit world. She isn't into channeling and reincarnation. She doesn't experiment with hands-on-healing and hardcore visualization. She doesn't practice yoga or Zen and she doesn't go around saying 'Whatever God does is for the best,' day after day." David stopped. "You know, sometimes I do get the feeling that Ariel is like Emily. Just last night she was chatting up a storm. I mean she spoke incessantly about the homeless veteran that parks in front of my building every morning. Did you know Ariel gives him a five-dollar bill each time she comes over? Now she's insisting on buying the guy boots. Another thing, in the lobby the other day Ariel bumped into Peter Dugan's wife and she spent an hour talking with Mary about her twins. I mean this thing for babies and panhandlers. Isn't that Emily to a T?" I started to make a comment. David interrupted. "Adam, I haven't told this to anyone. I mean this story makes it sound as if Ariel is as off the wall as Emily."

"Tell me!"

"Well, last week we passed an infirm lady on her hands and knees in front of a fire hydrant. Water was dripping from the hydrant's nozzle. The woman's hands were cupped to catch the dripping water, and when she caught it she sprayed it over numerous articles of clothing, which she then started washing. 'Be back in a sec,' Ariel shouted to me, and then she ran down the block. When she came back, she had two large bars of Ivory soap clenched in her fist. She knelt down on her hands and knees and started helping the woman with her washing. When I asked Ariel what made her react like that, she said something crazy. 'The woman didn't have a sand pail. She should have a sand pail.' Anyway, you know how sensitive Ariel is. How easily things set her off. I let it go at that." A moment later, David panicked. "What are you trying to tell me? That I'm going to lose Ariel like you lost Emily?"

Almost immediately my twin recovered his equilibrium. He spoke softly.

"I'm sorry. I'm a bit edgy these days. You know I think of Emily as family. I miss her, too."

I telephoned my best friend Johnny.

"This is Broadway Al," I said, using my code name.

"Hi Al. What can I do for you?"

"Give me a college line."

"There's only one college game being played tonight. It's a preseason NIT game in the Garden. Minnesota is one and one-half over Georgetown."

"Give me two dimes on Minnesota," I said.

In gambler's argot, a dollar is one hundred dollars. A dime is a thousand.

"Twenty dollars on the Golden Gophers of Minnesota to kick the ass of the Georgetown Hoyas," he said, trying to sound cute.

I returned to the typewriter. Sought answers. Pounded keys. Dancing didn't help. Margot was correct: Trying to discover what Ariel Warning was hiding, why she was lying, what it was that she wouldn't confess to was as difficult for me as grasping Emily's spirit world.

I tried rereading some of Shakespeare's plays and sonnets. Examined a magnificent folio that I had purchased at J.N. Bartfield of *The Tempest.* I waded through the arduous sixteenth-century script. Afterwards, I scribbled down all the key words that I had underlined in the tome which seemed to link up with Ariel's Warning's inadvertent revelations. I kept playing around with my own list of words, keys, codes, and symbols. Emily's name headed the list. The extent to which Ariel detested Em's name was reason enough for that. In the three additional hours consumed, everything which Margot or I had discovered was either diffused or dissolved. Everything I tried, refuted. My mind had exhausted just about all possibilities. I was without a clue as to where to turn.

I lost my wager. The Hoyas lost by one. I agonized over losing, cursing out the Golden Gophers. G.G. popped into my head: "Happy graduation, G.G." Golden Gopher was all I had to go on. I telephoned the University of Minnesota, was connected with an employee who assisted with public relations. I told this cheerful fellow I was a former student and that I needed a comprehensive list of the student body and graduate students for the past fifteen years. "Why?" the loquacious fellow asked.

I told him my film company was doing a documentary, something to do with cultural as well as health issues. "Believe me," I said, "the university will benefit financially, as will the people chosen." Within a few hours I received his fax. Not one person on the thirty page list was named Ariel.

I pulled from my library anything on the state I could find. I was searching for something that could possibly connect Ariel Warning to the State of Minnesota. Several minutes later I telephoned the Chamber of Commerce office in Minneapolis. The guy I was connected to spoke in officious tones as he explicated a multitude of things concerning the city and the Gopher State.

"We are the largest city in the Great State of Minnesota," he said, "and the county seat of Hennepin County. Since 1917, our fair city has been head of navigation on the Mississippi." He went on and on about the Gopher State. "Of course you know we're the land of ten thousand lakes…" He mentioned that the North Star State entered the Union as the thirty-second state and had two nicknames—which until that moment had confused me—Gopher State and North Star State. Its song, "Hail Minnesota." I was just about to hang up when he casually said, "Our tree is the Norwegian pine. Our flower, the cypipedium, more commonly known as the moccasin flower. And our bird, the loon."

I recalled the watercolors of the Norwegian pine forests, with loons and moccasin flowers, in Ariel's Warning's bedroom. For me, this provided sufficient impetus to continue to dwell on G.G. feeling it was possibly part of the puzzle.

Again I telephoned the University of Minnesota.

"If anyone can help you, Mister Remler," the operator said, "it is Anna Pedersen. Mrs. Pedersen is in charge of our alumni newsletter. For the past twelve years she's been keeping track of just about every student."

"I'm sorry the Golden Gophers let you down, Mister Remler," Mrs. Pedersen chuckled when I told her about my wager.

"Win some, lose some," I glibly responded.

Soon Mrs. Pedersen and I were on a first-name basis.

"Now, stop worrying. I'm sure I can be of help."

"I'm trying to locate an Ariel Warning. Her last name might have changed. It might be Olsen. But Warning is the name she's going by. Are you familiar with an Ariel Olsen? I'm almost certain she was either an undergrad or a graduate student. Anywhere from one to, let's say, eight years ago."

There was a prolonged silence on the other end of the line before Anna Pedersen began to think aloud. "Ariel Warning, Olsen…Ariel…Ariel, that's such a pretty name. I'm sorry, Mr. Remler. Can't say I remember. The only Ariel I ever came across was in a painting. Its title was *Ariel.*"

"What do you remember about the painting?" I asked. Not thinking too much about it, still having come this far, not wanting to leave anything unturned.

"Nothing!" Mrs. Pedersen answered. "The only reason I recalled the painting at all is my husband, Jonas, he wanted to name our first-born Ariel, but I wouldn't hear of it. I insisted on a good Norwegian name. Now I have two daughters, Armallie and Sigrid, but no Ariel," she chuckled. Her laugh was warm, infectious. I envied Jonas Pedersen. "Perhaps if Jonas and I have a third child, I'll surprise him and let him name it Ariel."

"The painting, Anna. Where did you see it?"

"It might have been at the Minneapolis Museum of Art. Then again it might have been at the Frederic R. Weisman Art Museum at our own university. I'm just not sure. It was many years ago. I'm sorry, I just can't be sure."

"What kind of painting was it? Was it a watercolor?"

"No, it wasn't. It was a rosemaling. We have many young artists in this part of the state who still do rosemalings. If you're interested in rosemalings, Adam, you know where you should go: Milan."

"Milan?" I said, thinking of *The Tempest*—Ariel, servant of Prospero, the deposed Duke of Milan. "Milan's a long way from Minnesota. Why would Milanese artists produce a Norwegian art form?"

Mrs. Petersen chuckled. "Oh, no, Adam," she said. "You have it all wrong. I mean Milan, Minnesota. It's about one hundred and fifty miles west of here. If you're interested, I'm sure you can find many, many fine rosemalings there. Milan is known as the rosemaling capital of Minnesota."

I telephoned the village clerk of Milan, Minnesota, a woman named Missy Stogartz. She was tight-lipped, suspicious.

"The population of Milan is 353…Yes. We do have an elementary school. Nope. No high school. No college. No hospital. If we need hospital care we go to Chippewa County at Montevido."

When I tried asking more direct questions, specifically if she knew of an Ariel Warning, Miss Stogartz hemmed and hawed. "Mister, I don't want to seem unfriendly, but anything else you need to know I suggest you call Old Man Whittier at the general store, or Sarabeth Xavier at the paper. And mister, I'd advise you to wait an hour or so before calling Luke Whittier. He takes his lunch break about this time. Won't pick up for anyone. And mister," Stogartz added. "If you think I'm close-mouthed, just wait till you speak to Luke Whittier."

I didn't feel calling some old-timer at a general store made any sense. I telephoned Sarabeth Xavier at the Xavier Herald.

"We put out an eight to twelve page paper, Mr. Remler. Of course, compared to a New York tabloid, it's not much…"

As soon as I heard Sarabeth Xavier's strident voice, I knew she would be difficult to deal with. There was an irritability in her tone. I tried fabricating small talk. When I figured I had established enough of a rapport, I cut to the chase.

"I'm sorry, I don't know any Ariel Warning or Uma Olsen," Sarabeth Xavier said. "And I'm surprised at you, Mr. Remler. Being an old newspaperman yourself, you should get your facts straight. Milan is not a town. It's a city. We were incorporated in 1971."

"What else should I know about Milan?"

"The only thing I'll tell you about Milan, Mr. Remler, is that we do not have any famous citizens or glamorous women, and the most controversial thing that's happened here over the past several years is the town meeting that Luke Whittier held to discuss whether we should replace the football coach. Oh yes, there's one more thing I can tell you," Sarabeth Xavier said, her glacial manner prevailing, sounding pissed.

"What is it," I asked.

"Unfortunately, Mr. Remler, it's not about Milan. It's about you. At the time you said you worked on the *New York Mirror*, it was defunct."

I awakened with a severe case of 'winter itch.' After applying a skin lotion, I telephoned Emily.

"You have to tell David."

"I can't. I just can't."

For a long while Emily remained silent. "Adam," she finally said. "I think it's because I'm not with you that you're doing this. If I were with you all of this would never have happened. I'm sorry I'm not with you, but I just couldn't give you what you needed." Emily paused.

"In a few minutes I have to hang up. Damon is watching Isaac. He…They need me."

So do I, so do I, I didn't say.

"You just don't understand," I said weakly instead.

"What, how guilty you feel? The pain you're in? Of course I do," Em said softly.

"No, it's not only that."

"What is it then?"

"Being a twin. What it's like."

Emily paused again. "You always said life was round. Now maybe it's my turn to help you. Remember, years ago, when I asked you what it was like being a twin? Remember your answer?" I tried to recall my words. I couldn't. "You said it was important I understand. And you went to your typewriter and typed out what it's like. Boy did you dance."

After a while I started to recall it. My voice echoed Em's words. "It's like having four hands and four eyes, and being two against one in every battle you face."

Emily interrupted me. "You also wrote: 'Even if you hurt your twin in the worst possible way you're still one with him. That's the way it is. From cradle to grave. You're one.' You see, Adam, you don't have to make Ariel Warning into a villain. You can tell David. You can."

When Emily and I finished speaking, I walked around the city, spent an hour at the Strand Book Store, hours at Tompkins's Square. It was almost one in the morning when I got home. I was still in a funk.

I walked into the bedroom. My answering machine was blinking. There were two messages. One was from David.

"In one hour I'm catching a flight to L.A. to meet up with Marcia Majors. I left my editorial suggestions on top of my desk. Don't panic, nothing major, they're all for the sake of clarity. And Adam, Thursday is…Thursday it will be twenty-three years since Mom passed. Keep Thursday open. We'll drive out to the cemetery. Visit Mom. And, Adam," my identical stammered, "how do you feel about me inviting Ariel to come along?"

The other was from Ariel Warning.

"Where are you? David just left for Kennedy. Call me as soon as you get in. Wake me if you must. I want to come over…"

I took two sleeping pills. Went to bed.

All that month my twin kept inviting me out with him and Ariel. I'd make up excuses. With each passing day, instead of becoming easier not to see Ariel, it became more difficult. She kept gnawing away at me. I could not stop myself from thinking about her. Still, I fought it. I did not call her. I tried to keep busy. I went to dinner several times with Margot Korman. On one of those occasions my uncle, Leo Solomon, came along. All through dinner he kept going on and on about his life. As a child I thought he was the greatest man in the world, later on loving him not because of himself but in spite of himself. As I matured I began to condemn him for the many mistresses he had, his double-dealings in business, his crass materialism.

Margot was surprisingly patient with my uncle's blabbering, but finally she said, "Adam, if we're going to make the film on time we have to leave now."

"What's your hurry, Margot Goil? Have some more lobster. You can go to the movies anytime. I want to get to know you. Adam boy tells me you're special. And so is Adam boy," my uncle said, flashing his gap-toothed smile. "No one knows as much about college basketball as he does, Margot Goil. My nephew put together an undercover organiza-tion that was pure genius. He was the best. He researched everything. Knew everything. Had outs and beards all over the country. He always found the best numbers. And he always managed every dollar perfectly. I'm telling you, Margot Goil, if my nephew ever took legitimate busi-ness seriously, he'd be in the Fortune 500. But to my nephew," this my uncle said as if he couldn't fathom the thought, "a guy like Les Wexner, who put together a multi-billion dollar business, The Limited, is no more than a shmata salesman who sells a pair of pants."

On each of these nights when I returned to my apartment, I'd check my answering machine for messages. Each night a large chunk of me was disappointed that Ariel Warning had not called.

❧

I stayed away from Ariel Warning. Didn't see her. Didn't spend any time with her. Nine weeks went by before I found a message on my machine:

"I called you because we have to talk. Meet me for lunch."

I walked through the winding corridors of the restaurant, failing to spot Ariel. I stopped in the Blue Room. A jazz pianist, Art Francis, was playing. I looked into elegant alcoves, as well as more than several glass-encased rooms of sparkling crystal. Finally I tried the garden. An immense pin oak, looking more like a Botero sculpture, was rooted at its center. The magnificent garden housed giant-leafed Elmwood trees, massive maples, Callery Pear, London plane, cascading shrubbery, paradisiacal flowers and plants. The scenic landscape provided the chattering customers with the kind of unnatural beauty only a natural park can offer. The majority of the people were seated inside because of the inclement weather. Still, a few were on the dance floor slow-dancing. Ariel was leaning against the trunk of a gnarled Norway maple, holding her favorite drink (I could tell by the color of the pomegranate syrup), grenadine and orange juice, in her left hand. She was talking to three males; one extremely handsome, the other two nondescript. I did not walk over. I sat by myself in the back of the garden, observing her. The wet drops of drizzle raining from the tops of the trees splashed the cream-colored sheer blouse she was wearing. The feelings inside of me now were not dissimilar from the boundless ones evoked during my airy days with Em. The difference was the degree of my ache.

Ariel spotted me. Walked over. Her large breasts bobbed underneath the cream-colored blouse. For the first time in months I felt alive. It wasn't only Ariel's bobbing breasts, or her scent of musk, it was everything about her. Simply put, her presence. We went through the motions. Sat down at a round table. Ordered lunch, from the dessert menu chocolate mousse.

The conversation lingered a while and then Ariel said, "I've tried to be fair and see your side of things. And I've left you alone as I promised I would, but I can't abide any longer with this altruism of yours. It's not altruism, it's impotence!" she exclaimed, her tone rising to accent the deprecatory word. "I'm withering. I can't help myself." She hesitated. "Can we go back to your apartment?"

"No."

There was a death-like silence. The only thing I could hear was Ariel's breathing.

"I'm not a monster," she said. "I've always told you I loved David. But my life with him isn't working any better than my life with you is working. It's only a life with both of you that will work for me. What I want is to tell David about us."

"Never!" I cried out.

"I love both of you. I'm in good faith that way. Hopefully, David will understand. If he can't handle it, my being with the two of you, I'll just walk away."

"You can't," I mouthed impulsively.

"I know this is going to be difficult for him. He loves the two of us. That's why both of us should go over right now and tell him together."

"No!" I repeated.

"All we have to do is be honest. Make him understand that for it all to work for me, I must be with the both of you. In time he'll come around. He'll begin to realize how unhappy I am. What I need."

"David wouldn't be able to handle it. He'd crack."

But it was I in fact who was really cracking. I was terrified of exposing myself to my twin brother. I kept dwelling on how self-destructively David had reacted when Thea died. But, I was really only thinking of myself. All those dead years I experienced after Emily Bloom abandoned me, before Ariel Warning had entered my life. And now I was renewed. My twin and I were both renewed, our lives enriched and made fuller by this very same woman. Compared to that, what did good intentions mean?

One constant dominated my mind. I knew I could walk away from all of this alive. Maybe feeling terribly empty, but alive. I was not certain my twin brother could.

I needed time to think. "I can't stay," I said. "I have another appointment. Come over to my place tonight. We'll discuss what to do then."

"I can't. I'm having dinner with David."

"Come over late."

When I opened the door, Ariel stood framed in the doorway in a long slick black raincoat with yellow buttons down to her ankles. For some reason I was certain she had nothing on underneath the coat. My immediate response was to peel open the coat from her throat to her ankles one shiny gold button at a time. At that moment my appetite for Ariel Warning was hardly dominated by good intentions. Or, what amounted to the same thing, by David. I slowly reached out to unfasten the top button of her coat's collar. As soon as I did I caught a glimpse of a flimsy silk blouse that she had on underneath.

Ariel laughed delightedly. "You thought I had no clothes on. You look disappointed."

She quickly stepped inside the door. Stripped off her coat.

"I feel like I'm bursting," she said, hugging me. She gazed at me. "I haven't made love to you in…" I started to say something. She placed her hand gently over my mouth. "Please, no talking. Just make love to me," she said. "And not anything kinky. Just sweet love. I want it to be special."

Why couldn't I say no? Did it, like everything else, have something to do with my being a twin? Not being my own person? Half a person? Ball and chain bound to another being? What was it? My makeup? A twin's makeup? The very stuff I (we) were molded from? As if the great sculptor had only enough clay to mold one, but his inspiration called for two. What was the Master forced to leave out of his creation, and what enmity resulted from this lack? What ambivalence. What competitiveness, jealousy, rivalry, and envy from this sibling tug-of-war. What self-hate and denial. What blindness. And also what love. What a piece of work is man, says the poet. What a piece of work are twins, I say. And at what cost twinship? What cost?

Again I tried staying away from Ariel.

"I can tell you one thing." Her voice was filled with emotion. "I know who I am and what I lost. Losing my twin was a big chunk of my life. You never lost anything. E. doesn't count. She wasn't attached to you. Maybe if you lose David, you'll finally understand how I feel." Her words were beginning to sound like a threat.

"For your sake, for all our sakes, I only hope you're strong enough to cope if you do."

"Margot, I'm exhausted. I have to get some sleep."

"You can't. Coleman said some awful things to me about our Ariel Project. He said it was built on false premises, and the danger in false premises is you end up with paper airplanes. And that paper airplanes do not carry weight. Well, you know me. Tell me I can't do something and I say we'll see about that."

I could only answer weakly, "Maybe Coleman's right."

A millisecond later: "I haven't told you yet the real reason I telephoned. Do you remember those case histories that disappeared? The ones Ariel fleeced. One of those histories is about these Miranda twins. Ring a bell? Miranda?" My first thought was the schoolteacher who disappeared in Bird City, Kansas, who loved Shakespeare. Her name was Miranda. "Adam, I've changed my mind. Warning is definitely trying to tell us something. I'm convinced she is. Adam, please investigate one more time. Check out those Miranda twins."

What had convinced me to investigate further was not only that the Miranda twins linked with the schoolteacher and Prospero's daughter, but also that "Miranda" and "Warning" also formed a kind of strange link. Miranda Warning. How many times did my best friend Johnny cry out to me: "The cops ain't kosher. They busted me without giving me my Miranda warning." Somehow my mind formulated a link between Miranda and Warning, the Miranda twins and the teacher and Prospero's daughter; all of it, as nebulous and far-reaching as it was, made some kind of weird mystical sense to me. Warning? Ariel was trying to tell us something.

I arrived at the Academy of Medicine at nine AM and began searching at once for the case history of the Miranda twins. Margot said she had come across it by accident, and that it wasn't an entire case history as she had originally inferred. By the end of our conversation she admitted to me it was more like a few sentences out of the mass of medical records she had waded through on conjoined twins. And so here I was searching medical records for a paragraph, possibly a single line. Thousands of case histories, volumes of medical books, replete with medical jargon. After six, possibly seven hours, getting absolutely nowhere, wiped out and discouraged, I left the Academy and returned home.

It was one thirty AM. I was pacing the terrace. My mind kept spinning. At two thirty I walked into the den. I glanced at my mother's bar mitzvah present. A Jacqueline Raphael sculpture of a twisted rope. I couldn't take my eyes from it. *"Do you know where the word 'twin' comes from, boys?"* my mom had asked us. *"It's derived from an Anglo-Saxon source meaning two strands twisted together."*

Out of the corner of my eye I noticed my answering machine was blinking.

"I've calmed down," Ariel Warning's voice intoned. "I've decided to be patient with you. Tomorrow David's going to be tied up all evening with some producer in town from the Coast." The machine kept playing. "That means I can personally say au revoir to you before you leave for England."

What made Ariel think I was leaving for England? I hadn't told her I was leaving. On second thought, I had. I'd told her if she kept pushing me I would escape the city. Take off for London. I'd also mentioned it to David: "I've been thinking of just traveling for a month or two. I need to think some things out." My twin's response was: "I read somewhere that the whole point of travel is to achieve some inner change. And you could doubtlessly benefit from that."

"Tomorrow night, we can spend it together," Ariel's message continued. "All of it."

I called Ariel back.

"I've moved up my flight. I'm leaving for Kennedy at sunup. Should be landing at Heathrow around eight. I'll see you when I get back. This will give us both time to think things through."

"I've done enough thinking," she lashed out. "It's time to tell David."

"Ariel, please, just wait until I get back from London. Two weeks".

"I told you, if David can't handle it, my being with the two of you, I'll just walk away."

"Two weeks."

Ariel viciously slammed down the phone.

"I don't know what your brother was thinking," the police officer said as he walked into the Intensive Care Unit. "I don't know if he was lookin' for a Gypsy cab or was headin' towards the subway. All I can tell you is he was walkin' north in the direction of 125th Street and he stumbled over this girl lying in a pool of blood in the gutter. Instead of splitting like most citizens would, he stopped. This girl was sliced up pretty bad. You know how these teenagers are nowadays. If it ain't a knife or gun they're carrying, it's a box-cutter with a removable razor blade, some of 'em with blades that snap out at the push of a button. Your brother kneeled down to help this cut girl, and she lunged at him with her box-cutter as if he were the one that cut her. Now I ask you—what was your brother thinking? I mean stopping in East Harlem like that to help some street girl at four in the morning? Oh yeah, that picture your twin is holdin'. He held it like it was Jesus on the Cross all the way to the hospital. I'm the one who put it back in his hand after the emergency surgery. I figured he'd want it."

The doctor said David didn't feel any pain. I wondered if it were possible that the pain from his body had passed into mine. Throughout my twin's time in the ICU, the recovery room, the tubes and bottles leaking liquid life into his veins, the days of leery anxiousness, I held his hand, clasped both of them, much of the time not sure where his left off and mine began. Sometimes David blinked his eyes at me. It was as if we were infants again, speaking in our own language. Once he muttered, "Adie." He hadn't called me Adie since elementary school.

An endless week went by before my brother started to improve. When my identical was well enough to leave his room, at his insistence, I wheeled him to the maternity ward. For hours he'd sit in front of a glass window observing the newborns.

"Ariel's right about having babies," he said in a weak voice. "As bad as it gets for people, it's good there."

Two days later I brought him home.

"Don't talk. Rest. You need to rest."

"I must tell you the whole story," my twin insisted.

"Sleep. You'll tell me everything when you're stronger."

After recovering for a few days, he was strong enough to talk.

"Where do you want to go? I don't know. I just want to get away. Get away from you. From everything. That's all I heard. And then, the day after you were supposed to leave for London, Ariel split," my twin said weakly. Then he proceeded to tell me the entire story.

It was midnight. Ariel had not come home. David had telephoned the superintendent of her building. He had no idea where she was. He paced his studio, back and forth. He looked out the window. Up to the heavens. *Where are you, Ariel? Are you safe? Even if you don't want to come home, call me, please! I must know that at least you're safe.*

"My mind kept jumping. I began to think the strangest thoughts. Had Ariel been unhappy with me? Did I do something wrong? I cried out in the pitch black night. Please—whoever you are—don't let anything happen to Ariel. Please, don't let anything change what we have. My mind kept jumping. I was self-centered. Did I impose my will? Did I force Ariel to placate me? Lie to me? Was she afraid to assert her true feelings? Her opinions? Was she scared to tell me what was wrong? Outside of the surface things I couldn't think of one thing. As far as I could tell, we were perfect together.

"Panic was setting in. I couldn't lose Ariel. Not now. It seemed to me as if in one mutilating night I had been pushed back to the black abyss where I had floundered when Thea died. I could feel the wonderful tranquility that Ariel had provided me escaping. I needed Ariel. I knew that as well as I knew anything.

"That night I did some insane things. I went looking for her in Central Park. I searched in hidden alcoves as well as the artificial lake where we had recently gone walking. I paced through the thick forestry surrounding the Sheep Meadow and Strawberry Fields. I walked into the park's most desolate areas, where more than a few women had been maimed, raped, murdered. Passed dozens and dozens of homeless people camping in cardboard boxes; squeezed up against each other on wooden benches and grass lawns, covering themselves with tawny newspapers stained by excrement where affluent Parkside residents' pampered dogs had defecated and urinated. Rank odors permeated the air. I searched each of these people's faces. Not one was Ariel. When it suddenly came to me where we had shared our first kiss, I raced twenty blocks down Central Park West and then cut back into the park. Under the giant sycamore tree was a young woman sleeping. It wasn't Ariel.

"After I left the park I decided to search the clubs. The Supper Club on 47th Street, between Broadway and Eighth, was my first stop. Chesky Records was throwing a private party to celebrate winning a Grammy. I went to Zero on 54th between Tenth and Eleventh next. Michella's down in the Twenties. Tuxedo in Tribeca; Caress in the meat-packing district. From there I grabbed a cab and taxied to Lafayette Street and checked out Gulag. Nothing! I went straight home. I checked my iPhone and my TAM for messages. None. I paced my studio, this time dwelling on the Parker twins. I became convinced that was where she'd gone. I dressed, and when I couldn't find a cab I flagged down a limousine. A coffee-colored Rastafarian with moptop dreadlocks was the driver. 'The Wagner Projects, 350 East 124th Street, driver. And hurry.' He turned to me, his blond dreads wriggling like swamp snakes. 'Mon, show your appreciation with a heavy tip,' he said.

"I pushed and prodded the livery driver to go faster. Faster. When we finally reached a half torn-down city-owned building, I got off at the southwest corner. I had to walk through the projects to get to the building the Parkers live in. Both elevators were down. I climbed the stairs. Pounded on the Parkers' door. When the twins unlocked the heavily bolted door they were standing in front of me half-naked. I can't describe to you the feeling I had when I actually saw them. Their heads and bodies were joined by a thick band of cartilage and flesh. Bart faced forward and Albert backward. I mean it jarred me. Adam, I could see over their shoulders into the project apartment. Standing in the shadows, maybe thirty feet into the apartment, was a woman. She had nothing on but a Cross-My-Heart bra and black panties. Her eyes were glazed as if she had been partying for days. Even at the distance I was standing from her I could smell alcohol on her breath. See a bottle of Wild Irish Rose in her hand. An old wax recording of Caruso was playing on an RCA Victrola. Shutting off the music, the woman strode over. 'Bart', she said, 'I don't do friends, and your money is only good for another half hour. And your next disability check don't come for three weeks. So you won't be seein' me for three weeks.' She grinned. 'Besides, who other than me is gonna listen to your crummy records. Fuck you without a condom.'

"'Don't sweat it, Pia, I got another fifty,' Bart said.

"'Let me see it,' she retorted.

"'Bart has it, Pia,' Albert squealed. 'I know he does.' Pia smiled.

"I tried to explain the situation to the Parkers. Why I was in such a state of panic. When I finished, Bart, the twin facing me, sneered.

"'Stop all this woman's talk, Remler. Ariel's been complaining to us about you since you first met her. It's not the way you treat her. And it's not that you refuse to go clubbing or skiing with her, or that she loves foreign films and you don't. It's just that she needs more space. She's no different from any other woman. Besides, it ain't the first time Ariel will be spending the night in some strange dude's house. And believe me, Remler, if she's like other women, it won't be the last.'

"'Why are you speaking about Ms. Warning like that?' Albert stammered. 'She's a decent woman. She's not a tramp.'

"Within a split second Albert became extremely emotional. Began stuttering. Collecting himself, he said, 'You know, Mr. Remler, Ms. Warning confides in me. I mean she tells me things about herself and her friendship with you that you might not want to hear.'

"'Like what?' I asked.

"'For one thing you have a neighbor who has twins.'

"'That's correct. Peter Dugan and his wife, Mary. Actually, now with the twins they have four boys. Ariel can't get enough of those kids.'

"'Well, they're the reason she was so terribly late the night you had theater tickets. She told me you were so mad you ripped the tickets up.'

"'That's true.'

"'Well, Mr. Remler, you might not agree with Ms. Warning's priorities, but you'd better understand that they're important to her.'

"'Priorities? What are you trying to tell me?'

"'I'm telling you Mrs. Dugan's children are important to Ms. Warning. She's been helping her out just about every day. One of the twins has been real sick. That day you had tickets to the theater Ms. Warning had to go 'cross town to a children's pharmacy for Mrs. Dugan. The traffic, she told me, was bumper to bumper. Her cab couldn't move. That's why she didn't make it to the theater on time. Priorities, Mr. Remler. Ms. Warning's priorities. They're not Broadway theater. Or the ballet or books or writing movies. They're children.'

"I tried to find out from Bart Remler where I might look for Ariel.

"Bart rubbed his beady eyes. Cocking his head to look up at me, he said, 'What about your brother? Did you ever think that she might be with him? Seems to me she had a thing for him as well as you.'

"'Why do you say that?' I asked.

"'It's the way she talks about him.'

"Albert said, 'Bart's making an excellent point, Mr. Remler. Look at my brother and me. Ms. Warning had us fighting over her. And believe me, it's not because either of us ever touched her. It's just the way Ms. Warning is. She came between us.'

"Bart burst into piercing hysterical laughter. 'Yeah, she really came between us. You can see that. Can't you!'

"'I'm trying to tell you, Remler,' Bart continued, composing himself. 'She's out there partying. I can't tell you where or with whom, but I sure as hell can tell you why. Ariel called me. That's correct. She telephoned. Not only to find out how we were doing, but because she's down on herself real bad. She wouldn't tell me or my brother why. But she's real depressed.'

"'I'll give you some serious advice, Mr. Remler,' Albert volunteered. 'If you really are serious about Ms. Warning, you should give her a baby.'

"Bart growled. 'Stop sweating. She ain't been with me or my brother, though both of us wish she had. But, as they say, that's neither here nor there. What is, is that she's with some new dude shacking up for a few days. But I'm telling you, as soon as she gets tired of the dude she'll come back, not because she loves you, but because she can't do no better. She knows with you and your twin she got a good deal. Better than she'd have with me and mine.' Albert signaled his brother to shift positions. They nimbly moved their feet, a whirling of the toes. When they completed their pirouette, Albert said, 'Ms. Warning said something about feeling abandoned. That's what she said. Strange, isn't it? You're right here. Why should Ms. Warning say she felt abandoned?'"

David paused for a moment. Then he said, "Adam, you know how I am with Ariel. There wasn't a minute that went by when I felt I didn't have to walk on eggshells. I mean I had always sensed from the beginning that one moment of pressure, of disapproval, of harsh comment, of insensitivity, of misinterpreted communication, and she'd be gone. It wasn't because I felt she loved me less than Thea did. It was because I believed she was troubled more. It never mattered. Until Ariel, inside, I was always empty. I don't want to be empty anymore. But Adam, I'm frightened. Really frightened." He peered straight into my eyes, "Tell me. Do you know anything about any of this?"

He waited. I couldn't believe how panicky I felt. Did David know? Was he testing me? Now was the time to tell him.

He's too weak, I told myself. This isn't me, I told myself. I'm a better person than this. That's what I wanted to believe as I stood so very close to my identical, remaining silent, observing myself. I was as much aware of my shortcomings as an impotent man is of his limitations in the

bedroom. Aware of every pretense, each putrid gesture, all of the hid-
eous justifications I affected. I knew what I was doing. Yes, I knew. I
remained standing there, violating my twin. Explain it to me if you can:
I loved my twin brother. For me he isn't the other. Another. He's my
genetically identical twin, my other-self.

David gripped my wrist. "I don't care what the problem is. Just find
Ariel. Tell her she's right about having a family. As bad as it gets it's good
there. Bring her home," he said, finally letting go of my wrist.

"I'll find her," I said. "I promise."

For one week the only thing I did about my actions, or lack of, my
pusillanimous lamenting, my pathetic wordy whining, was write. And
then I awakened from my self-regarding despair, psyching myself,
rationalizing that if I found something out, was able to tell David
some truly insightful piece of news, it would work out. I returned to
the Academy of Medicine, marched to the main desk and asked for
assistance. The people at the library were cooperative. One young
woman took the time to show me how to operate the library's computer
and program it so that all of the Academy's records on conjoined twins
would appear. Soon I had compiled printouts on everything the library
offered. I tore off all the sheets, holding the sheets of printed paper
rolled up in the shape of a baton in my fist. I walked slowly around the
austere room, ignoring the thousands of volumes of medical records,
selecting only the volumes identified by the files I held in my hand on
conjoined twins. Locating text after text, I carried at least a dozen or
more heavy volumes back to the desk I had been assigned, desk number
18; waded through each thick text, sometimes beginning by looking
through the indexes for "Miranda twins," and then, when disappointed
at not finding Miranda in the index, thumbing through the books
themselves, searching at random for whatever.

I scanned much of the purely theoretical material, as well as read many specific Siamese twins case histories, but found nothing on the Mirandas. Five hours flew by. I was about to give up when I opened the next to the last volume I had gathered. I flipped the pages indiscriminately, happened to glance at page 317. In the middle of the page my eyes focused on a heading: SIAMESE TWINS. EXTRAORDINARY SEPARATIONS. I read the text that followed. "Although this corrective surgery is unique, many pediatric surgeons who have previously tried to separate twins having a common heart have noted that only a few have made it through surgery and even fewer survived beyond six months...'I certainly wish the little Miranda girl well, and if she turns out to be a long-term survivor, I'd be the first to congratulate Dr. Miller's team, but experience has shown that death within the first week is likely.'" The man being quoted was Dr. Eric Habbaz, surgeon in chief at the Anderson Children's Hospital in Baltimore. "I've performed two such operations myself," Dr. Habbaz said, "neither of which resulted in long-term survival—and remember in the cases I performed surgery, neither twin shared her heart to the same extent as the Miranda girls, which theoretically made the separations easier."

I returned to page one. Went through the entire medical text again, searching for additional references to the Mirandas. On page 612, paragraph two: DEPARTMENT OF PEDIATRICS, MINISTRY TAIWAN, HOSPITAL NO. 9. "The eight-week-old Miranda twins relied on a common heart. And as we know, only rarely have surgeons successfully divided twins who shared this vital organ. Furthermore, with these particular Siamese twin girls, not only did they share a common heart, with multiple congenital abnormalities, they also shared a single liver. Many of the most eminent pediatric surgeons in the world advised Dr. Miller against the surgery, saying one child would certainly die and the other would have as little as a one percent chance of surviving. But Dr. William Miller felt there was a chance. He consulted the foremost medical ethicist in the United States, Dr. Margaret Collins Kessler, Chief of Neonatology, Boston Medical Center. In this situation, where the doctors feel there is a chance and the family's all for it, I think we have to respect the family's choice for intervention, just as we would respect their choice if they requested we stop treatment. It's evident that Dr. Miller understood the gravity of the situation, acted responsibly. He continued to brief the parents on the Miranda twins. It has been documented that he spoke to them just about on a daily basis, spelling out to Alice and George Miranda that Siamese twins joined at the head or at the chest are in general the most difficult to separate.

"Ultimately Alice and George Miranda insisted the surgery be performed on their twin girls, Jane and Janice, and Dr. Miller agreed to try."

I read on, searching for more personal information on the Mirandas. For example, where did Alice and George Miranda live? On page 773, I found another reference to the Mirandas: "I hope the best for the little girls, and if they turn out to be long term survivors, that would be impressive, but experience has shown that death within a few days is quite likely in this kind of surgery. Yes, I told this to both George and Alice Miranda before they left the States," Dr. Frederick Lindstrom was quoted as saying. A line here. Another there. "It was a bittersweet triumph, since, as had been predicted before surgery, Jane Miranda had to give up her life so that her sister, Janice, might have a chance to live. With the help of some highly technical creative surgery, Janice Miranda has so far beaten the odds. Obviously it is too early to predict with certainly what the outcome will be, but it is encouraging to have come this far," Dr. Miller, who headed the team that separated the twins, said at a news conference after the operation. "At this time Janice is stable and comfortable, and we hope this will continue. Obviously we are sad that Jane could not continue with her sister."

I kept searching for information that would tell me more than the medical particulars. On page 1197, the Miranda twins were again identified by name. No whereabouts were given. When I finished with that volume, there was one more tome to look at. I had placed it under my seat because of insufficient room on my desk. On page 811, I found something: "Prenatal diagnoses of the Miranda twins was difficult, and was unable to be accomplished, as the rural facility Alice Miranda first attended did not have sonography at its disposal."

That was it. When I returned to my penthouse I telephoned the Department of Pediatrics, Ministry Taiwan, Hospital Number Nine. Asked to speak to Dr. William Miller, the staff member who headed the sixteen-man team that performed the surgery on the Miranda twins. I was told that Dr. Miller had left Taiwan after the operation and that there was no forwarding address on record. None of the other members of the team would speak to me. I asked to be connected to Social Services. The social worker, Li Qui Liang, with whom I was connected, politely told me I'd need written permission from the Miranda twins' parents, Alice and George Miranda, to pursue the inquiry.

"Where can I reach them?"

"You don't know? You are not a family member?" Li stammered. "I'm very sorry, this is a confidential record, Mr. Remler. I'm afraid I've told you too much already."

I was not sure what lesson to take from the Miranda twins. All I was certain of was that I would investigate further.

PART III

THE INVESTIGATION

Way before I was a handicapper, my school friends called me Anatomy. I always had a penchant for objective analysis, whether it was numbers, players, games, teams, theater, political issues, films or books. I decided to push aside *The Tempest*, to just allow my natural swing to take over. I told myself: Just handicap. Didn't I write the basketball rating handbook which critically evaluated every player in the history of the NBA? Didn't I begin handicapping college basketball with a bank roll of two hundred and fifty dollars? A twenty-five-dollar wager. The stormy winter night I won a monster bet, felt I escalated to an out-of-wack economic bracket. "Became free!" I recalled, screaming my lungs out, jumping for joy on my panoramic rooftop. I knew I had accumulated sufficient Franklins for a lifetime. "Screw you, world! I'm FREE!" Didn't I win…Win…Win!!

My mind was still going around in circles. The rural facility the Miranda twins' mother attended did not have sonography at its disposal. What was more rural than Milan?

As obsessed as if I were on a losing streak, compulsively betting one game after another, I telephoned American Airlines.

"Get me on the next flight to Minneapolis."

If I was a tormented soul cursed by spiritual poverty, a man who desperately needed to piece together his own divided identity, I was not yet completely conscious of my motives. I still hung on to the notion that I was only searching for Ariel Warning, yet, now, in retrospect, it's clear the reason I was so obsessed with finding her, learning who she really was, was my own existential quest (call it what you will—a crucial voyage of self-discovery, a search for a unified self, a psychological awakening.) To find it somewhere in the void: myself.

Two hours later I was at LaGuardia. And then I was flying over the Twin Cities, circling the St. Paul-Minneapolis Airport. From there I rented a silver blue Toyota Land Cruiser and drove to Milan. Milan, population 353, is 150 miles west of the Twin Cities.

Luke Whittier refused to talk to me for two days. He said he had nothing to say, was indisposed. I remained in Milan. Milan had a church, a post office, a school, Luke Whittier's general store, many gray-haired grandmas, and Sarabeth Xavier. I tried to make an appointment with Miss Xavier, but she was travelling through Europe. On the third day I again visited Luke Whittier's general store. This time he invited me in. He had a goiter under his chin, a full head of wooly white hair, bushy eyebrows, leathery skin. He looked as if he could be in his late seventies; then again, he could have been an octogenarian. His words came out in a machine gun cackle.

"Wait just a minute, sonny. Milan did have one family made the news. Made quite a fuss roun' these parts. Hey, Keeler," Luke Whittier yelled out. "Come over here for a minute."

Joe Keeler was a beefy man, ponderous and slow moving. He carefully put down the Xavier Herald newspaper he was reading. Took his time ambling over.

"Bout time you got here, Keeler. Now what I want is for you to tell my friend from New York here what caused all the excitement we had a few years back."

"It wasn't a few years back. It's been over ten years. And what you mean is the Miranda twins."

"That's it," Luke Whittier wheezed, slapping his knees. "Thanks, Keeler. I knew you were good for somethin'!"

Luke peered across the counter. "Milan sure enough made the news with them Miranda twins, sonny. They were what you call conjoined. Real horrible situation. Don't want to make light of it."

"Did you know Alice and George Miranda?"

"Nope, but I did hear they were jus' kids themselves," he cackled. He stopped to slurp down his cappuccino. "Maybe you should see Fred Lindstrom. He's probably doin' some diddlin' at Montevido Hospital. He's the one who would be familiar with the Miranda twins. Fred's my age, but he's still hangin' 'round the hospital. I suppose he's waitin' for me to show up, but I've been foolin' him for a lot of years. We got a wager goin', you know. Who goes first. We made it back in ninth grade. In them days, one day we were morbid and the next we were curious. Today neither of us is morbid and we sure as hell ain't curious. Neither one of us wants to go anywhere but fishin'."

I filled Dr. Lindstrom in on how I managed to get this far, confessing a bit more than I wanted.

"When was the last time you liked yourself, young fella?" he said, swinging the gold chain of his Howard pocketwatch back and forth.

"Dr. Lindstrom," I persevered, disregarding his question. "This woman who works with me in New York. How should I put this…I think she's lost her identity."

Lindstrom removed his spectacles. "Delicate balance between courage and cowardice. Never met a body that didn't go through it. And that's what all this sounds like to me. Then again it could be a kind of amnesia this friend of yours is experiencing. Mental strain, the most severe kind, mind you, can bring on the sort of behavior you've been describing. I've known patients through the years who, while in a fugue state, experienced some of the strangest episodes imaginable."

"Tell me, Doctor. How long can one block out their memory?"

"No telling. Some say it depends on the degree of trauma in their past. How long it takes for the mind to sort of come to grips with all the hell it's been through. Then again, a body could snap out of it in a week. Had one patient it took a month, another five years. One man from Duluth, it took him twenty-three years to come out of it. When he did, he took one look at his wife, recognized her, and went straight back." Dr. Lindstrom chortled. "I don't always have that kind of gallows humor, young fella, but I just couldn't help myself. You're a serious New York fella. Anything less decent than your spying bothering you?" The way he accented the word "decent" made me feel as if he knew. Knew what? Knew everything. He squinted at me hard. "I'm sorry, young fella. There's just no way of telling about the time it takes to come out of a fugue. People are people. Everyone's on their own schedule. Drugs. Does this woman friend of yours imbibe drugs?"

"Why do you ask?"

"It's not only something devilish that can cause a body to block things out. Nowadays no tellin' what kind of damage a body might do to itself."

"I don't think it's drugs. What makes most sense is what you inferred. Some past trauma."

"And now you're thinking it's connected to the Miranda twins. Is that it?" he said, putting his glasses back on. "Have a photograph of this woman?" I removed from my wallet a picture of Ariel with David. "That's you, of course. But that's not Alice Miranda. If that's what you've been thinking, you've been yanking down the wrong skirt. Anyone blind could tell you this gal is a full-bodied woman in the prime of health. Kinda voluptuous, you might say. Alice Miranda, she was as delicate as a spider's web. Stigmata, you know. Poor Alice, she was as pale as chalk and as reedy as Luke Whittier's fishin' pole."

I thought about Emily's metamorphosis. The night we met: blotchy paste-colored skin, bone thin. I stopped Dr. Lindstrom right there. I wanted to know the color of Alice Miranda's eyes. I think, looking back, that if he'd have said brown eyes I would have given up. Why? Perhaps at that moment I, too, wanted to go fishing.

"Alice's eyes were her best feature. She had wondrous eyes. They were azure blue."

I began to question Dr. Lindstrom about the Miranda babies. Delving into their case history. Discussing Alice Miranda. Something was there: Miranda, Prospero's daughter, azure blue eyes. Something was there.

I stayed over in Milan. Slept on a cot in the back of Luke Whittier's general store. Before I went to sleep the two of us chatted. "I'll tell you what I think of today's doctors. They're businessmen with stethoscopes. Fred Lindstrom, he's a doctor. He made house calls. You know what that is, sonny? He made thousands of them and I mean after midnight in snow and sleet and frost, and when his car stalled, he'd pull out his Schwinn bike from the trunk and keep going."

In the morning I returned to Montevido Hospital, to Dr. Lindstrom's backroom office.

"You see, young fella, Alice never came over to Montevido for her prenatal care. She never had a sonogram. When I saw her for the first time, she was already in her seventh month. She didn't have a clue at the time that she was ready to give birth to conjoined twins." Dr. Lindstrom went on to advise me that early diagnosis and assessment of the degree of conjoining would have given the Mirandas the option for pregnancy termination via vaginal delivery. "If it were even a few months earlier I could have done something."

Dr. Lindstrom stood up. "One thing I give them credit for. The two of them wanted to raise a family, they were looking forward to that." Sitting down again at his desk he wrung his spotted hands. "I tell you, it was a ghoulish time. I had to tell them this awful news." He peered directly at me, his eyes pale and watery.

After Dr. Lindstrom made some more tea, we continued talking.

"Alice never did confide in me her family history. Just that her parents were deceased and that she had been living with George Miranda for a long time. And he, too, as far as I could tell, had no family support. Even then she referred to herself as Mrs. Miranda. I didn't know if she were lying or tellin' the truth. But at least that much was straightened out. They got hitched during all the ruckus that month. The day Alice turned eighteen, to be exact. I remember the day well. I was one of their witnesses. The two of them wore identical periwinkle sweaters. Well, that ain't the point. What is, is that they didn't come to see me for much too long."

He sipped his tea, returning his spotted hands to his lap as he continued.

"After the twins were born, I pulled some strings and had the chief of surgery of Minneapolis Central examine them. He said Janice was considerably healthier than Jane and had more fully developed organs. When conjoined twins are chest to chest and rely on a common heart, Mr. Remler, it is not unusual to have to make a choice as to which one you're going to roll the dice with and which one you're going to sacrifice. After our consultation my emphasis was on trying to save Janice at once. No responsible physician would have said different. But George Miranda kept insisting he wanted to try and save both girls. He got it into his head that there was some specialist out there who could separate his twins and keep both alive. He kept searching for that man. George Miranda was as hard-headed as Luke Whittier is. The only difference is old Luke got some sense. He'll let go of something before it ends up biting his head off. Not George Miranda. He was the kind that squeezes all the juice out of the lemon. He had some friend who worked for Bruegger's Bagels in Burlington. George investigated. Discovered that Burlington had a center that was doing some progressive things with conjoined twins. So he dragged Alice and his twins over there. They stayed in a motel. Alice told me it wasn't that bad. She liked looking out at Lake Champlain every morning. That's about the extent of her happiness as far as I know. After that, Miranda read somewhere about these two surgeons, Miller and Doblin, who were doing outstanding work with conjoined twins with common hearts. Mind you, these men were in Taiwan, but that didn't stop George Miranda. Soon he was telling Alice he wanted to take the twins to Taiwan. Alice didn't want any part of it. Said she had resigned herself to losing Jane. She had opted to try and save Janice. The Mirandas fought bitterly over it. Alice even left George. She took the twins and ran off. But he tracked her down. Brought her back. I think by that time he, too, was just about resigned, and then this William Miller fella called from Taiwan. He had heard about their dilemma from a colleague practicing in Burlington. Miller recommended immediate surgery. Was anxious to perform it, he said. Next thing you know, Doctors Miller and Doblin show up in Milan."

I had only read about Dr. William Miller at the Academy of Medicine library.

"Peculiar, isn't it—not one word was mentioned about Dr. Doblin in all the texts I read."

Dr. Lindstrom squinted obliquely at me, an obtuse look in his crystalline blue eyes. There was a suppressed hostility in his voice as he said, "I'd say Henry Doblin was more than just a colleague."

"What do you mean?"

A subtle smile came to his face. "You're a twin, Remler. Them two, seemed to me, were also more like twins than colleagues. The same yet totally different people. William Miller was the outgoing one. He postured all the opinions. Doblin was the quiet one. He was taciturn and dignified. Kind of shy. Both of them were real spiffy dressers, though. Henry Doblin wore what looked to me like Saville Row. Miller was a bit more foppish. Liked wearing mocha-colored Balmain suits and polka-dot bowties." Lindstrom grinned. "Surprised you, huh? I spent some time in Paris. Got to know a few things about fashion. All empty things, but I got to know 'em." He grumbled. "Rather go fishin' with Luke Whittier in Montevido Pond than stare out at the Seine to tell you the truth."

I steered Lindstrom back onto Miller and Doblin. "Peculiar, them two. As far as I could tell they had no bond or connection outside of medicine, that certain flexibility in their sexual behavior, and Alice Miranda."

"What do you mean, Alice Miranda?"

"They both seemed to take a shine to her. It was as if they were rivals for her attention." His lips pursed. "That's the way it seemed to me at least." Dr. Lindstrom stopped to reflect. "To be fair, Miller did work well with Doblin. They were a good medical team." He placed his spotted hands on his knees. "Anyway, William Miller soon convinced George Miranda he could save both his twins. He was real keen about that. What could I say? I wasn't chief of surgery at an esteemed children's hospital in the Far East, and I certainly never divided twins who shared a vital organ. The only damn thing I could do was continue to advise the Mirandas that even with the advanced technical surgery it was unlikely that either twin would survive."

He paused to calm himself. Drank some tea. "A week later, after Miller and Doblin returned to Taiwan, Alice still had her doubts. She was petrified that she'd lose both girls on the table, but George kept going at her, trying to bully her into taking off for Taiwan. He insisted trying to save Janice and not Jane made no sense at all. That they belonged together, either here or with God." Lindstrom shook his head. "I've seen a lot of frightened people in my time, but no one looked more scared than Alice Miranda. For days she kept stalling. One flimsy excuse after another. Finally, exhausted, she gave in. Collapsed is a better word for it. It wasn't that she didn't have strength. But there's just so much a body can take. I felt sorry for her. For George Miranda, too. Both of them were dealt a nasty hand, especially considering how young they were. Finally, they flew to Taiwan. And William Miller, this surgical wizard who promised miracles, along with Doblin assisting, performed the operation. Sure enough, Jane had to be sacrificed on the table. But Miller did save Janice, and of course that in itself was a miracle. You know what William Miller said when he was asked at the news conference if the surgery were a miracle? He replied, 'I don't think anything we achieve in science is a miracle; it's a product of talent and hard work.' The man was filled with himself. Considering his profession, it isn't that uncommon, I suppose."

At my request, Dr. Lindstrom went on to describe in some detail the extraordinary separation performed. In the sixteen and one half hour operation, Dr. Miller first divided the girls' common liver. Then he and Dr. Doblin restructured the heart and rerouted its blood supply, severing the vital vessels that led to and from Jane's body. Although a normal heart has four chambers, the Miranda girls were born with a six-chambered heart, which included only one left ventricle, the principle pumping chamber. They had a congenital heart defect and unfortunately only enough heart tissue matter for Janice, which was the reason Jane had to give up her life so that her sister Janice might have a chance to live.

"When the Mirandas returned to Milan, the two of them were still teenagers, yet they looked old. I mean real old. Alice was coping, though. She kept telling George that thanks to God they still had one child. A healthy daughter. But George Miranda wouldn't hear any of it. There were screams in the night, Remler. Did you ever hear a man howl for a lost child? And then a few months later, as if things weren't bad enough, complications set in with Janice. George insisted on telephoning that same fella, William Miller. But he was no longer in Taiwan. He and his associate," Lindstrom chafed, "he and his 'friend,' Doblin, were now teaching at Stanford. Didn't have much gusto left for the scalpel, I suspect, after what they had done. Anyway, soon after that, George Miranda took off with the baby. Then Alice started losing it, started quoting Shakespeare and things of that nature. And it wasn't long after that she disappeared. I suspected they lost Janice, too. Wasn't much hope to save her. And I sort of figured when Janice was gone, the two of them just sort of drifted."

Land of a thousand lakes…How many times had I made a wager on a game because of a gut feeling? Many times something as ephemeral as an ESPN play of the day was all I needed to sway me. I thought of the list of revelations: Shipwrecked malefactors came to mind. Played a hunch. Was it a hunch or a bad habit?

"Dr. Lindstrom, is there any place in these parts where one can go sailing?"

"Emily," Lindstrom proclaimed.

"Emily?"

"It's a resort town, Mr. Remler. Not far from here. Emily's north of St. Paul by a hundred and sixty miles. Real good sailing there."

I took my time driving from Milan to Emily, stopping for a cheeseburger in Crosby, which was eighteen miles from Emily.

"Nothing that great about Crosby, mister," the frazzled waitress with a red bow in her blue hair said. "We got our Bernie Madoffs, too. We're people." The week before, the waitress reported, thirteen hard-working families were scammed out of their entire life savings.

"No, we ain't got no artist community and I don't know of anyone aroun' here who does watercolors or rosemaling. No, we ain't got no galleries. Hey mister, we don't even have a shopping center. And there ain't one in Emily, either. Emily does have a meeting hall, though. And when they schedule a meeting just about the entire county shows up."

Leaving Crosby I drove along a bumpy road and soon was driving past a golden pond. I looked over. The sun was shining on some fish-eating loons diving for food. Their cries were the weird call of the Great Northern Diver. Alongside the pond I noticed two yearlings nibbling on moccasin plants with pink and yellow flowers. They were definitely shaped like a lady's slipper. All of it reminded me of the watercolors in Ariel Warning's bedroom. This made me step on the gas.

When I arrived in Emily I went straight to the city clerk's office. The person who I was directed to see was a stout no-neck female in her middle fifties. "Emily's population is 613, Mr. Remler. Mostly we do timber logging. That's correct, most outsiders who come here do so because we are a resort city. You can rent yourself a cabin. Go fishing. Sailing. We have plenty of lakes."

Finally, after more small talk, I said, "I'm looking for someone."

"Who might that be?" the woman replied, as if she had suspected I was after something all along.

"George Miranda."

"Don't know him," she said, crisscrossing her plump arms, crossing her thick legs.

"Maybe you remember his wife. She gave birth to conjoined twins. It was about twelve years ago."

"No one from Emily has ever had conjoined twins. Mrs. Lagerlof had triplets."

I took out a Franklin.

"Oh, you mean George," she said, stuffing the bill inside her considerable cleavage. "How'd you know I was making up the story about the triplets?"

"Percentages," I said. "Conjoined twins and triplets? What do you make the odds on that happening between Milan and Emily?"

She nodded her head. Looked impressed.

"Many years ago, George Miranda had some trouble on the lake. The story goes he crashed his boat into another boat. I didn't know his wife. She never lived in Emily."

"Where can I find the sheriff?"

Her eyes narrowed. "You might want to talk to Pete. He's our church's basketball coach, as well as Sheriff Ally's deputy, as well as about the only friend George Miranda had in Emily. You can find him at Allison's Fish and Tackle down the street."

"When I was a little tyke, my pop took me to see the greatest basketball team ever assembled, the Minneapolis Lakers, win back-to-back championships. Old Number 99, he was somethin' else, and Mikan's front-court mates, Mikkelsen from Hamline College and Pollard from Stanford, none better. These days people talk about Kobe and Lebron. What about Jim Pollard? He dunked with either hand, seen him do it in practice a thousand times, but in them days, during the game, guys didn't showboat. Know what I mean?"

After our breaking-the-ice sports talk, Pete Allison admitted, "Yeah, it was my wife who steered you over here. Don't look like that, mister. You weren't hustled. I can tell you a hell of a lot more about George Miranda and the raw deal he got than Allison could. That's right, mister. Allison Allison. You won't be forgettin' my wife's name I'd wager." He pulled out a fresh pack of Camels from his Levi's pocket and lit a cigarette, loosely holding it between the thumb and forefinger of his left hand.

"Dr. William Miller? George couldn't testify to what happened to him. He was killed when his boat crashed into Miranda's. The state didn't give poor George a chance in hell," Pete Allison said, rubbing the grey stubble under his chin. "The State indicted George Miranda because of the circumstances. The motive the defense attorney built his case on was vengeance. He charged him with involuntary manslaughter. Said he was jeopardizing human life because of all the pills and liquor he had been taking. George's lawyer was out of the Public Defender's office. You know the type. Bad posture, twigs for legs…She did all the talkin'. George just sat in the court room starin' into space. He refused to say a word during the whole trial. Acted as if he were deaf and dumb."

One question led to another.

"You're correct about that. When Miranda first showed up in Emily he had a sick baby with him, but that problem was cleared up in a jiffy. We all thought that what helped was the water. You know we got all of these sparkling lakes. The air's good. Anyway, after a week or two, once the infant's problem cleared up, George felt a whole lot better. He decided to stay for the entire summer. Trouble is I heard he was also sellin'…well, you know, chemicals."

"Drugs?"

"You said it, mister. Not me. All I can tell you is, George Miranda was an unhappy man from the first time I laid eyes on him. That's why I guess we took up with each other. Both of us was grieving. I was coming off my first wife's death to cancer. She had been chewed up by the monster. That's right, mister. Allison's my second wife. Well, getting back to that summer. What I'm trying to tell you is what I pieced together. It was near to the end of that summer when his infant again took sick on him. He telephoned Dr. Miller. Pleaded with him to fly down. That's correct. From Stanford. The way I figure is, Dr. Miller showed up too damn late. George's baby was already gone. He was out on Lake Doubtful brooding. Must have had some liquor in him. Maybe some chemicals. Anyway, he damn well ignored the Coast Guard warnings about this here tempest we had comin'. And Dr. Miller must have done the same. He musta grabbed a boat and raced out on Lake Doubtful lookin' for George. He didn't have no idea the baby was already gone. And that's when they crashed. Well, that's why the State charged George Miranda with manslaughter."

I asked Pete Allison about Alice Miranda. Didn't Alice Miranda show up in Emily? "Didn't she join her husband?" I asked.

Pete Allison stood straight up. His frame was as threadlike thin as his wife's was squat and stout. "She might have been here. There's plenty of cabins on these lakes. But I never seen her." He took a drag on his Camel. "Come to think of it, the two of them could have been livin' in one of them log cabins all summer without me or anyone else running into them. I always figured a woman to be with George. I mean someone had to be taking care of his baby and all." He stopped to light another Camel. "The only woman I saw for certain from Milan that weekend was the publisher of the Xavier Herald."

"You mean Sarabeth Xavier?"

"That's correct."

"Who was she with?"

"Didn't recognize the man. Weren't no one from Milan, Crosby or Emily. That's for sure."

"What makes you say that?"

"Mister, Sarabeth Xavier is an unmarried woman and quite a celebrity in these parts. People around here, we might look the other way when there's a little hanky panky goin' on. As long as it's not with one of our own." He puffed on his cigarette. "If she were with someone from roun' here, there would have been a whole lot of gossipin' goin' on in church on Sunday. You know how it is with townies." He squinted at me. "No, I guess you don't." I returned to Alice Miranda. "If George were shacking up with his wife and not a townie, I can tell you one thing for certain. She would have been as frantic as he was when the baby went into convulsions. And when the baby died, his wife would have freaked, too." He leaned his rough hand against the counter of his fish and tackle. "You know what my theory is? Want to hear it?" I nodded that I did. "George Miranda was out on the lake thinking about doing himself in. I always thought that way. Why else would he have been staying out there on Lake Doubtful with the tempest warnings comin' down? And then William Miller shows up from the West. He hears about what happened. In his own mind he feels responsible. He goes after George. The two of them just got caught up in the tempest, mister. Now remember, it was a real gale that hit Lake Doubtful that night. And the lawyer with the twigs for legs, she didn't even bring up that William Miller didn't heed the Coast Guard warnings. Or that he had rented this here cabin cruiser from Jack Keel the size of a shark, and went out there in that storm where you couldn't see five feet in front of your face. The way they told it in court, it sounded as if George Miranda crashed an aircraft carrier into Miller's cabin cruiser rather than a motorboat the size of a minnow. No sir, mister. No one including the State is going to make me believe that Miller and Miranda didn't accidentally get blown into each other."

Pete Allison took a last drag on his cigarette before extinguishing it. He quickly lit another. "You know what the State hung him on? Made a big deal about? They found a letter in George's desk that he composed to his wife that he never got to mailing. He didn't know for sure where his wife was at, so he never got to sending it off. In that letter, each time he spoke about his twins, or Dr. Miller, he used symbols. Happy faces, sunshine, things like that. The D.A. built much of his case around them symbols. Now I ask ya, mister, is that reason to hang a man?" He shook his head. "George Miranda wasn't the kind of man to kill in cold blood. Geez, many a mornin' that summer, he and I at five AM, we'd go fishin' on Lake Doubtful. George's eyes would be bulging with joy as he cast his reel in the water, cooed to his baby, talked to the Lord. Damn, mister, George wouldn't even keep the fish he caught. He'd throw them back in the water." Pete Allison puffed on his cigarette. "Maybe on that particular night he took a few drinks too many, and too many of them there pills, too. But that's understandable. Ain't it? With all he'd been through?"

I reached into my wallet, taking out my photograph of Ariel and David.

Allison fixed his eyes on the picture. "You got George Miranda's intense eyes," he said, puffing, on the cigarette, "but that ain't Alice. That woman looks more like one of them Philadelphia heiresses who attended finishing school than a Minnesota town girl." He continued squinting at the photograph. "Nope, don't look nothing like any of the pictures George showed me of Alice." He turned to me. "Strange, George Miranda ending up in Sandstone Prison and his wife disappearing like she done. I mean, they were once a family. Had conjoined twins. They'd gone through a lot together. You'd a thought she'd stand up for him. Show up at the trial. What's it all mean? Don't you ask yourself that once in a while?"

The shop door opened.

"Hi, Sheriff. How you doing?" Pete Allison cheerfully yelled out to Allison Allison, who was now sporting a badge on her ponderous bosom while entering his fish and tackle.

"I just came over, Pete, to remind you that you promised to take me dancing tonight." Sheriff Allison glanced at her watch. "Got to get over to my office." She swiveled her no-neck. "Want to walk with me?"

By the time we arrived at the office, our conversation turned precise.

"A forensic psychiatrist talked to George Miranda. It wasn't anything preternatural. I saw his report. Miranda wasn't ill. Despondent, yes. He lost his two babies in less than a year, his wife had abandoned him, rage had been building up in him for quite some time. He was a walking time bomb, the psychiatrist said."

"Did Miranda take a lie-detector test?" I asked.

"He took it. Just the same don't mean a thing. I've seen saints fail and sinners pass."

"Just tell me what the results were," I snapped.

Allison Allison gave me a cold stare. "The results were inconclusive."

"What else did the psychiatrist hypothesize?" I asked, this time more gently.

"The D.A. did his job. He requisitioned Miranda's psychiatric records from Sheriff Gissing in Crosby."

"Crosby? Why not Milan?" I asked.

"There ain't no sheriff in Milan. As I was saying, the man had problems here, too. Before the twins' birth he had already threatened to do away with them."

This was true enough. According to Dr. Lindstrom, George Miranda had coerced Alice into making the trip to Taiwan. "If you don't go along with trying to save both Jane and Janice, I'm going to put them both down," he had said.

"Mr. Remler," Sheriff Allison said, walking towards me, offering me a chubby hand. "Let's stop this smallness. It just made a whole lot of sense, what happened. The trial went right."

"Where would I find the D.A.? I'd also like to speak to the public defender who represented George Miranda."

"You can't talk to Mike Blowers. We buried him in his seersucker suit seven years ago. As for the lady who defended George Miranda, she passed last year."

I persevered with more questions.

"I guess it's possible that Miranda's wife witnessed the accident. Anything's possible. Anyway, if she was here in Emily for a day or a month, she sure enough disappeared before the trial. And she never showed up when they buried her baby either. I know that for a fact. Had Pete do surveillance. Distasteful job, but I felt it was needed. Yes, Pete testified at the trial that George Miranda was the only parent who showed up at the funeral. If you like I can show you a video of the funeral. We do a pretty thorough job around here. I bet you sorta think we wouldn't."

"Did Miranda mention any relatives? Maybe an aunt or a great aunt? A schoolteacher who might have taught school in Bird City, Kansas, with a predilection for Shakespeare?"

Allison Allison walked over to a filing cabinet. Perused the file.

"No relatives mentioned outside of Alice Miranda. Last address I got on her is still in Milan. Hasn't turned up on any computer since. I have a wedding picture of her and George Miranda. Want to see it?"

Alice Miranda definitely looked as if she was carrying twins. Her face was distorted, her body misshapen. Even her mouth was dissimilar from Ariel Warning's. The only similarity between the two women seemed to be in their eyes, but here, too, Alice Miranda's were off. There was no sparkle in them whatsoever, more like David's eyes after Thea died.

"People just don't disappear in a vacuum, Sheriff. Where do you think she is?"

The flab under her chin shimmied. "None of my business. Alice Miranda didn't break any laws. The way I heard it from Sheriff Gissing, she just drifted away from Milan the same way she drifted away from her husband and former life. Maybe into oblivion."

Sheriff Allison heaved a huge sigh. "Let me spell it out for you, Mr. Remler. It went something like this. The Mirandas couldn't offer each other much of any kind of comfort after the first twin died. And then George Miranda loses the second. And somewhere along the way his wife abandons him. Well, Mr. Remler, I don't care how strong a fella is, people snap. As for William Miller, things even out, I always say."

"What about getting to see Miranda?"

"Far as I know he's still in Sandstone Prison."

Allison informed me that Sandstone was a low-level federal correctional institution housing almost as many inmates as the entire population of Emily and Milan combined. It was located approximately sixty miles from the Twin Cities. "To see Miranda, you have to write Howard Puris," she said. "He's the executive assistant over at Sandstone. He'd have to ask Miranda if he wants to speak to you." Sheriff Allison paused. "I know you'd like to expedite this, but calling won't do you no good.

You have to write."

"Can we send a fax?

"Mine's broke."

"How about a wire?"

☙

I was advised that George Miranda had been released six months prior to my arriving at Sandstone. I asked permission to interview Rodney Meeks, Miranda's cellmate. Howard Puris asked the man if he'd speak to me. The prisoner said he would.

Rodney Meeks was serving time for killing his wife's white lover with a MAC-10 machine pistol. He had fired twelve rounds into the man.

"The only thing you can do for me is get me some books. The library here isn't all it should be," he said, placing his enormous hands on his prison overalls, gripping his knees. His requests ranged from Gebreselassie's *American Cities are the Black Man's Vengeance* to Jesse Redmon Fauset's *Comedy American Style*. I recommended Bret Elllis' *American Psycho*, Ralph Ellison's *The Invisible Man.* "The two sound like books I'd be interested in," he said, "but what about Balzac's *The Human Comedy*?" Meeks then explained, "There was a French fella serving time here. He's the one who told me about Balzac. Said he got it down better 'n the existentialists. One thing Frenchie kept drilling into me is something I sort of have stuck to my ribs now, but it took a lot of years."

"What's that?"

"Laugh. You got to laugh. Every day." Meeks placed his huge hands on the glass panel that separated us, leaned closer to the window. "Will Balzac make me laugh?"

"He'll do more than that," I answered. "He'll make you think and cry."

"That's good," Meeks replied. "In fact, it's great. But I don't think you understand what I'm saying. Will he make me laugh?"

There was none of the "I want to be happy" in his somber eyes. What I saw in his eyes was an understanding of what it means to laugh. Not only the good feelings it releases, but the suffering it originates from. A fuller perspective beyond the tears. "He'll do that, too," I said. "Every day."

We spoke about George Miranda.

"Never could get him to laugh."

"How about Miranda's wife?"

"Eleven years George was in my cell. Never talked about her. Not once."

"What about phone calls? Did he make any? Get any?"

"Every now and then he'd call to the outside. Them telephone calls could have been to his wife. Not saying they were, but they could've been."

I took a deep breath. "Can you tell me where Miranda is?"

"As far as I know he's living in Bemidji. He said he was going to try and find a job at the state college. Has an aunt living in a nursing home near there, I think."

"How do you spell Bemidji?"

"B-E-M-I-D-J-I. It's four hours north of the Twin Cities. The state college is about thirty minutes from Emily." I started to leave. Meeks yelled out, "Add one more book to our list."

"Name it."

"Yours!" he said, laughing.

When I arrived in Bemidji, my intention was to try and locate Miranda's aunt first. After that I was going to visit Bemidji State College, try and find him. I asked around. "Is there a nursing home in Bemidji? I don't mean a fancy institution. Just some place where an old woman might get some care." Finally I got lucky.

"Oh, you mean Ruth Ramsey's. Mrs. Ramsey lives about two miles down the road. She takes care of a few old folks who have nowhere to go." The young woman smiled warmly at me. "We don't call it a nursing home. We like to think of it more as a fun house for the elderly."

In a trembling voice, the imposing old woman said: "This is not Alice Miranda." I continued holding Ariel Warning's photograph to the light, certain that Simone Miranda, the schoolteacher from Bird City, Kansas, would be able to identify it. "Please take another look," I said.

"I should tell you, Mr. Remler, Alice is a real beauty. Not so obviously sexual at all. A frail beauty is what my niece is." Simone Miranda was extremely tall and skeletal, had steel gray eyes, powdery skin, long arms, a stately carriage. The white silk blouse she wore luminously caught the silvery moon as she swayed in a rocking chair on the front porch of Ruth Ramsey's "fun house for the elderly." What was ironic was that she had on a wide-brimmed hat, its brim decorated with a nosegay of yellow orchids shaped like a lady's slipper. I thought of the painting in Ariel Warning's bedroom, the woman with long arms dressed in a white frock with a high collar who was wearing a pendant, which looked like a heirloom, signed by 'U.'

"My niece is still quite young, Mr. Remler." She enunciated each word as if they were letters in a spelling bee contest. "Alice won't turn thirty till July."

Simone Miranda answered each question I put to her. She was pithy. Extremely open. At times quite sharp. Other times severely oblique. I attributed much of this inconsistency to her advanced age.

"Alice had an unfortunate beginning. She lost her twin—" I was certain Mrs. Miranda was going to say Roberta or Bobbi, "—Amy, to crib death. It took years of hard work, but finally with my help, she overcame her twin sister's unfortunate passing." She nodded her head. "What really helped was Peter Townsend's opera, Tommy."

"Tommy?" I said, surprised. A victim of my own provincialism.

"Do you know the story of Tommy?" she asked.

The Broadway version had been reinvented, though the basic tale remained that of a boy turned by childhood trauma into a deaf, dumb and blind kid, only to emerge from his hurt as a gifted and glorified pinball-playing star.

"I'm not sure if I can put it into words," I answered.

"The story is as basic as dirt, Mr. Remler," she said, swaying in her rocking chair. "Which of us doesn't go through it, where we want to just take off, retreat to a hideaway, shut out the whole world. What takes maturity and courage is coming back and dealing with things in a kindly way. That's what I tried to teach my Alice." Simone nodded her head with conviction. "I taught Alice the story of Tommy so well, Mr. Remler, eventually she became an expert at ignoring her pain. It was a good lesson for her to learn. Especially when she experienced her second, third, and fourth tragedies." She nodded again. "Alice was a wonderful child. Did everything I asked of her." A chill was in the air. Simone Miranda vigorously rubbed her hands. "Did you know it was Alice's decision to sacrifice Jane? Her husband didn't have the stomach to give it. It was Alice who had to sign the papers. That's why all the insurance claims George filed were turned down. But I suspect you learned all of that by doing your research. What you didn't learn talking to others, I suspect, is what happened on Lake Doubtful."

"I heard some of it," I said.

I was furiously trying to keep the facts straight. Four tragedies: Amy, Jane, Janice. What was the fourth? My mind continued to turn over the facts. As I knew the facts: Ariel's mother was Uma Olsen. Her father's name was Chris. He had run off when Ariel's twin died in her sixth week from SIDS. Just couldn't take it. Ariel's grandfather—I couldn't recall his name—loved basketball. Was reckless. Ariel told me something her grandfather had said: "Don't feel sorry for me, Ariel. I lived seven hundred years in my seventy plus." For some reason I was certain of that. Funny how certain things stick in your head.

Another thing that stuck in my head: Simone was very old. In her eighties. She would have been close to sixty when she started raising George and Alice. Was Alice's mother much younger than her sister? Was the father of George Miranda much younger than she? The age thing felt way off.

"Was your sister much younger than you?" I asked.

Her face pinched. A thousand lines. "Yes, she was. So were all the men in my life," she said, her lined face breaking into a toothless grin as she lifted her eyes to face mine.

"Did your sister do watercolors?"

"She did wonderful work with rosemaling. Her work is still exhibited at the Minneapolis Institute of Art." A moment later, Simone Miranda smiled almost wickedly at me. "I'm not without accomplishment myself, you know. I've written two musicals. Neither one conventional. I wasn't one of them happy-in-the-dark bourgeois songwriters, you know. I was sort of a radical. There were nude bodies all over my stage, but it was my sister Victoria who was the really gifted member of our clan. My sister was a marvelous painter."

"Wasn't your sister Uma Olsen? Didn't she win the Winslow Homer Award? Wasn't she a watercolorist?"

"My sister was a fine painter, Mr. Remler. Her married name was Frohman. Her Christian one, Victoria. Some called her V." Was the U a V? It must have been. "As I said, she did stylized floral designs. You see, Mr. Remler, rosemaling must conform to specified standards. It has very little realism, too. For that reason, Victoria did some experimenting with watercolors. But nothing of much consequence. A great many self-portraits."

Most of the time I could not ask Simone Miranda direct questions, or prompt her to answer those I asked. She'd ramble on, talk to herself as much as to me. Another significant problem was that Simone Miranda was hard of hearing.

"When I gave up teaching school and moved to Milan with my stepson, it wasn't that I wanted to. It was a responsibility I felt I had to assume. Victoria had lost Amy Roberta—"An explanation for the name at last, "—and then her husband, Budd Frohman, abandoned her. She was unable to cope. Someone had to pitch in and help my sister out." The front porch overlooked a wooded area. There must have been a pond nearby as I could hear the strange cry of the Great Northern Diver. "You see, Victoria's husband just left her. Budd Frohman was not a man of strong character. Neither one of us ever had much luck with men. I, too, was a widow at the time. Well, when Budd Frohman deserted my sister, as I said, she couldn't cope. So I resigned my post at Bird City, wrapped George in some blankets, and drove straight to Milan."

"Was Frohman's Christian name Chris?"

"It was," Simone said, before pausing for a moment, gazing at the stars above. It was a clear evening, and stars were sparkling like jewels in the night sky of Bemidji, Minnesota.

"My sister was a fine painter, Mr. Remler, but she was never one to cope with pressure. She was extremely delicate. And with the death of the newborn, I knew I had to make a decision in a hurry. Her husband, that bigamist," she said, her voice curdling, "leaving her like he did. So I came up from Kansas to take care of Victoria and help with baby Alice. I'm sure if it weren't for my taking over, Victoria would never have made it through the first year. Delicate girl, my sister. Depression always seemed to take her over in times of crisis. Victoria took her own life, you know. Alice found her in our vegetable patch."

There it was. The fourth tragedy. Simone Miranda torqued her body around so that she was looking directly at me.

"Now do you understand why it was so imperative for Alice to become an expert at ignoring pain?" She peered at me with steely gray eyes. "Four major tragedies suffered in such a young life." She spoke in a measured, almost insurgent tone. "I was the one who prepared Alice for life."

When Simone Miranda finished speaking, the two of us remained still for a while, both staring out at the wooded area, listening to the cry of the Great Northern Diver, gazing at the stars above. I reflected on what Simone had said: Chris 'Budd' Frohman was a bigamist.

As Simone Miranda continued to gaze up at the starry night, a tiny smile, like a wistful memory, creased her withered face.

"I raised Alice and George as if they were my own. They grew up as brother and sister. Possibly more like twins. Then, when Alice became pregnant," a sudden flash of anger crossed her powdery face, "some intimated that George was Alice's uterine brother. It wasn't true, of course, but some whispered that it was." She knotted her gnarled hands. "George is not related to Alice or me by blood. My third husband was his father. As for Alice, she is not Victoria's birth child. She's Uma Olsen's. Christopher Frohman's child by Uma Olsen. I told you he was a bigamist. He was!"

The anger returned to Simone's face as she said, "Budd Frohman sired the twins and he married Uma Olsen illegally the day after she told him she was pregnant. He never said one word to her about his legal marriage to Victoria. By the time Uma Olsen discovered Frohman was married to Victoria, she was already in her sixth month. She told him she never wanted to have a baby to begin with, and that now she'd never consider bringing one up on her own. Being an artist was difficult enough, she said. And that's what she did. She gave birth to the twins and walked out on them. It was Victoria who had to collect Alice and Amy from the hospital, bring them home." Simone Miranda arched her back. "You know what my sister said when she did? 'I prayed for two beautiful twin angels, and the Good Lord answered my prayer.'"

I inquired about Uma Olsen. I was intrigued. In truth, I identified with her artistic temperament. Her selfishness.

Simone scowled. "She was a reckless, indulgent woman boiling over with self-hate. The Winslow Homer Award, her fame in the art world, none of it meant a damn to me the way she acted. As for Budd Frohman, he stood there that last day and he told my sister straight up that Uma Olsen and he were right for each other. She was an artist and the only thing she needed was her work and his body. He said he didn't want to be needed and he didn't deserve a wife who was his best friend. Mr. Remler, do you believe in group reincarnation? I do. When Uma Olsen and Budd Frohman get themselves reincarnated, guaranteed the two of them come back with horns."

The next thing Simone Miranda said was sufficiently connected to make me think the puzzle was ready to be solved.

"Did you know my favorite play is *The Tempest*?"

At that moment Mrs. Ramsey quietly opened the squeaking screen door, stepping out to the porch. "You want to jabber some more, Simone, or should I chase this suitor off?"

"It's a beautiful evening, Ruth. I'm fine. Just fine. Besides, I feel like jabbering."

"In that case I brought you a shawl," Mrs. Ramsey said, placing a fine-spun wool shawl carefully around Simone's frail shoulders. When she finished she motioned for me to join her. I followed Ruth Ramsey to the far end of the porch. "Mrs. Miranda's well past ninety, Mr. Remler. I do think you might be overtaxing her a bit. She's not used to this much conversation. Hardly gets a visit nowadays other than Dr. Seeberg and her son. Now that he's around."

"What's George Miranda like?" I asked.

Ruth Ramsey's visage went from light to dark. "I don't trust men like him," she said.

When I returned to Simone Miranda's side, I asked:

"How did your niece get interested in studying the Bard?"

"Alice was a precocious child," she answered without blinking. "And I would recite Shakespeare's sonnets to her every night. She was enamored of them. Those sonnets would supersede bedtime stories in our house. By the time Alice was twelve I was reading *The Tempest* to her. On Alice's thirteenth birthday I took her to see *The Tempest* for the first time. After that, for years, we'd try and catch a Shakespeare play on her birthday, and if we couldn't find one, the two of us would recite the sonnets together, or read from *The Tempest*. After that we'd always exchange birthday gifts."

"Why exchange?" I asked.

"Alice and George's birthdays fell two days apart. July tenth and twelfth. I told you they were like twins," she said.

"The year you took Alice to see *The Tempest* for the first time. Do you remember the birthday present you gave her?"

"My memory's not what it used to be," she said. "But I'm quite certain it was something special. It was her eighth birthday, you know. A prodigious accomplishment for an eight-year-old. Sitting through Hamlet. Don't you think?" Was it senility? Alzheimer's? It could simply have been fatigue. At any rate I felt frustrated. Thwarted. Confused by the convolutions, discouraged. I decided once more to show Ariel Warning's photograph to Simone Miranda. I held the photograph in front of her. Turned her rocker to the moonlight.

"Have a good look," I said. "Take your time."

"This woman is definitely not Alice," she said. "This woman might have cerulean blue eyes but she looks hard. Maybe not hard but sophisticated. Like one of those chic New York ladies. As if she's experienced it all." Simone Miranda gazed up at me. "I haven't seen my niece in almost thirteen years, Mr. Remler, but I assure you she couldn't be that hard. It wasn't her nature. She was a shy child. If she weren't as lovely as she was, people would have called her a wallflower." She paused. "My stepson, George, was just about the only person in the entire world she'd talk to."

The way Simone Miranda shifted nervously in her rocking chair made it seem to me as if she didn't want to continue. I was wrong.

"I got it," she said.

"Got what?"

"The birthday gift for Alice's thirteenth birthday. It was a Royal typewriter."

I recalled the typewriter in Ariel Warning's flat. "Are you absolutely sure it was a Royal?"

"I'm sure," Simone said. "It was a second-hand machine. Bought the Royal from Clancy's fix-it shop. Circa 1961. I remember that year for a fact because it was the year of the Berlin Wall. What a year that was."

It couldn't be mere coincidence. There were just too many special connections to Ariel Warning. Alice Miranda had to be Ariel Warning. She had to be.

The old woman took the photograph from me. Held it in front of her eyes. "This woman doesn't have the bearing of a writer. Besides, she has cruel eyes. Alice's eyes were kind."

"Mrs. Miranda, this woman is a writer. Her name is Ariel Warning. I am trying to find out her identity." I filled Simone Miranda in, concluded by saying: "I think what happened to Alice is that when she lost both her babies the mental strain was too much for her. She suffered a form of amnesia." I proceeded to explain some of the more obvious links between Ariel Warning and Alice Miranda. The old woman interrupted me.

"I'm sure there's a great many circa 1961 Royals still in circulation, Mr. Remler. And my sister wasn't the only one who did watercolors of me. I was in an artistic enclave back then. In fact Uma Olsen, as well as the artist Kana Outfuji, must have done fifty watercolors between them of me wearing a hat almost identical to this one I have on. And they sold every one of them. That's a fact."

Stymied. Refuted. Losing patience, I exclaimed, "Can you explain to me why Alice Miranda disappeared?"

Simone Miranda deliberated for a long while. Finally she said, "It wasn't only her grief over the twins. I'm sure George had himself another woman." She shook her head. "Eighteen and burdened with an unfaithful husband and conjoined twins. She never had a chance to fulfill her dreams."

"Where do you think your niece is now?"

Fine lines multiplied on each side of Simone Miranda's prominent mouth. Her ancient face grew even more taut. "I never had my own children. George and Alice, both of them disappointed me. The fact they were not consanguined does not excuse their behavior." She pointed a crooked finger at me. "Their love was not out of a fairy tale, Mr. Remler. Once I discovered Alice's predicament, I insisted they marry at once. When they didn't I asked them to leave my house." She smiled. "You might find that a bit of a contradiction. I mean, considering the kind of radical plays I told you I had written. But in my personal life I was a bit of a prude." She fixed her steel grey eyes on me. "You do understand, though, they were not related by blood." A yellowjacket buzzing around landed on Simone's hoary hand. "I love bees," she said. "So did Alice."

I began thinking, where to next?

"One day Alice will come home. I pray when she does," Simone said, touching her crucifix, "she has put behind her, like Tommy did, all that has happened."

These were the last words I heard from Simone Miranda. She fell asleep a moment later.

PART IV

A LIFE IN THE MIND

When I handicapped I had to make sense out of the chaos of gambling stats and figures, odds and prices, and calculate with precision and predict with certainty at least some of the games that were put on the board for the nation's addiction. I did so by using my will and desire, my own methodology and approach, and by revamping my character. It seems such a simple plan: to gear one's intelligence to spot the flaw, the error in the professional point spread and price line. It was simple, and yet, to the best of my knowledge, no one else had ever done it before; if anyone had done it, or was currently doing it, it was certainly a well-kept secret. Adam Remler—The Handicapper.

At dawn I stepped out of the log cabin, gazed out at Lake Doubtful, which was directly in front of my cabin—the lake where George Miranda's boat had crashed into Dr. William Miller's, killing him. On a passing sailing ship two lovers with flaxen hair were kissing. They spotted me and waved. I waved back. I sat down on the moist sand. Removed my boots. Extended my feet into the cold black water. I could feel the lake's detritus, fragments of rock, the disintegration. Once again I began to concentrate on the investigation of Ariel Warning. I contemplated the cast of characters I had located. The information they had communicated. I tried to fit these new pieces of information into the puzzle. Splashing my feet in Lake Doubtful, I began to think: possibly David already knows. Accepts my violation. Our separateness. I removed my bare feet from the icy-cold water. It was a matter of making sense out of the pieces. Finding more pieces that fit snugly into the lost identity I was trying to piece together.

I walked back to the log cabin to retrieve a manual typewriter, then returned to the lakeside. "Detective Story," I typed. Stared at the words. They felt concrete. Implied a solvable ending. That there were answers.

I continued dancing. I had to find more pieces that fit the puzzle. THEY WILL FIT, I typed out in capital letters. I felt better. I would remain on the Ariel Project trail. I would not lose what was left of my unraveling sanity by detaching from it. By giving in to myself. Admitting that the voyage was complex and meandering, that my own identity, though not resolved, was at least not in danger of being further ruptured, entwisted, shrunken or stolen, I felt relieved. I hunched down and focused on Jane.

Doctors Miller and Doblin sacrificed Jane because the infant didn't have sufficient heart tissue substance to continue. George and Alice Miranda gave them permission to sacrifice Jane in order to try and save Janice. Actually they had no choice in doing this. The eminent surgeons insisted—medical science prevailed. What about sacrificing identities? Who stands tall with those kind of decisions? Who makes that decision for twins? I tapped out, "We must look inside Lake Doubtful, go deep, that's where the monsters reside, in the deep." I looked up from the machine. Once more read what I had written. Murmured, "That's where the monsters reside. In the deep." Then I typed, "No, that's not what I'm searching for. It's finding the lake that leads to the river that runs to the sea. It's discovering the ultimate universal dumping ground which shines and glistens and ripples on the surface, appears calm and beautiful, but is foul. I must continue the search. Who has the answers?

Is anyone who and what they seem to be? Who of us, certainly not I, has the courage to plummet the depths?"

Stepping away from my typewriter, I began to scribble notes. I did not want to forget any of the concrete pieces I had uncovered. When I finished my note-taking I returned to the machine, tried to use these notes to help explore the cast of characters that were unfolding. George Miranda: A young man not blissfully happy, I wrote down. Married too young. I used Margot Korman as an example. With Margot a scintilla of difference and her life would have taken a different turn. Her legs diminutive rather than unending, her voice nasal rather than mellifluous, her eyes dull rather than intelligent, her waist thick rather than a snug handful. Any single part of Margot, just a trace different, a particle, and Coleman would never have gotten involved. When you're young you make damaging mistakes. You're dominated by hormones, libido, not hardly by wisdom gained through experience. Unfortunately, for many, this kind of grace-laden maturity arrives too late.

I looked over what I had written, and an idea came to my mind—George Miranda was pulled in many directions. Alice Miranda was just a girl. He was bursting with testosterone, she was a wallflower, definitely shy, reticent, possibly frigid. Didn't Simone Miranda infer as much when she said he had been unfaithful? Was she correct? Did George Miranda gravitate to someone else? And if he did seek someone else, did he do so before he became cognizant of Alice's pregnancy? Or was theirs an Arcadian life and did it only happen later on, when he suffered the full impact of what it meant to have conjoined twins in her womb? Jane and Janice. Who was it he went to?

Next Alice Miranda: Who was Alice Miranda? Was she Ariel—seventeen and pregnant? Simone Miranda had said Alice wouldn't be thirty until July. Ariel said she was twenty-four. Was she lying? Why was it I felt so strongly that Ariel Warning was her? Next I typed out: Birthday gift. Royal typewriter. Circa 1961. Coincidence or psychic influence? I thought this not about Alice Miranda and Ariel Warning and the Royal, but about the Remler twins and our own Smith-Coronas.

David was lecturing in East Lansing, Michigan, at the time. As a surprise gift for me he decided to bring home a Smith-Corona. At the same time, I was in Germany for the Frankfurt Book Fair. As a surprise gift for him, I, too, purchased the very same archaic Smith-Corona model. My mind jumped to my identical. What was David thinking? Did he know of my betrayal? Had Ariel told him? Had he figured it out by himself? Should I telephone David? What should I say?

Get back to the Mirandas, I told myself, grabbing the machine and jerking it closer to my chest. Didn't the old woman with the wide-brimmed hat say that George and Alice were not Romeo and Juliet? Without romantic love what is it that keeps young people together? Obligations. Economics. Good sex. But as I already said, Alice Miranda was a wallflower. Possibly frigid. Yes, Simone Miranda must be correct. There had to be another woman. I started tinkering with that possibility. Milan. Population 353. How many nubile women were there in Milan to investigate? Not many, I suspected.

My mind returned to my twin. "When you two were maybe two months old, you'd speak to each other. You had your own language. I couldn't understand you, but you were talking," our mother had told us. How was it possible that my identical didn't know? Our whole lives we'd looked into each other's faces and known. If I didn't see David for a week, a month, I'd know where he was, what he was doing, what he was thinking. I'd just know. We didn't have to be told what the other was feeling. Thinking. We didn't have to talk. We knew. How many times had I received a telephone call from David (in the light of day, in the dark of night) when I had taken ill? How did he know? He just knew! I began to shiver as I sat on the moist moraines in front of Lake Doubtful. David knew. He was waiting for me to confess.

I shut myself off from thinking. The omnipresent guilt I was feeling was too painful. I forced myself to return to the Ariel Project. The puzzle, I shouted to myself. Concentrate on the puzzle. I told myself that before returning to Bemidji, I'd make some calls. Get a list of Milan's female citizenry. I jotted down, call Sarabeth Xavier at the Herald. I slipped another sheet of paper into the portable, typing out the names Henry Doblin and William Miller. What about these two men? Dr. Lindstrom had strongly suggested they were gay, but in the same breath he said they were both enamored of Alice Miranda. It was possible. Millions of people were bisexual. Of course Alice was burdened with a tragic problem, but that probably only brought Miller and Doblin closer to her. "Ariel Warning has the bloom of youth," Margot had said. They could have been rivals for Alice Miranda's attention. A wallflower is likely to appear gentle, sweet-natured. Of pure heart. Aren't those some of the qualities I was originally vulnerable to in Emily Bloom?

Additional convolutions entered my mind: I'd rather betray God than betray my brother. I don't know God. I can live without God. I cannot live without my identical. So how could I have betrayed him? I continued dancing. A million swirling tadpoles in my brain. All of them to be considered. Not only pieces to fit into the puzzle, but pieces giving birth to pieces. More pieces coming alive. One after the other. I had to make them fit. Watching the shimmering black water, I thought of my father: "You're thirteen. You must lay tefellin." "It doesn't make any sense. None of it does. Uncle Leo says, and I agree, we should judge a man by deeds not prayers." "Leo Solomon: That big shot! That gambler!"

My father had distinguishable pillars. Like rocks. Pillars of stone. His dread was relieved. Suddenly I saw my father in his synagogue, on the dais, leading his congregation in prayer; Cantor Remler wrapped in a prayer shawl with the traditional fringes. His head covered by a high hat. His voice commiserating with melodious melancholy. Did God really exist for my father? Did it matter? He had his congregation. His flock gathered around him with compliments pouring from their lips, with adoration in their eyes. We know so little, we have to believe in something. My father prayed to his God. It alleviated the dread. What did I have? What did I believe in? Was that why I was what I was? As a fiction writer my commitment was to pursue truth, but as a man I lived a lie. Contradictions. I reeked with contradictions. I still used type-writers. I lived on the edge. An arroyo is a dry gully, a rivulet, a stream. Contradictions are in all of us.

I thought of Emily. "Remember the time you visited me at Mount Sinai? Well, something flashed through my mind at the time I never told you. I thought the next time I'd be in the hospital, it would be to have your baby....I'm sure about it now. One day I want to have your baby. You're the only person in the entire world I'll ever say that to."

I took an oath: "No more contradictions. No more lying." I would confess to David as soon as I returned to the city. I was certain I would keep that promise. As sure about that as I was certain my identical already knew. I could feel it. He also knew I knew he knew. I could feel that, too.

"Ariel's returned," David said, sounding euphoric. He proceeded to fill me in.

"I was walking by the Delacorte Theatre, and standing in front of *The Tempest* sculpture, there she was."

'David, I didn't run away because I don't love you. I was just de-pressed and confused. And I can't even tell you exactly why. Besides, something inside me told me the way you feel. And I'm not returning because of what Bart Parker said. This you can believe. It's not because I have nowhere else to go. I've come back because I care about you.'" My twin paused. When he continued he was still euphoric. "It wasn't ten minutes before Ariel was insisting we go back to my studio to make love. Now, Adam, fill me in."

I lied. "You know how Ariel always spoke about how much she loved the University of Kansas? I had a hunch that's where she went. I'm in Lawrence. I guess the best thing for me to do now is take off for London."

"If that's what you want. Right now I have to get to a meeting, but hold on, Ariel wants to say hello."

"Call me back on my Blackberry," she instructed. When I called back Ariel spoke in measured tones. The hysteria in her voice, that trilling sound, that warble on the edge. "All of us are ticking time bombs and then one day, when we least expect, we explode. It's over. We're gone. I don't want to waste the time I have. I want both of you." She stopped. "Come home," she said. "If you don't, what has all this been for?" She stopped again. "You think you're connected to your twin? You'd be shocked at some of the things he's doing. Did you know that since the incident in Harlem, he's been carrying the Glock automatic I gave him? Come home. We can face David together," she said, her voice picking up frenzied steam. "One week," Ariel Warning screamed, her voice tinged again with that trilling sound at the edge. "One week," she cried out, smashing the phone handle against her palm. Three times she smashed it. "You think I'm a fool. I know what's going on. You better get back or I'm warning you. Both you and that meddlesome Margot Korman will be sorry. One week! One week!"

I telephoned Margot.

"I think Warning's been stalking me. Last night I noticed her across the street from my building. And this morning when I took Boggie for a romp on Riverside Drive, I saw her again. Adam, hold on…It's Jason Wyler on my other line. I must speak to him. Call me later."

When I called back, Margot insisted on discussing in detail what I had actually uncovered. I mentioned the Royal typewriter. The fact that both Alice Miranda and Ariel Warning preferred writing in longhand to using a keyboard with a ribbon, or a computer. The fact that they both used the same words. "It feels more sensuous" as the reason why.

"I've been reading up on cosmic twins," Margot said. "Sounds to me as if that's what Ariel and Alice are. Cosmic twins."

"Please, Margot. Just stop with the cosmic twins."

Margot stopped. But what came out was just more Margot. "I've done so little with my life," she sighed. "Maybe I'll teach and give back what I've learned. Maybe I'll work on somebody's farm. Maybe…" She was also upset with me. David had called. Told her that Ariel had disappeared. Returned. "I'm sorry for not telling you," I said. Apologies are a big thing with Margot. Her misgivings dissolved.

"Here's something I think you should follow up on."

"What?"

"Your other woman theory. Whoever that other woman is, she could very well be our main character. Don't knock chemistry. Passion is everything."

"I'll telephone you after I track down George Miranda."

"I'll be waiting," she said.

Before driving to Bemidji State College, I telephoned Dr. Henry Doblin in Stanford, California.

"Where were you at the time of Dr. Miller's death?"

"I was at Toso Pavilion. I remember because it was the first home game of the season for the Stanford Cardinals."

Was he lying? Toso Pavilion was the band box where Santa Clara played its home games. Stanford also played its basketball games in a small arena, but not quite the cage Santa Clara did. Maples Pavilion, where Stanford competed, probably could fit in seventy-five hundred to Toso's five thousand. I was perplexed. I thought it possible Dr. Doblin had gotten his pavilions mixed up.

"Dr. Doblin," I said. "You got your pavilions confused. Santa Clara plays its home games at Toso. Stanford plays at Maples."

"My mind sometimes gets muddled," he said. "It's enormously disconcerting."

Before I could ask another question, Dr. Doblin stammered, "I prefer to think that the explosion killed Bill, Mr. Remler. You see, if Bill drowned, it would have been an agonizing death. He would have swallowed the lake water until his respiration stopped."

I inquired about Alice Miranda.

"Alice was a wonderful person. Beautiful in a fragile way. I truly admired her. So did Bill."

I asked about George Miranda.

"George Miranda was a difficult man. When Bill consented to go to Emily, it was only because Alice had called. Miranda had been harassing Bill that entire summer. He telephoned him almost weekly. Threatened to kill him if he didn't come down to Emily to examine the baby. Bill ignored his threats. After all, Bill realized his behavior, inappropriate as it was, was understandable. He had lost one infant because of…" He stopped himself. "It was understandable," he repeated.

"What about you?"

"I, too, ignored George Miranda's threats. But then, on that Labor Day weekend, Alice telephoned. She informed Bill she had received an emergency call from her husband. Janice's health had deteriorated once again. She told Bill that she was very concerned and that she was leaving immediately for Emily. She pleaded with Bill to meet her there."

"Why did she desert her husband and the baby? Disappear? What was that all about?" I asked.

"Bill said when he questioned Alice as to why she had relinquished the baby earlier that summer, she became almost hysterical. It must have sounded to Alice as if he were accusing her. The ordeal she had been through. In my opinion it was too much for her. She needed a rest desperately. A breakdown was a strong possibility. Bill didn't agree with me, but I recommended to Alice that she get away. I told her to take some of the money that had been donated to the family to cover the twins' medical costs and to use it for her own needs. I told Alice she had been through too much. George Miranda, too, had been through too much. Do you understand?"

What went through my mind was: Pete Allison said they found an unmailed letter in George Miranda's desk that he had composed to his wife. He didn't know where she was residing. When Alice Miranda left Milan, no one knew where she had gone off to. How did her husband find her?

"I can't answer all your questions, Mr. Remler. I'm sorry. Is there anything else?" As I tried to think of something, Henry Doblin stammered, "If it were only George Miranda who telephoned, I'm certain Bill would have never gone to Emily. The collision would never have happened." He hesitated. "It was Bill's decision to visit. The two of us were giving a lecture that week in Madison, Wisconsin. Bill insisted it wasn't that big an inconvenience for the two of us to get over to Emily. What am I saying? Bill was the one who visited. Not I. I stayed in Madison."

First the man said he was attending a Stanford home game at Toso—which he wasn't. Now he was in Madison. Not only was it impossible for him to be in two places at once, it finally hit me that it would have been impossible for him to be attending a Stanford basketball game. It was the Labor Day weekend. The college basketball season didn't begin until November.

I confronted him on the contradictions.

"I'm sorry, Mr. Remler. Since Bill died I become confused quite easily. Events get tangled in my mind." He spluttered. "You must understand, Bill and I, we were extremely close."

Henry Doblin rambled on speaking about William Miller being a championship swimmer. "Three times Bill prepared to swim the English

Channel. Not once, but on three separate occasions. Do you know how many people have attempted that swim? Only 4,300."

The last thing Dr. Doblin said to me was, "There are days, many of them, Mr. Remler, I don't want to go on."

I decided to return to Milan and visit Sarabeth Xavier. When I arrived at the Herald I was kept waiting. I took the time to look around. There were dozens of photographs on the wall. The one that captured my attention was of a superb woman with filmy green eyes and two extremely attractive men. Were they Doctors Miller and Doblin? High school swimming trophies were encased in glass cabinets, Sarabeth's name carved into the identifying bronze plates. Evidence that she had been a championship swimmer during her school days.

"Ms. Xavier will see you now," the intern announced, ushering me through a vestibule that exhibited a moose head into the publisher's private domain. I was surprised. I wasn't prepared to find a cosmopolitan woman in that rustic newspaper office.

"I made the grand tour, Mr. Remler. Germany. France. England." She curled her lip. "Some of us do leave Milan. We do travel."

Sarabeth Xavier insisted I explain why I was in Milan.

"It's simple," I said. "I'm trying to go back twelve years. Put together the pieces."

"What do you expect to find?"

"I'm not sure. George Miranda lived in Milan. Do you happen to know where he worked?"

"Schwan's Sales Enterprises. They're an outfit out of Marshall, Minnesota. They operate over 2,300 computerized vans that deliver frozen food, including meat, vegetables, and juices, to customers' homes. George Miranda drove one of their yellow vehicles. They have a swan logo. If you saw one you'd probably describe them as traveling 7-Elevens." She didn't stop for a breath. "Is there anything else?" she said in an impatient tone.

"What I need from you is a list of all the young women in Milan during the time of Alice Miranda's pregnancy."

"That's none of your business," she said.

"My hunch is that George Miranda was having an affair with some woman from Milan, and that woman went with him to Emily."

"It's still none of your business."

With long, polished fingernails she drummed on an emerald green edition of Lillian Hellman's novel, *Pentimento*, which lay near the edge of her dita bark, devil tree desk. Glowered at me with a defiant haughty mien. "Is there anything else?"

"I spoke to Dr. Doblin." Her expression changed radically. I wondered about a connection between these two. "He said George Miranda took the baby with him because his wife couldn't care for the infant."

"Did Dr. Doblin say anything else?" she asked.

"No," I said. "He seemed out of sorts. Losing his colleague seems to have taken a great toll on him." She nodded. "How about that picture of you in the hall? Those men with their arms around you—are they Doctors Miller and Doblin?"

"I don't have time for this," she railed.

I took out the photograph of Ariel Warning. "Is this Alice Miranda?" I asked.

"I haven't seen Alice Miranda in over twelve years. It certainly doesn't look like her." She stood up. "That's it, Mr. Remler. I'm busy. Good day to you."

◎◎

It was late evening, quiet and dull, as I paced my let room. Between steps a gusting rain began to fall, rattling the windowpanes. I stared at the blank walls, peered at an empty bottle of Stolichnaya vodka that was left in the room. At an arrangement of dead flowers. It was the cadaverish flowers that made me return to Ariel Warning.

I remembered what Ariel had said to me. "You never lost anything. E. doesn't count. She wasn't attached to you. Maybe if you lose your twin brother you'll finally know how I feel." I had a sudden sense that David was in danger. I reached for my iPhone. Took a deep breath. Dialed.

"I'm on my phone. I'm speaking to Marcia Majors. I think we finally have a deal. Hold on. Ariel wants to say something."

Her voice was venomous. That trilling sound, that warble at the edge.

"Your week is up."

"Three days. I'll be returning to the city in three days."

A long lethal silence passed as Ariel Warning measured her words. "Seventy-two hours," she hissed.

I paced my let room, thinking. What would I do if David was gone? I'd be more alone then when Emily Bloom left me. And I knew myself. I could not be alone. I'd always had David. What was wrong with me? Even after betraying David, I was indulging myself in self-pity. David needed protection. Ariel could...

After an hour I rinsed my flushed face with lukewarm water and went down to the inn's sitting room. Inside, a Japanese woman was reading Naoya Shiga's *A Dark Night Passing*. We chatted for a while. She had lived in New York. "New York makes you forget things you were born knowing." Forty-five minutes later I returned to my room.

Before driving to Bemidji State College I filled Margot in. Before too long she was telling me:

"Dr. Porder has volunteered to help us solve the puzzle. We're fortunate to have him. More than thirty years ago he helped translate the oldest known record of a murder trial, in which three Sumerians were sentenced to death in 1850 B.C."

"What did he say?"

"He said for him translating the murder trial was like life itself. Full of conundrums."

"What did he say about our investigation?"

"Follow your dreams, he advised. That is if thou seekest clarity instead of murk." Margot asked, "Have any weird dreams of late?"

I mentioned several. Margot clamored.

"Think them through. Interpret them. And call me after you speak to George Miranda." Margot paused. "You know, Adam, that newspaper publisher, Xavier. We shouldn't rule her out as the one having the affair with Miranda."

"What makes you say that?"

"You're such a plodder," she sighed. "You're the one who likened her to the witch, Sycorax. Not me."

I asked Margot to get in touch with Sarabeth Xavier. "Maybe a woman can get something out of her that I can't."

I was directed to the lower depths of the BSC administrative building to speak to the person in charge of maintenance engineering.

"I'm looking for George Miranda."

"Today's his day off."

"Do you know where he lives?"

"You his parole officer?" the man asked, eyeing me suspiciously.

"A friend."

"Sorry. Can't help you."

As I walked down the hall a porcine maintenance worker raced up to me. He was wearing freshly laundered blue overalls with a cardboard crease which seemed in direct contradiction to his tangled shoulder-length hair. "Hey, mister," he said, puffing. "Wait up. I heard you speaking to my sup. Steiner's got a rod up his ass. You a friend of Miranda?"

"We knew each other in Sandstone," I said.

He looked at me as if I were the kind of guy who would carry a pen protractor in his pocket. "Who was his cellmate?"

"Rodney Meeks."

He smiled. "He's probably over at JJ's. Just follow the road south. You can't miss JJ's. It's all lit up." A dry laugh. "And bring your money. You might find something you want."

When I arrived JJ was tending bar with another more appealing woman. The younger, leaner woman had a smooth red garnet pierced into her tongue. She was handing out shots of hard liquor to several underage girls, impressing on the girls that the drinks were on the house, and always would be, compliments of JJ. I had to fork over a twenty to JJ before I was taken to the back room where George Miranda was. Two lines of coke were spread out in front of him.

"This here is Remler. The dude who visited Simone," JJ said, leaving us alone.

Miranda had the thousand-yard stare. Men coming out of combat have it, veterans who have seen men killed and worse—much worse.

"I've been expecting you. Sit down." He sniffed his coke.

I examined his face. The punctuated indentations near his brain where the drilling took place were neatly covered, but if you looked closely you could see through the deception. A gray scar starting over his eye, from his brow to his jawbone, dominated his face. You couldn't help noticing that the entire side had been cosmetically improved. His jawbone was still a bit off center, jutting out more than it should have.

Miranda looked up from the coke. Caught me staring.

"Additional parts of my body were torn asunder by that collision. Want to see the damage?" he asked, pulling up his pantleg. "Some of the shambles is right here." He pointed to his knee. "This ain't my kneecap," he said.

I took a stab. "There's one thing about my girlfriend that annoys the life out of me."

He took the bait. "What's that?"

"She uses the expression 'listen up' all the time. You have any idea how that expression can get on your nerves?"

He peered at me. "My wife Alice used the same expression. So do I. Don't everyone?"

Right then I noticed something that disturbed me about George Miranda. He was a man whose eyes never blinked. My uncle Leo had warned me about men who never blink. "Never trust them. They're cold and they're brutal," he said.

I mumbled something about Rodney Meeks sending his regards from Sandstone. Mentioned Pete Allison. His version of the trial. I brought up the letter to his wife that the State had found in his desk drawer. I inquired about the symbols.

"Don't you sometimes put things out of your mind? Things that you just can't talk about. Lies that you can't even admit to yourself. How else do you get by? Denial is the best defense we have. And mine weren't even conscious. I mean I might have felt like killing William Miller, but that's not what I wrote in that letter to my wife which I never even mailed. But maybe they're right. Maybe that's why I did use clowns and happy faces when it came to writing Dr. Miller's name. Maybe I couldn't even get myself to admit that I really wanted him dead. As for my twin girls. I just didn't have the heart to spell out their names."

After Emily and I separated I went back to work on *Confessions*.

During the entire period of obsessive work, for over two years, I could not spell out Em's name. Instead I would just type five asterisks.

"People used symbols all the time, my lawyer told the jury. But the State made a hell of a case against me. They brought in criminologists, alienists, handwriting experts, all of them swore up and down that I was in a state of denial. Their interpretation was that in the letter I wrote and never mailed I couldn't admit to myself that I wanted to kill Dr. Miller. They made such a stench with them symbols it had to affect the jury's thinking."

Miranda paused. My mind flashed to Uncle Leo's words. How many clichés have I heard over a lifetime? A lifetime engulfed by a multitude of flawed people spewing out platitudinous rhetoric. Remain open, I told myself.

"I knew they wanted to hang me. I mean I was scared. Because of how scared I was I couldn't think straight all through the trial. I even went so far as to see a priest. I insisted the Father hear my last confession and give me absolution. Did you ever feel that kind of fear?" he asked, looking directly at me. When I didn't respond Miranda intoned, "Happy faces, sunshine, a couple of clowns. You know what it added up to? Twelve years."

Miranda sniffed from another vial of coke before going on, slurring his words like a corpulent drinking man in need of sleep. "The doctors testified that both Alice and I had been prescribed mood-altering drugs since the death of Jane. My lawyer told the court I didn't take any for at least two weeks before the collision. She said I might have been in a state of withdrawal, went so far as to say that it had caused emotional instability. That along with my brooding over the loss of my second daughter, Janice—" Here Miranda became completely unintelligible. "An enfant for an enfant," he uttered under his breath.

One meaning I think I understood. Jane for Janice. But a more ominous one could have been "an eye for an eye."

"An enfant for an enfant," he uttered again before continuing. "And well now, you might have justification for building up a case for manslaughter two, but certainly not murder one. And that's what the State tried to charge me with. My lawyer stuck her ground. She said No Way and she meant it. She insisted that missing out on them drugs caused my temporary insanity, and that's how she pleaded my case. So, thanks to her, they ended up charging me with voluntary manslaughter."

"Look at this photograph," I said. "It's a woman I think you'll recognize." I thrust the photo in front of Miranda's face. He squinted with his glazed eyes at the picture. Then at me. Then he passed out, hitting the floor with a thud. JJ walked in. "Happens all the time," she said.

Miranda revived after several minutes, JJ rubbing his neck and forehead with dry ice. He tried standing up. His legs were wobbly. His cola-colored eyes were bloodshot, bags under them, his face flushed, his nostrils dripping snot congealed with blood, but, despite it all, he was feeling better. The lean woman who had been tending bar with JJ walked in.

"Penny," George Miranda yelled out. "This here is my friend. He's come all the way from New York to find Alice."

Penny strolled over to Miranda. Slowly unbuttoned his shirt. Yelled out to JJ, "Look at him. He's as hairy as a bear." She rubbed up against him. "I'm telling you, JJ, George here is the prettiest male in Bemidji." Penny stroked Miranda's crotch. "This stud can be our lover forever if he applies himself."

Miranda turned to me, his face grim.

"My wife was nothing like these two."

JJ stuck her hand in Miranda's pocket, removing some smoke, blow, and a few Tuinals.

"George, you and your friend are welcome to come upstairs." She turned to Penny. "You come up, too, Pen. I'll have Teddy tend bar. We'll party."

"I'm for that," George Miranda intoned metallically.

George Miranda and I ended up on the Bemidji State campus at a student hangout named Abracadabra. Bright-eyed campus scholars were drinking beer from giant mugs, devouring cheeseburgers, fast-dancing. One coed with braids down to her shoulder blades was sitting alone, an iPad in front of her. I looked more closely at the girl. She had a scrubbed-clean, cleansed-of-emotion, boyish face. When she noticed me scoping her, she stared back, her untenanted face absent of feeling. As clean as Lucite, a fugue, or my Grandma Eva's kitchen floor.

At our checker-clothed table I sobered Miranda up on black coffee, tried to get him to eat something solid. "Some soup is all I'm good for," he said, peering at the student with the braids. "Pigtails don't mean a warm heart," he muttered.

An hour later he had ostensibly recovered. If Ariel Warning and Alice Miranda were two different people, cosmic twins, George Miranda was Jekyll and Hyde.

"I know you didn't see it back there at JJ's, but that's not me. I'm truly changing. I got a friend. She's a Seventh Day Adventist. She's been working on me. My friend says what I need to do is find some peace. Now how do you do that, I asked? She said you got to believe in the Lord. Well, Remler, I've been trying. But sometimes I think too much of all that's happened and it gets pretty darn hard."

He asked to see one of my business cards. I handed one over. He scrutinized it for several seconds. "It's important for you to establish the identity of that woman you showed me the picture of. Isn't it?"

I said it was. I told him the truth. "I think the woman's your wife."

He asked to see the photograph again. I removed the dog-eared picture of Ariel with David from my wallet. He studied it. Scrutinized me. "If you'll be straight with me. I'll be straight with you." His eyes were no longer glazed. "One question, Remler. Do you love this woman?"

At Lake Doubtful I had sworn an oath. No more lies. It was a beginning.

"My twin brother does," I answered. "That's him in the photograph. I'm not sure I can love anybody," I tried to explain.

Miranda nodded. "Sometimes when you lose your heart, you also lose your identity," he said.

He studied the picture of Ariel Warning again. And then in an unsteady voice: "Don't look like Alice. But it's Alice," he said.

To this day I find it strange, but my reaction was to revert to type. To handicap. What I mean to say is, when you're on a winning streak you don't stop. You maximize the streak's potential. You just keep going. I think that is why, when I finally discovered that Ariel Warning was Alice Miranda, I just kept going. To explain further how I felt at that moment is not easy. Ariel Warning was Alice Miranda, my brain digested. But handicapping is a large chunk of me. And what came to my mind to clarify it, I mean, was the World Series. You win the first game and you still need three more out of a possible seven. I felt as if George Miranda identifying Alice Miranda was just one game. I still needed to keep playing-slash-investigating to win the entire series.

Miranda chewed on his cheek. "Mind if I ask you another question?" he said shyly, some red coming to his ears. "Did you ever notice Alice wearing a periwinkle knit pullover sweater? You see Alice knit his-and-hers sweaters for our wedding day. We promised we'd never take them off. Now I never expected her to go that far. But I was wondering, does she still have it?" The crimson blush that had started at his ears now covered his entire face.

"She wears it just about all the time," I lied.

"Ariel…Ariel Warning," he rolled over on his tongue. "Ariel figures. Warning, too. The first time Alice and I made love was on the Auf Passen bridge right outside of Montevido."

"I don't understand."

"Auf Passen. In German it means, 'watch out.'" He grinned. "We were pressed up twenty yards from the northern end of the bridge. All of a sudden the supports give and the two of us were splashing around in the water with tadpoles and minnows squishing around in our clothes. For months I told Alice, from now on we better watch out for the Auf Passen." Miranda laughed. "Not my Alice." A crease crossed the terrible scar on his face. "Alice would remember that day," he said huskily.

"Ariel Warning won't remember," I said. "That's the reason for my investigation. Why I'm here. She's lost her memory."

I excused myself to go to the toilet. When I returned, Miranda said, "I've heard about your investigation. I've received calls. Not only from Simone. Sarabeth Xavier has e-mailed me half a dozen times. She's pissed." He paused. Reflected. "Yeah, you've been doing your home-work. Yet, with all your investigating, the only thing you've been filled in on is the terrible things that happened to Alice and me. Not on how close we were. In the evening we'd tangle our legs together and lay in bed reading." He ran his hand through his thick black hair. "We had sweet days. Now all I have are memories."

Words? Deeds? Heart? What defines a man? I could feel the glowing pride George Miranda felt as he spoke of his wife. I sensed that, like me, he too had to expiate his feelings, affirm who he was by recalling what he had shared.

"No one I ever knew had an imagination like Alice. She would al-ways be telling me stories. From the time we were five she made 'em up." Tears began forming at the corners of George Miranda's blood-filled eyes. "When we were tykes, both of us chewed our cheeks, sucked our thumbs, cried when we were left alone." He wiped his nose with the back of his hand. "Both of us were susceptible to nightmares and loaded with fears. We needed to be together all the time. Especially through the night." He looked up at me. "You spoke to Simone. She's correct. We were like twins."

He stopped to collect himself, and while doing so he glanced at the business card I had given him, eyeing me with suspicion. "If you have a film company like you say you do, Alice is the right person for you to have hired. She devoured everything she could find on the film business. By the time she was sixteen, she taught herself how to write film scripts." He examined the elaborately designed, showy card. "You say you and your twin are writer-producers. What have you two done?"

"Nothing we developed has reached the screen yet. But we're close."

His eyes narrowed. "I hope you two big-city guys aren't taking advantage of my Alice. Nothing like that, is it?"

"It's not like that. My brother wants to marry Ariel. I'm concerned."

"She's still married to me. Anyway I think she is." He chewed his cheek. "Is it possible she could have divorced me while I was in Sandstone? Is that possible?"

Suddenly his head slumped down to his chest. I assumed he was feeling dizzy from all the drugs he had consumed earlier.

"My brain's a bit fuzzy," he said. "It's been like this with me ever since that damn collision on Lake Doubtful. Doctors tell me there's not a chance in hell of it getting any better." I poured him a glass of water. He drank it down with two pills.

"If Alice wants, I'll let her go. I won't stop her," he said. I poured him a second glass of water. Again he drank it all. "I'm sure Alice still loves me in her heart like I do her. But when Jane died something in both of us died, too."

"It's obvious you still love Alice," I said.

"When we first married I believed in them words," he said. "They're beautiful words. Till death do us part, in sickness and in health, for richer or poorer, but them beautiful words faded out of our lives real fast. Still, I feel them. I feel them inside of me for Alice right now," he said, tapping his heart. "Right here."

I couldn't believe that this man would steer his boat in cold blood into William Miller. I kept thinking that this man wasn't a murderer. That he was a decent man capable of love. I looked into his eyes. Sandstone Prison. Twelve years. There but for the grace of a left turn rather than a right go I. I probed myself. What made a seemingly responsible adult with reasonable intelligence deteriorate as I had? Each interpretation I conjured up in my mind, when analyzed and assessed, turned into an odious justification. Who knows all of it, I told myself. Why are some people courageous, others cowards. Genetics? Nurturing? Environment? The debate goes on. Reasons aren't the only reasons. Answers aren't the only answers.

"What's best for Alice is what's best for me," George Miranda concluded.

We left the Abracadabra. Trouble on the road. I had to brake suddenly, swerving off the dusty road onto a gravelly dirt shoulder, in order to dodge a shiny-eyed white-tailed deer. Further on down the road I had more trouble. I was stopped for speeding. The broad-shouldered trooper marching out of the shadows into the moonlight boomed, "Sir, step out of the car," illuminating first mine, than Miranda's taut face with his flashlight. He stood threateningly at the side of the vehicle: a large rough-hewn, granite-jawed, arctic-eyed police officer.

A vein on George Miranda's forehead swelled, punctuating a pulsating line in his temple. "Don't look at me that way," he lashed out, glaring at the unprepared trooper. "I'm not going to do anything crazy. And neither are you. You want to put me back in the slammer so I can get my joint slopped. Do it: I've had it with you guys. I don't give a fuck!"

Observing the hate in Miranda's piercing eyes at that moment, it was impossible to believe Simone Miranda: When George and Alice were children, Alice would take her BB gun and hunt down jackrabbits. George would grab his first aid kit—bandages and gauze—and conscientiously mend the rabbits Alice maimed. In this moment, it was easy to believe he had steered his small craft into William Miller's cabin cruiser.

We arrived at Seventh Day Adventist, Sally Cummings' property, late that night. A lone piebald calf was munching on the grass. Adjacent to the main house Miranda leased a crawl space above an oversized tool shed that was fenced off from a small garage. When he first arrived from Sandstone, he had been living in the more comfortable garret above the garage, he said, but he was asked to move by Sally Cummings' husband, Luke, so that he could let the loft to a Bemidji theologian devoted to the Lord. In his cramped quarters there was a large sofa that converted into a bed; a small desk with a hinged lid that opened up for writing. Four framed photographs lay flat atop the desk. One photograph of Jane and Janice, another of Simone Miranda, a third a sepia photograph of a woman with wavy chestnut hair, thirtyish; her beatific countenance and weary eyes, dreamy and melancholic, made me feel that if she bumped into George Miranda's rickety chair she'd be the one doing the apologizing. The fourth photograph was partially damaged: it was of Alice and George as teenagers. They were dressed as Romeo and Juliet, possibly for Halloween; the two of them looked angelic and gloriously happy.

We continued talking.

"George—did you steer your boat intentionally into Dr. Miller's cabin cruiser?"

Miranda's corded arms involuntarily jerked. "Is that what you think? That I'm a murderer? The truth is I don't know what happened that night. When Janice died I did feel like hurtin' someone. I wandered 'round. Ended up on my boat. I remember drifting around the lake. I admit I took some pills. I was cloudy. But some things I can recall. Like praying for Janice's soul and seeing Dr. Miller waving, and waving back. And he wasn't standing at the helm. Now I'm not saying that his boat couldn't have been on automatic pilot, but someone else could have been steering it as well." He paused. "I'm no murderer, Mr. Remler. At least I don't think I am."

I convinced George Miranda to go over the entire summer one more time.

"When I arrived in Emily I arranged for Sally Cummings to care for the baby. It wasn't till later, when she and her husband split up legally, that I was getting a little on the side. Nothin' much, mind you. It was just convenient for Sally having me around. Now she's a changed woman and I'm a changed man."

It crossed my mind that a distraught Luke Cummings could have been on Emily's waters. Did he intentionally ram into Miranda? Destroy William Miller in the process?

"It was during the time I was finishing up my last year at Sandstone when Sally and Luke decided on getting back together again. They confessed their sins and forgave each other. Fortunately all three of us were able to stay friends."

He swallowed smoke, began pacing.

"Now I'm thinking maybe I should've taken what I had with Sally Cummings more seriously. Ah, what the hell," he said a second later. "She's better off without me. Besides, Sally's been a real good friend. It's because of her encouragement that I've been changing. And I have been changing," he said, his earnest eyes challenging me. "I'm beginning to put my binges behind me."

He moved restlessly about the confined space. Snatched a bottle of red from the floor; stopped again for a steel-handled corkscrew under the dresser; turned the corkscrew, freeing the cork from the wine bottle; sank down on the floor in the far corner of the hazy room, dark strands of hair shaped like a curl dropping over his brow. Gazed at me as if he were a celestial choirboy, that gaze making me feel as if I were his Father Confessor.

"When I go to JJ's and start carrying on like you seen me do, it's them ghosts getting the best of me. But each day the temptation to go down to JJ's seems to get less." A moment later his expression changed from choirboy to somber recalcitrant. "And just because I was doin' drugs doesn't make me a lowlife, either."

He again reached under the dresser, this time pulling out a tangerine. "Want one? I have two." The way he unpeeled the fruit, using his thumbnail to apply pressure at the top and popping the skin, was the same technique I had seen Ariel Warning use. He swallowed the fruit whole. Poured himself some red. Reached for his stash of potent weed.

"You know in prison some guys, to pass the time, lift weights, some play cards, some look for trouble. Some play with birds or roaches or with men. You know what I did? I spent my time thinking about establishing a career. It kept me going."

George Miranda served nearly twelve years at Sandstone Prison. I checked. The State never actually proved premeditation. Those symbols adversely influenced the case, but didn't do sufficient damage to place Miranda in a coffin. Manslaughter had a sentence of seven to fifteen, and with good behavior, the probability of less. He served twelve years.

Miranda gulped down the red. "Now I have plans," he continued. "Ever since I was a boy my goal has been to be a journalist. And for me it's going to work out," he said, his dark blood-suffused eyes looking at me defiantly. "I made Sally Cummings a promise. I'm going to stay here in Bemidji for a year or two. Save my money. My plan is to enroll at the college and take some journalism courses. Maybe even get my degree. Then I'm going to head back to Milan. I think I can persuade Sarabeth into giving me a job. She owes me."

"Why does she owe you?"

"If it weren't for me she wouldn't be scheming now to be Milan's mayor."

"Why does she owe you?" I repeated.

"She just does. It's between her and me," was his sullen rejoinder.

I didn't press. When he went to the toilet I tried to put it together. First premise: Sarabeth Xavier was the witch Sycorax. Two: William Miller had come to Emily, as I had originally suspected, with romantic intentions, to ask Alice to fly back to Stanford with him. Third: While Dr. Miller was in Emily on Lake Doubtful, things became tangled, like twins are tangled. Fourth: Sarabeth Xavier crashed Miller's boat into Miranda's. Hence the explosion.

My mind took off. I did go dancing. When Alice Miranda heard that her baby took a turn for the worse, she rushed to Emily. Now, she, too, was on her husband's boat, grieving beside him on Lake Doubtful. Sarabeth Xavier was also in Emily for a clandestine affair with William Miller. It made sense. Especially if Margot was correct and Xavier was the one who had an affair with George Miranda when he and Alice first became estranged. Then, when Dr. Miller came to Milan to examine the conjoined twins, Xavier dumped Miranda and took up with him. Dr. Miller did not only go to Emily to save Janice Miranda. He was there on Lake Doubtful to rendezvous with Sarabeth Xavier. William Miller had good intentions—I wasn't selling him short. He did want to save Janice. But when he got there Sarabeth Xavier jumped all over him. Demanded he marry her. He wasn't prepared for that. My second premise: he longed for Alice Miranda. From what Dr. Doblin had said, that was a distinct possibility. William Miller always had strong feelings for Alice. Now here he was on Lake Doubtful. A glowering Sarabeth. The two of them on the cabin cruiser. Sycorax pressuring him to marry. He said no. They got into a violent argument. When things exploded, Xavier panicked. A life destroyed.

My mind jumped to Emily Bloom. One glimpse and my heart went out to her. Was it that way when William Miller glimpsed Alice Miranda (not George) waving in the moonlight? Was it at that moment that he told Sycorax he was finished with her? I kept dancing. When William Miller spotted Miranda's boat and waved, Sarabeth could have been below. No one saw her. A moment later at the wheel. Yes, it made sense. It wasn't George Miranda who crashed into William Miller, causing the explosion. It was Sarabeth Xavier who steered Dr. Miller's cabin cruiser into Miranda's tiny boat. Xavier was a high school swimming champion. Before impact she dove off the cruiser and swam undetected the many miles to shore. When the two boats collided, George Miranda suffered serious injury. But that isn't the reason he can't recall what happened. He wasn't up to par, as the State proved, because of the prescribed drugs he supposedly hadn't been taking. Alice Miranda, too, was shell-shocked. She had been since the time she had disappeared from Milan. Possibly before that, since the death of infant Jane in Taiwan. Wasn't it Dr. Henry Doblin who said Alice Miranda wasn't functioning properly back then? Now, with the death of her second infant, there was little left of Alice Miranda/Ariel Warning.

Monstrous Sarabeth Xavier reacted quickly. Somehow she made contact with George Miranda; told him she had been on the cabin cruiser; saw everything that had happened. Told him she had seen his wife intentionally steer his boat into William Miller's. Convinced him that once Alice came out of her trance she would want to confess to what she had done. It was her character. She was a person of (as Simone Miranda advised) immense integrity. George Miranda believed it was true. He believed his wife had purposefully killed Dr. Miller. It would go down as murder one. He reasoned that if he went to trial instead, he would not be indicted for murder one. His lawyer could use the fact that he was unstable. Prove it by the chemicals he supposedly wasn't taking. The most the State could sentence him for would be manslaughter two. A couple of years' prison term was all he anticipated receiving. In his mind it was not only his selflessness, but Sarabeth's cunning, that made it possible for Alice Miranda to get off scot-free. That was why he couldn't tell me what it was that Sycorax owed him. He wouldn't dare tell anyone that she, Sarabeth Xavier, was on the cruiser. The Coast Guard never had a clue about her being there.

I kept dancing. Xavier probably promised Miranda a position on the Herald, maybe a lot more. At this time he was posing. That's what all of this was. A pose. He was waiting for the appropriate time to cash in. I decided I, too, had to pose. When Miranda returned from the toilet I pointed an indicting finger at him.

"Alice was the one who murdered Dr. Miller. Not you."

"Why are you bringing up Alice? She's got nothing to do with any of this. It was me. Me!" he shouted. "I did it. I served my time. It's over!"

A jumpy Luke Cummings knocked on the door.

"George. Sally's water broke. She don't want me to do the driving. Says I'm too jittery. Besides, she says she wants you at the hospital. Says she promised you you'd see your godson born along with the Lord."

All night I kept hearing George Miranda's rebuttal. "I did it! I served my time! It's over!" His apprehension: "Why are you bringing up Alice?"

A fifth premise conjured in my head: Alice Miranda ran away not only because of her anguish. She also escaped because of her guilt. A subtle distinction. The way I now had it pieced together, at the onset of the summer, not only because of her distress, but because of her culpability, she ran away from it all. Her memory (as Miranda's memory because of the prescribed drugs he *wasn't* taking) was shattered to begin with. As I said, the tranquilizers, pain killers—these chemicals in Alice's system since Taiwan—could cause profound problems. Loss of memory, intermittent violence. Add the heartfelt state of denial that inevitably occurred with the loss of Janice. The fact that Alice was still a teenager. All of it overwhelmed her. Alice Miranda simply detached from everything. Her brain stopped functioning. She couldn't remember anything that happened on Lake Doubtful, including her culpability. I told myself it was the reason Ariel Warning let slip all those revelations. Subconscious guilt. Not that different from when I sat at the Smith-Corona exorcising my own demons. Only in Ariel Warning/Alice Miranda's case, it was the murder of William Miller her mind was trying to escape. With me, it was the heathen betrayal of my identical twin.

All through the night I told myself I had to confess to David. Confess. Confess. What was it Ariel Warning had to confess? She had threatened me. Threatened Margot as well. Her voice was menacing. Ariel Warning was dangerous. She was real. What if she was the one? Was she the one? Had she steered Miranda's boat into William Miller? Was she the murderer?

I made a decision. I would stay over in Bemidji, let a room for an additional few days. Do more probing. Immediately after renting a room I telephoned Margot.

"Adam, stop ranting. I will follow up on your premise. In the meantime, why don't you call Dr. Porder. I've caught him up on everything that has transpired."

"Cosmic twins. *The Tempest.* Mysticism. Rubbish!" Dr. Porder growled, letting out a wheezing bark. "Remember your Goethe, young man: 'It is easier to perceive error than to find truth, for the former lies on the surface and is easily seen, while the latter lies in the depths where few are willing to search for it.'"

It was only a minute or so later when Dr. Porder and I began discussing Ariel Warning.

"Has Ms. Warning ever mentioned having dreams?"

I recalled something Ariel had said to me once: "I've been having this dream. It's about twins conjoined like the Parkers. Only they're girl-twins."

"Dreams such as you described could be a piece of her memory returning," Porder said. "In that case she may not be psychotic. It's very possible she might be borderline."

Dr. Porder stopped to take a phone call. Upon finishing, he continued: "One thing you and your twin brother did correctly, you gave this woman time to recover. You didn't push her to remember. And from what I gather, she hasn't pressed herself. That's all in her favor. Any therapist will tell you, let it come back naturally. As for those flashes of anger you mentioned, it's possible she's acting out of unconscious hostility....How can I tell you what to expect? Expect everything. Expect nothing. From what you've told me, here's my prediction. You and your identical had better be prepared. Ariel Warning will be getting a lot more hostile before she gets better. Yet once she regains her memory, everything which happened during this transient period will disappear. She'll only recall her life before the fugue blocked it out. And in all likelihood she'll be regaining her identity in the very near future and will return immediately to her past life."

I deliberated on "a lot more hostile before she gets better" while Dr. Porder took another phone call. When he got off the phone, he summed up, "As life, conclusions evolve. I'm confident all the answers you're seeking will evolve."

"Adam, delete premises one through four. Sarabeth Xavier wasn't on board William Miller's cabin cruiser. She was on the yacht of one of the most powerful businessmen in the State of Minnesota. That's why Sarabeth was spotted in Emily by George Miranda's buddy. The fish and tackle guy. That's what that was all about. Not betrayal."

"Margot, how did you pick up on all of that from the little I said?"

"This guy and I go all the way back to when I was doing a series for the *Village Voice* on organized crime. I have files on this pharisaic thicker than a Webster's. Anyway, when I checked my files, the information sure enough corroborated what I already thought. This crumb was on Lake

Doubtful that weekend. I always felt this guy had a girlfriend on Lake Doubtful that summer. I just never knew who the woman was. You just triggered the idea in my mind that it might be this Xavier woman. So I investigated. Turns out I was dead wrong. Sarabeth Xavier was in Emily all right. But she was there to do a feature on this crumb…Of course I have proof. I had a source of mine fax me the Sunday feature story Xavier wrote for the Herald. Her byline out front. When you shuffle it all up it tells you something, doesn't it? Sarabeth Xavier wasn't onboard William Miller's boat, and she didn't murder him or cause the crash."

I asked Margot to do more checking on my Fifth Premise—Alice Miranda escaped because of her guilt.

"I'll get back to you in twenty-four hours," she grumbled.

Twenty-four hours to the minute, responsible Margot telephoned.

"I did a thorough investigation. Not only with the Coast Guard, but also with the National Weather Service. It was an extremely foggy night." As Margot spoke about fog, I thought, David trusts me with his life, and I walk through it as if it were fog.

Margot continued spewing forth torrents of information.

"I also checked with the marina representative. The vessel Dr. Miller leased was ship-shape. I asked about the explosion, and he said, 'Water will stop an alcohol blaze, but not gasoline. Keep your extinguishers freshly filled and know how to use them. That will take all the hazard out of the fire.'" Then she added, "George Miranda obviously didn't have the wherewithal to use his extinguisher. I checked. According to the Coast Guard records, when he was picked up he was in a drug-related stupor. I also checked out William Miller's capabilities. This same marina fellow told me that his files indicated he spoke to Dr. Miller at length before he leased the boat to him. In his opinion Miller was a knowledgeable seaman. If his vessel had a gasoline leak, he should have known ordinary soap would temporarily seal it."

I heard Margot shuffling papers. I could imagine what her desk looked like. Cluttered, yet organized, everything she needed at her fingertips.

"From the dossier I compiled on Dr. William Miller, he was the kind of veteran seaman that would spend the extra few minutes it takes to go over all the nuts and bolts of his engine with a wrench. Lag screws holding the motor down are particularly prone to loosen up with vibration. I'm certain Dr. Miller was cognizant of that. I would also have to believe he knew that gasoline tanks should be provided with tight fillers to the deck…"

What makes us speak from the head rather than from the heart? Is it that man's fundamental condition is inherently insecure? How could I be annoyed with barren Margot? Was she speaking from her mind for any less cowardly reasons than myself?

Finally Margot brought up my fifth premise: that Alice Miranda was on board her husband's boat. Her culpability.

"Alice Miranda is not mentioned in the Coast Guard records. No one saw her. So if your theory's correct, she had to be lying at the bottom of the boat. Curled up. There wasn't much room. And she would have had to put on a life jacket to allow her to escape. It makes sense." Margot explained, "According to the Coast Guard records, two life preservers were listed as being on board. George Miranda was found floating on driftwood. He was wearing one jacket. There was still one more. It makes sense," Margot repeated. "As much sense as the fact that Dr. Miller's body was never properly identified."

"What do you mean?"

"The Coast Guard advised me that because of the fire, positive I.D. was never made. Still, much of the wreckage was eventually recovered and by association used to identify Dr. Miller: a silver scalpel along with a Rolex watch somehow surfaced near the beach. My theory is that swirling waters or possibly a turtle or other sea animal had carried the scalpel and timepiece to where they were spotted glistening beneath the lake water by two twelve-year-old boys fishing along the sylvan shore. The engraved inscription on the Rolex identified the owner: 'To William Miller with respect, from Ministry Taiwan Hospital #9. For humane work with all our children.'"

"When the State made a more thorough search of the area, they found additional identification. A Snickers bar wrapper, along with several joints of his fingers. Lab reports identified the digits as Miller's. On one digit, still attached, a ring: NCAA swimming champion, Stanford, 1976."

When I again initiated speculation on Alice Miranda, Margot immediately cut me short. Soon she was discussing bells, bow lites, side lites, stern lites, whistles, horns, flame arresters, first aid essentials, pistols that shoot parachute-type flares, anchor lines, boat hooks, mooring lines. I could hear Margot shuffling papers.

"What's your conclusion?" I asked, needless to say impatiently.

"George Miranda's lawyer was inept. The law specifically states: 'Such a rate of speed as will enable a vessel after discovering another vessel meeting her to stop and reverse engines in sufficient time to prevent any collision from taking place.' Who can prove that George Miranda didn't obey the law? There's reasonable doubt here. With reasonable doubt, any dunce has a formidable defense. You see, Adam, visibility varies with atmospheric conditions. Sometimes it's impossible to clearly see objects below the horizon. An object, let's say a log, an oar, or even the remnants of an iceberg, could have contributed to Miranda losing control of the wheel. The truth is, a major jostling of any kind might have induced his eighteen-footer to swerve off course. We have established that neither seaman had any other problems. The fish and tackle guy's theory is wrong. The tempest he spoke of blew over. That's why there weren't any mayday calls to the Coast Guard. Besides, even

if there had been a storm, their radios were in good working order. I
checked. Both boats were sound. What's left? The fog! The two men
didn't consider the extent of the fog. Their visibility was extremely limited. What they didn't have was good judgment. And Mr. Miranda's pro
bono lawyer's defense was even worse. My conclusion: The smashup
was an accident."

"What about the State's position? Miranda was on drugs. Went berserk. Wanted vengeance. Took it."

"It was never proved. Of course there are several more things I want
to investigate. And I will when I get back."

"Get back?"

"Coleman's birthday is coming up. To celebrate we've decided to
take off for an extended weekend. Coleman's become a mensch. We're
biblical again."

That night, along with two bottles of a good red wine, I visited George
Miranda again. He had on the periwinkle sweater Alice Miranda had
knitted for him. "It's getting hot in here," he said, removing the pullover.
Tossing it in an open dresser drawer. The T-shirt he wore showed off
his blacksmith's arms, which were in direct contradiction to his scarred,
gaunt face. I pulled a Snickers bar from my shoulder bag. "Want one?"

Miranda grinned. "When Alice and me were kids, every day, even if
it were ten below, I'd run down to Old Man Stiloski's candy store and
buy her half a dozen." He began speaking enthusiastically about Sally
Cummings and the male child she had given birth to. I cut him off.

"I've heard a great many things about you and Alice," I said. "What
surprises me more than anything is how mature and sober the two
of you were. I mean the two of you were teenagers. You had to go all
the way to Taiwan. I know the money for the trip and everything else
was contributed by many different community sources. But still, the

pressure you two were under. Both of you acting so responsibly."

Miranda nodded. "It ain't maturity, it's reality that does it. We had no choice but to handle it. But the two of us paid a heavy toll. Know what I mean?"

There were several loose ends still bothering me concerning Ariel Warning.

"Where did Alice get the money to attend the University of Kansas? How did she arrange for that?"

Miranda smiled. "Alice never attended Kansas U. That's all wishful thinking. That's all that is. When the two of us split Milan, Alice did go down to Lawrence for that one summer. At the time we weren't sure if we'd stay apart or get back together. The only thing we knew for sure was that Alice was unable to care for the baby. That was why I agreed to take Janice with me to Emily in the first place."

Another loose end bothering me was that if Ariel Warning grew up in Milan, Minnesota, and Bobby Cover lived his entire life near Middle Beaver Creek in Cheyenne, Kansas, how was it possible that their paths crossed?

"That's easy to explain," he said, answering my query, pinching a cyst on the side of his neck and draining the suppuration. "When Alice and I were fifteen, Simone took us back to Rawlins to visit family. It was at that time she met Cover." He rubbed the wen. "Remember what you said about your friend not being able to lie? Alice, too, wasn't a liar. But that one summer she did. I didn't find out about Bobby Cover till the day we got hitched. It was then that she confessed. Other than that one time, far as I know, Alice was always straight with me."

"Be straight with me, George. You're the one who told Alice to take off. Invent a new life."

"Whatever you want to think, you're welcome to," he said, his face suddenly appearing much older. He poured himself some red. Drank it down. "The best thing I can do for myself is to let go. As Alice let go. As far as Alice's detaching goes, it was the only way for her to remain sane." He drained a second glass before lamenting that he wasn't the person he had been.

"I'm like a prize fighter who's been in the ring with a killer champion," he said. "What's left of me is unrecognizable." He leaned over, snatching from the bureau the framed photograph of him and Alice as Romeo and Juliet. He dropped it in the process, the protective glass splintering on the floor. For a moment he squinted at the jagged pieces. "When Alice and I left Taiwan, I wasn't sure who I was. I was hardly capable of asking questions correctly, let alone answering them. I felt powerless. Out of control. As if my mind was gone." His voice trailed off. As I gazed at him I thought of how I had obsessed over Emily Bloom, walking the streets till five in the morning. Or I would be in a bar of laughing people, and inadvertently one of them would say something that would trigger me off. I'd begin to weep like a lost child. I'd go home with strangers.

"Don't mind me. When I get down I begin to feel I need a lifetime of sleep, but then I pick myself right up."

"How do you accomplish that?" I asked, recognizing I'd never had that kind of strength.

"I focus on being out of prison. And how I'm going to change my life." He continued, "You know who was worse off than me? Henry Doblin. You should have seen him at the trial. Just imagine how you would feel, losing your lover." Miranda reached underneath the rumpled bed he was sitting on, pushed aside a butterfly dish, picked up a pinewood cross. "Without faith in a higher power it's near impossible to make peace with oneself. I've seen it at Sandstone. The guys who come back are the ones who believe. Believing in God is the only chance we have."

I thought of my father. Miranda peered at me. He fondled the cross.

"You remind me of Henry Doblin. There weren't no bad blood

between us. It wasn't him I blamed." He paused. "If I were writing a profile on Henry Doblin, I'd describe him as conflicted, divided and dark." Miranda reflected on what he had said. Grinned sheepishly. I suspected he was the kind of man who felt uncomfortable being labeled anything but blue collar. "Even then Henry Doblin carried a lot of baggage. He would talk to me about what he called his 'relationship struggles.' Sometimes he would sit with me and murmur, as if it were a prayer he was reciting, that William Miller was an egoist and would eventually experience despair. I never could figure out if he was talking about this lifetime or the next. But as I said, Henry and me got to know each other pretty good, like you and me are doing, Remy, and we ended up exchanging confessions like men do."

Miranda had started calling me Remy. I think it was his way of extending warmth.

Miranda gulped down more red. Stretched. "I think I'll have that Snickers bar now." I took one out of my shoulder bag. He grabbed it, gobbled it up. "Got another? But as I told you, Remy, Henry Doblin was an all right fella. He taught me a whole lot, especially about preparin' to be a father of twins. He said with twins…here, let me show you. What was the first word you ever spoke?"

"Tree," I answered.

"Then your brother's was something less rooted, like car, maybe airplane, something like that."

David's was taxi, I acknowledged.

"See, Remy, Doblin was correct. He said if a twin's first word was one thing, his brother's would be the opposite. Something to do with yin and yang. Henry said he and William Miller were a lot like twins." He brushed back his thick black hair. "Henry told me that when he and Miller were in college they swapped lovers all the time with boys they dated. Talking about swappinging lovers. What 'bout your twin and Emily?"

"Are you crazy?" I cried out.

He hesitated, drained what was left of his glass of red. "The other day at Abracadabra you mentioned your twin's wife died. What did you say her name was?"

"Thea," I answered, recalling Thea's raised fist. Two men, one fist, she loved to say, raising her fist at us.

"What about your conduct with Thea?"

I shuddered. "Thea's gone."

He finished off the second Snickers bar, brewed coffee.

After that he started talking again about the eight-pound baby boy Sally Cummings gave birth to. He seemed to take enormous pleasure in describing the miracle of birth. It took a while, but eventually I steered him back to Doblin and Miller.

"Truth is, Remy, Henry, he did have a problem." Miranda shrugged. "We all have a dark side. Lovers, like twins, are symbiotic," he muttered, as if that was a definitive answer. "I always calculated that Henry's ambivalence for Miller had something to do with them being gay and symbiotic. But that Henry," he rolled his cola-colored eyes, "he was a strange one. He'd say weird things, like he had come to believe it was his own arrogance that had him believing that by the act of thinking, reasoning, he would be able to become a whole person. Be more. He would then pound his fist and say he wasn't more. He was less. When I asked him what made a successful guy like him feel like such a loser, he'd just look at me. It was the same kind of helpless look my wife and I had when he informed us that there was only enough heart tissue to save Janice. That Jane would have to be sacrificed."

The corners of Miranda's mouth tightened. "At the news conference after the operation Henry didn't say a word, he just stood at William Miller's side. It was Miller who did all the talking." He picked up the steel corkscrew beside him and unconsciously ground it into his palm. Blood trickled from the spot.

"At this time, Janice is stable and comfortable, and we hope this will continue. Obviously we are sad that Jane could not continue with her sister," he whispered, that thousand-yard stare etched on his face, eerily uttering Dr. Miller's exact words to himself, continuing to grind the corkscrew into his palm.

Recovering his composure, he wiped the blood on his shirt. "I never could get Henry Doblin to go further. Lookin' into someone's heart is dangerous. So I left it at that."

Miranda wrapped his hand in a dirty handkerchief, gulped down two pills.

"Remy, let me ask you a question. How do you think your twin would react if Alice comes out of her fugue? Explains what she's gone through and then tells him she has to leave him?"

I didn't have to answer George Miranda's question. He nodded off.

That night something popped into my head that Dr. Doblin had said:

"It wasn't only Bill that was hooked on sweets. Both of us were notorious chocolate addicts." Immediately I thought of the Snickers wrapper found floating on the lake water. I started thinking about Henry Doblin. What if he was faking? I had detected inconsistencies in his statements: The Toso-Maples lie, as well as the fact that the college basketball season didn't begin until November, and the murderous incident on Lake Doubtful had taken place during a Labor Day weekend. Did these contradictions seem a bit forced? Perhaps contrived?

Dr. Doblin was a brilliant man. He was associate chief of surgery, Hospital #9, Department of Pediatrics at Ministry Taiwan. Why would a man of his stature promulgate arguments that were blatantly wrong? And then I thought: Homosexuals, like twins, live with drives and tensions that alienate them from the rest of society. Many identical twins and gay lovers suffer from halved or diminished self-esteem.

Betrayal is a way to assert their will, their autonomy; a drastic means of rebelling against their other half/lover. My Henry Doblin theory gained momentum: Henry Doblin destroyed William Miller. Was this hypothesis any less logical than my clenching a silver dollar when I phoned in a bet? My parents lighting candles on Friday night? Emily's Zen chants?

I began to think of *The Tempest*. For some reason the play had conjured up in my mind some strange, brave new world as I tried to separate from my identical. It certainly wasn't because *The Tempest* had become a matrix for the mystery. There had been no definitive reason established by Margot, or by myself, as to why Ariel Warning/Alice Miranda would be so besotted by this play that it would become another reality for her. Nothing I could think of made the matrix feasible—yet here I was, dwelling on the Bard's creation. By the art of Prospero the usurper's son, Ferdinand, is wrecked on the island. Wrecked!

"William Miller," I said. Doblin wrecks Miller. Was Henry Doblin posturing his grief? I thought of something George Miranda had said: "Sometimes when Henry spoke about Miller he had the same kind of rage in his eyes I usta see in them soulless zombies in the yard at Sandstone." I concentrated on Henry Doblin. Why? To fill up the day. To avoid going inside myself. Returning to New York City. Looking David in the eye.

I decided to pay a visit to Henry Doblin in Palo Alto.

I recognized Dr. Doblin at once from the photograph I had seen in the vestibule at the Xavier Herald. He had a topknot in his hair like a Sumo wrestler, was wearing an elegant beige cashmere robe, inelegant powder-blue cotton pajamas. The aging houseboy who was feather-dusting folios whispered softly, "Dr. Doblin has a way to go before he's fully recovered."

Henry Doblin's library was designed in rosewood. In fact his entire home was done in rich, warm, very exotic woods. Everything in Dr. Doblin's abode was designer made, painted or sculpted. The walls were paneled; the ceilings beveled. The rooms looked more like they belonged to what the Japanese call "a living soul" than to a grieving surgeon living a solitary life amongst the giant redwoods on a woody mountaintop outside of Palo Alto.

As I entered Doblin's immense library, it became evident that he was an art collector. Paintings by Picabia, Tanguy, Egon Schiele hung near artifacts of ancient Greece and Rome; a similar sculpture of antiquity stood alongside a modern bronze. Possibly it was Melissa Joy Tobin's Mother with Six Tongues, or its identical twin. The work that especially caught my eye was a framed daguerreotype on the wall of Chang and Eng, perhaps at six months of age. Dr. Doblin motioned for me to sit.

"I'm glad you came early," he said, offering me some apple juice. I accepted. Once we began, Henry Doblin did most of the talking.

"Bill and myself were trying to be useful. Our entire careers we tried to be useful. We started out two earnest young doctors." He wiped his brow.

I asked Dr. Doblin what he could remember of the past twelve years. "I can tell you the first two things I recalled when I came out of this fog I've been in. I remembered I was a doctor. And, more importantly, how I felt about Bill." He reached for a framed photograph of William Miller. Caressing it, he placed it on his lap. I had the feeling that if William Miller were alive with AIDS lesions covering his body, Henry Doblin would have caressed those lesions, too.

"From the beginning, Mr. Remler, I was against the kind of unorthodox surgery Bill wanted to try. I kept demanding we do the more conventional surgery. Creative surgery is a turn-on for you, I told him. It's exciting. Once you start experimenting there's no stopping you. It's ego over patient every time. I insisted it was only Janice who could possibly be saved. I felt if we did the more accepted surgery, and Janice survived to childhood, the quality of her life would be excellent because her brain and other organs were normal. Everyone on our team agreed with me. If you polled them, they would tell you to a man that when conjoined twins are chest to chest, and without two good hearts, it is only logical that a choice be made as to which one you're going to prioritize, which one you are going to sacrifice."

I recalled Dr. Lindstrom telling me that Janice Miranda was significantly healthier than Jane, and had more fully developed organs. That it was Dr. Doblin's idea, an orthodox one, to take bone tissue from Jane (an enfant for an enfant) to repair defects in Janice after the separation.

"I kept demanding we do the more customary surgery," Henry Doblin repeated, while stroking William Miller's photograph and continuing to explain himself. It seemed he could not stop doing either.

"Bill, your way is without precedent, I told him. My way, at least we have guidelines, and there is a good chance to save one of them. Bill, I argued, even if Janice survived the surgery, death would most likely occur within three days. He remained adamant. I dissented—I said, I'm sorry, Bill, glory can wait. I won't gamble with Janice Miranda's life. It's up to the Mirandas, Bill reluctantly reminded me. It's their decision. And so, before we left Milan, the two of us spelled out all the facts to the Mirandas. 'Let's go for it,' George Miranda said. Those were his exact words, Mr. Remler. He passionately wanted Bill's surgery performed."

Henry Doblin glanced at William Miller's photograph. Continued. "By the time the Mirandas got to Taiwan, Bill and I were at each other's throats. 'I'll do everything in my power to stop you. Get a court order if I have to.' Bill continued urging everyone concerned that we must attempt to save both twins. In his opinion, it was the sanest thing to do. He strongly felt there was a chance. Almost as good a chance as saving only Janice. The operation was put off for one day. Then, when our dispute continued, Bill was forced to postpone indefinitely. You do realize, Mr. Remler, each day postponed was critical." Again Henry Doblin caressed Miller's photograph. "By this time all of us were conferring on a daily basis at Hospital Number Nine. Alice Miranda was exhausted, on more than one occasion disoriented. As for George Miranda, well, people become anxious. Desperate. 'Do something' is what you eventually hear.

"Bill waited. Four days later George Miranda asked to confer with him privately. He told Bill he had thought it over in his heart and his head. He again emphatically stated he wanted to try and save both daughters. Bill told George Miranda we still needed his wife's permission. George said he would talk to her again. Alice Miranda continued to despair. Bill didn't reschedule the surgery. Finally, two days later in the hospital chapel, while the Mirandas were on their knees praying side by side, Alice Miranda gave her permission to go along with her husband's decision. It was only then Bill rescheduled the separation surgery. Ultimately, it came down to the fact that Alice Miranda, like her husband, couldn't accept doing nothing. She had to try and do something even if the operation wasn't likely to succeed. Of course she continued to have trepidation. Who wouldn't? And of course she continued to pray. The Mirandas gave their written consent to try and save both twins. Separate Jane and Janice Bill's way. His way!"

Dr. Doblin walked over to a window. Gazed out at the giant redwoods. A cryptic smile crossed his face as he muttered, "A fork in the road. A left turn. A right. A yes. A no."

The cryptic smile had disappeared from his face when he turned to me. "Thirty minutes before the surgery was to begin I went to Bill. 'I've put in a court order to stop you. You'll be getting the injunction within minutes.' 'I can save both infants,' Bill shouted, turning away from me." Dr. Doblin paused. "I asked Bill to leave the operating room. 'What's wrong with you? Your plan is reckless and unworthy.' It wasn't just my words, Mr. Remler. It was the way I said them. Bill was unworthy. When you tell your closest friend, the person who knows you better than you know yourself, when you look him straight in the eye and tell him he's unworthy. The person I was closest to in the world I stopped. You must understand, our combined skills were needed." One without the other came to mind.

At that instant, Dr. Doblin seemed to lose it. As if the stuffing was knocked out of him. "You know what I testified at the trial," he said, his voice cracking.

"Do you still think your judgment against George Miranda was the correct one?" I asked.

"I'm not certain," he stammered. When he regained his composure, he said: "The authorities said George Miranda was alone on the boat. Of course I'm aware that no one saw Alice there. But you know, Mr. Remler, I had many long conversations with George Miranda. More than once he said to me that when he and Alice went sailing, it was always she who took charge. You see, Mr. Remler, George Miranda told me that he never felt comfortable steering a boat."

Carrying a ripe watermelon, I knocked on George Miranda's door. I was still of the opinion that he was not the guilty party. The way I felt was as subjective, as sentimental, as oblique as the romantic notion I held in my heart that Emily Bloom still loved me, one day would return. Henry Doblin's pronouncement: "Man is an egotist and must experience despair," stuck in my mind. Or was it Kierkegaard? Only with George Miranda it wasn't my ego. It was simply a strong intuitive feeling. Perhaps Henry Doblin and or the cerebral Dane knew more.

Miranda opened the door. In his left hand he held a gray metal strongbox. "Come in. Bring the watermelon with you. I'm on the phone." He hurried inside. "Stop worrying. Got them valuables right here," he said in a low voice, tapping the metal box. Then he murmured something into the phone I couldn't quite grasp.

As soon as Miranda was off the phone I asked him what was in-side the strongbox. "Memories," he answered. A second later he checked his watch. Clicked on the TV. Beyoncé was gyrating. He sat down on a rickety chair in front of the TV. "I'm a big Beyoncé fan," he yelled out. Soon he was quoting from King Henry VI. "Could I come near your beauty with my nails."

Once again it was difficult for me to believe that Miranda could encompass so many extremes. Sometimes sounding like the proverbial sailor, other times like a Shakespearean scholar.

After Beyoncé finished, Miranda peered up at me. He must have guessed what I was thinking. "I know the way I act and talk, sometimes it's hard to believe I can quote the Bard. But I sure can. You see, Remy, Simone made me as well as Alice listen to her recite all those iambic pentameters and rhymed speeches from his plays all them years we were growing up. I might not love them sonnets and tragedies like Alice does, but I know them." He grinned. "Just think of it this way, Remy. Me quoting the Bard is not so different than some twelve-year-old kid rattlin' off the batting averages of his favorite players on his favorite team. You still remember them batting averages of your favorite Yankee teams. Don't ya, Remy?"

I noticed a sand pail in the far corner. Walked over. Picked it up.

"That Simone," Miranda said. "She insisted on washing the family laundry. She did it by hand, on her knees. Used Alice's beach bucket and a washboard. And then she along with Alice would carry the wash to our backyard and hang the laundry on clotheslines out to dry. That's the bucket," he said, pointing to the sand pail.

He slid off the rickety chair, slumped down on the planked floor, the watermelon beside him. He rummaged through his back pockets for a switchblade. Cut open the melon. Swallowed a chunk. Stared at the blade. "When Alice and me were eleven, as I lay under the covers one night, we quarreled. She picked up this here blade to frighten me. Not realizing my leg was under the blanket, she stabbed the blanket. The blade stuck into my ankle. Alice started to cry. 'Don't cry,' I said. 'It don't hurt.' And I proceeded to grit my teeth and pull the saber out. Later, the doc told us it had missed a vein by a quarter of an inch." Suddenly, like a live wire, Miranda jumped up. Tossed an empty bottle into the sand pail. Sat down once again in the rickety chair. "The person for me was Alice. She's the only woman I could ever talk to. Really talk to. We'd clasp hands and talk from dawn to dusk." Miranda paused. "After we married my wife and I would lay in bed together, side by side. And clasp hands. That connection was everything to me. I could hold Alice's hand forever," he said in a husky voice, closing his eyes.

Miranda turned to me. His haggard face was wild with a faraway look. For several minutes he continued speaking as much to himself as to me. Then he vigorously splashed his face with brown sink water, shook his head, and his faraway look dissolved. "Maybe one day, if I get myself together, I'll come to New York City and look Alice up."

I commented on the way I felt about Emily. He looked directly at me. "You're different than most," he said. His voice years younger than his scarred face. "Today, more than ever, people get caught up with surface beauty, not people. What you saw in that woman," he nodded. "I felt the very same way about my Alice. Still do. Them feelings haven't changed. Got detoured for a while, both of us got detoured, but one day, as I said, I just might look Alice up. There's still a large chunk of me that believes inside we're going to end up together." He sipped some coffee. "The other day you asked me if I still loved Alice. Yeah, Remy, I still love her."

I would never have abandoned Emily Bloom. How could George Miranda have deserted his wife? Taken the baby and run off to Emily?

"George. Be straight with me. Why did you take the baby and split?

Miranda spoke in a restrained voice.

"The truth is after Jane was lost on the table, I couldn't look at Alice without thinking of Jane. I told Alice it was my fault and that because of my evil I was afraid I had cast a spell on us. Alice tried to hold onto me. She might have been frail, but she wasn't one for quitting. She kept telling me that everything was going to be all right. But I was so riddled with guilt by then, I started seeing the devil's face in my cornflakes every morning. And then, because of my guilt and Alice, I started heading towards contrition. I got myself baptized. It didn't calm me." Miranda blinked. "I would sit for hours reciting the Jesus Prayer. For weeks I stayed in the house and wept. One day I seemed to be coming out of it. I held Janice in my arms and I felt content. But then it got real bad again. I remember thinking, That Man, he'll probably open the door for me." He looked up at me. Grimaced. "You were right, I took up with Sarabeth. But I weren't for her. And she weren't for me. After I told Alice about it, the two of us just crumbled. Soon after I packed my bags and left."

My mind began whirling. I felt as if I was in the middle of a losing streak. The kind you can't walk away from.

"George, listen for a minute—is this what happened on Lake Doubtful? Alice spotted Dr. Miller waving from the bridge of his cabin cruiser. She was overwhelmed with rage. She grabbed the wheel, not you. Your wife slammed into him. When it was over you convinced her that it was you. She disappeared. Now all these years later Ariel Warning is unaware of what transpired."

Miranda remained silent. Mute.

"Stop protecting Alice!" I shouted. "Stop lying! You can. I'm not sure if Ariel Warning can."

"That isn't the way it was," he finally answered. "I'm no hero. You're correct about one thing, though. My having an affair with Sarabeth."

"What made you?"

"We first started up right after Alice was examined by Doc Lind-strom and found out she was going to birth Siamese twins. That's when both of us felt betrayed."

"Betrayed? By whom?"

"Each other," he said, shrugging his shoulders. "We both felt tricked. As if we couldn't trust each other or our bodies any longer. We felt queasy toward each other all the time. That's why!"

He reached for a bottle of wine. Stopped himself. Poured more coffee.

"You want to know how Alice reacted when she found out that she was going to have conjoined twins? First she tried taking pills. When that didn't work she tried a long needle. I was able to stop her. Then all she did all day was stare at a wall. When she wasn't starin', she was chanting from *The Tempest*…What is past is prologue…He that dies pays all debts…My ending is despair…It was as if she were talking to the Holy Ghost, Remy. Our relationship unraveled something fierce. So I messed up, took up with Sarabeth. But as I said, it ended as quickly as it started." Miranda's face went dark. "I tried to turn it around with Alice. But after what happened in Taiwan, it was impossible."

He drained the remains from his coffee cup.

"Both of us died in Taiwan, Remy. Whatever was left of us jus' died. Now, as I said, I still love Alice in my heart, and I think she loves me in hers. But fate and Dr. Miller ruined us for each other. I told you the State wasn't that wrong when they said I wanted to kill him. I did…But I didn't."

"George. The truth. Was it Alice?"

"No, it wasn't. It couldn't have been."

"Why not?"

"By the time William Miller's boat appeared, Alice had passed out. I had already wrapped her in a blanket. She was fast asleep on the deck of my boat."

I thought: Statistics. You can prove anything you want by stats. Even a lie. Especially a lie.

Miranda picked his coffee cup off the floor. Sipped. Gave me a vulpine look. Quoted the Bard: "Suspicion always haunts the guilty mind. The thief doth fear each bush an officer." He took another sip. "The one thing I learned at Sandstone, besides how to take a leak straight into a cup, is it's a lie to expect man to be coherent. Lies, like irrationality, are as much a part of our makeup as war is. Look at you," he said, giving me another vulpine look. "Are you that different?"

He didn't pursue the question. I did. I'm obsessed with betrayal. Why was it I never accused Emily Bloom of betraying me? She was the one who abandoned me, not I her.

"You must have done something damn awful, Remy, to be here. It ain't just because of my wife's identity. That kind of generous Samaritan you ain't. Excuse the ain't." He squinted at me. "Isn't it about time you started telling me the whole truth?"

I swallowed hard.

"Come on, Remy. 'Fess up. Who did you destroy?"

I confessed it was David whom I'd betrayed, and that now I didn't have the courage to return home and face him.

"I'm sad for you and your twin," he said.

After a minute or so he continued. "One thing I'm going to do. Seek out a good woman. I want kids." He gazed at me with black somber eyes. "What about you?" he inquired.

"You're right. A man without a family doesn't have much of a life."

"You know what I think?" George Miranda asked, grinning. "You stay in Bemidji a little longer and you and me, we're going to end up real good friends."

❧

Betrayal might have been the predominant reason for my escapist journey, but my twin brother was in love with Ariel Warning. Was Alice Miranda/Ariel Warning a murderer? Who was? Who wasn't? I pursued the loose ends.

"George, you still haven't cleared up why Sarabeth owed you."

"'Cause of what I done for her. She got herself pregnant. Had to take her to a buddy of mine in Crosby. Kept my mouth shut. She owes me. Now let go of it. You've been drilling me long enough. I'm bushed. I need some shut-eye." He gazed at me. "You won, Remy," he said softly. "What you came after you found. You discovered who Ariel Warning is. You won," he repeated. "Now let go of it."

Win! I felt as empty as I did losing a bet. The next day you're wagering again.

Miranda must have sensed how I was feeling.

"What I learned in Sandstone is kind of tricky. When I first arrived I told everyone in the prison I wasn't guilty. Everyone laughed. It was when I told them I was guilty, that's when they believed me. The same thing with the parole board. That's when they said I reformed." I appeared puzzled. "All people know they're guilty," Miranda explained. "It's when you can admit to them you also are, that's the time you become a member of their club. That's when they'll set you free."

He walked over and placed his scarred hands on my shoulder.

"You already admitted that much to yourself. Now you must tell your twin. Don't matter if he already knows. It's for yourself you'll be doing it." Miranda paused. "I'd say you're ready, Remy," he said, nodding his head up and down. "You're ready!"

Minutes later he reached for two of the framed photographs that remained on top of the chest. One of them was of the conjoined twins, the second of the beautiful woman with wavy chestnut hair.

"Remy, will you do me a favor? Give these photographs to Alice." He stopped as he looked at the pictures. Swallowed. And then handed me the photograph of Jane and Janice, as well as the second one.

"Who's the woman?" I asked.

"It's Alice's birth mother, Uma Olsen."

His eyes focused on the periwinkle pullover sweater Alice had knitted for him. Slowly he walked over to the open dresser and snatched the bulky garment from the top drawer. "I want you to do me one more favor. Give this here sweater to Alice. Tell her it no longer belongs to me. Tell her that I hope that real soon she'll be feeling real good about herself and that she should knit another sweater for the man she chooses to be with for the rest of her life. Tell her that. Will you?" He touched his brow with his long fingers, wiped his eyes. He was crying.

A short while later I reached into my jacket pocket. Took out my checkbook.

"I don't want your money."

"It's not for you, George. It's for me. Besides, if you don't take it, I'll probably just gamble it away." I wrote a check out for his BSC tuition. I did feel more human. But did it really matter? Either way—conscience or generosity—I wrote the check.

"I have to get back to New York," I said, standing up groggily at the door.

"Hopefully Ariel Warning will be getting her memory back real soon," Miranda said.

"When her mind is ready, she will," I acknowledged. We both stood quietly. Our hands hanging limply at our sides. "One more question, George. If Alice came back to you, are you sure you would want her?"

"Would you want Emily?" was his rejoinder.

As I reached the Toyota, George Miranda yelled out: "I won't be contestin' any divorce. If Alice didn't already get one, tell her to file. I'm lookin' ahead, too," he said, gritting his teeth. Impulsively he trotted up to me. He took my hand, peered directly into my face with sinless, sober eyes. "You think I'm doing the right thing?" he asked.

"Better than me," I answered.

We embraced.

PART V

MATCHSTICKS

For seven years Charles Darwin studied barnacles. Barnacles! That's it. Much of his groundbreaking theory was based on what he had learned from focusing on barnacles. Back at the let room I started packing, dwelling. I kept stringing pieces together, assessing and adjusting my scenarios, trying to make the pieces fit. Going back twelve years is not easy. Especially without all the pieces. Particularly with an imperfect mind. I took out a pad and commenced scribbling down all the incidental information I had gathered on Dr. William Miller. What was found: A Rolex watch. Several finger joints, on one digit the NCAA championship ring. A Snickers bar wrapper. A silver scalpel. Whatever else came to mind.

I was a handicapper again. No! I was a gambler again. Obsessed. Fusing known facts with wishful thinking. With dreams of winning the big one. As confused as my mind was, I kept thinking George Miranda was vis-à-vis "The Good Twin." Alice, Iago. What was I thinking? Was this all part of my guilt defusing, leaking? There are things a man can't control or change or hide during his lifetime: his color, his heart, his nature, his fingers, his passion, his crime, his lies, his guilt. All of these are uncontrollable over a lifetime, as uncontrollable as the ineluctable reality of a final (losing) score.

I experienced a stab to the heart—*David knows.*

My mind returned to George Miranda. He believed his wife caused the collision. He was drinking. On pills. He was aware of her troubled state. He knew she was at the wheel, she would be faulted for ramming the cabin cruiser. He truly believed Alice/Ariel was to blame. He convinced his wife to escape as I originally had thought. George Miranda was a hero. He stayed. The Coast Guard found him just about semi-conscious drifting on the lake. He had on a life jacket. I suspected Alice Miranda somehow grabbed the second jacket. Of course, credit that critical detail to Margot, her meticulous accounting. The Coast Guard also found William Miller. That is, his joints, ring, timepiece, scalpel and other identifying possessions. George Miranda was examined for drugs. Chemicals showed up in his urine. Not the ones prescribed. The State made a point of impressing on the jury, besides the chemicals, that the marijuana he had been smoking was "today's weed," which was ten times more potent than the weed smoked in the sixties. It did not take much more than the chemicals, the weed, and the symbols to convince the jurors that it was George Miranda who had crashed into William Miller. I went over every detail. I examined all the facts at the jury's disposal: "Conclusions evolve!"

The more I kept thinking about the jury's decision, the more sense it made. The more I became confused. It didn't make sense. Something was still missing. It couldn't have been George Miranda. He couldn't have been the one who so violently attacked William Miller. He was more like David. "Deva" in Hindu mythology, a deity of good spirit. Alice Miranda was more like me. "Deva": in Zoroastrian mythology, a demon of evil spirit. From all I had learned about George Miranda, it wasn't in his nature. He was like my beloved brother. I took a deep breath. Everything was there. All the barnacles. All I had to do was power rate them correctly. See the entire picture. Make the correct number for the game. Pick the game.

"Deciphering takes time. One must have patience and the analytical powers to break ambiguity down," Margot had advised. At the time

I resented what she had said. I felt it was a put-down. What I wanted from Margot was applicable answers. I wanted to know who the murderer was if it wasn't George Miranda. I wanted the kind of plausible solutions you receive when you watch nighttime TV mysteries. Clean. Precise. Simple. One scene logically segueing into the next. A predictable, sequential flow. A few surprises along the way, but ultimately common sense wins the day. Solves the enigma. And you go to sleep satisfied. I learned while gambling you don't get those kind of answers. There was as much chance for those kind of answers as winning consistently in Las Vegas.

I kept thinking: Twins do not destroy each other. Themselves, yes. But not each other. And then what came to mind was that George and Alice were like twins. Twins. Head and tails. Yin and yang. George Miranda would not have been able to go on if he was the one responsible for betraying Alice. How can I explain it? Betraying your twin. It's betraying yourself. Destroying the best of who you are. Your moorings. Your sanity. The reason a twin can get up in the morning is because he knows his other half is there. People leave you. Parents, friends, even Emily leaves. A twin stays through all of it; betrayal and fury, disillusionment and enmity; through inconceivable disappointments; through the many silent bitter sorrows; a twin bites his lip and stays. Forever! And at that moment the message that made most sense to me was: Together! George and Alice Miranda had conspired together. Planned William Miller's murder, together.

And, then, because of the word "together," I wasn't confused any longer—or perhaps more confused.

"You're not alone. You still have me," David had said, when Emily Bloom left me.

"That's like having me," I answered. "It doesn't count."

For a moment my tormented mind took hold. I glimpsed that what I had lost with my identical had been replaced by a journey to myself.

Then my weak-willed mind took flight and it was as if I were back as an imaginative child in a Times Square penny arcade in front of one of those distortion mirrors. It was frightening yet familiar. George Miranda? Alice Miranda? Was I correct? Was I wrong? Was there such a thing as being correct and wrong, wrong and correct—as if tangible deeds as cognitive dissonance, conjoined twins, lovers, could be essentially contradictory and unifying at the same time; interlocking parts of a clashing dual psychological system; as interlocked as when one arranges the two (twin) parts of a mechanical system so that they cannot move independently of one another. To be connected in this way. Handicap the Mirandas, I uttered to myself. All the content in the world doesn't replace the one spiritual bloom—Jane and Janice—that was missing. Let go! Move on! All the talk about moving on. You'll find yourself again. What I found was…My miracle was Emily Bloom. Grow up! But grown-ups play a role. Pose. A weary body does not necessarily mean a wizened heart. My heart was aching not to play by seasoned, dead-of-winter rules. I craved what I had shared with Emily Bloom. What she evoked in me. A wondrous humanizing renewal. I didn't lie or cheat or betray Emily Bloom. I tried to compensate for her loss with Ariel Warning. Soon I realized how heinous was my pursuit. More than ever I was painfully aware of how intensely inspired and open and genuinely committed David was to her. Those past months in the city, it was as if I were floundering in the black waters of Lake Doubtful on the murky night of the collision, and Ariel Warning was a life preserver to cling to, as I had clung, and was still clinging, to Emily Bloom.

"It's because you're a coward!" David chronically lamented. "Stop all that romantic nonsense. My life with Thea was a life. We were moral equivalents. We shared something real. With Emily you were play-acting Jesus, walking on water. You gave her a life, and she, like the Romans, took a life."

And what about George and Alice Miranda? Their miracle was not exclusively each other. It was likewise the creation of Jane and Janice. Destroyed!

My mind took another flip-flop: Ariel Warning will be coming out of her fugue. Leaving David. David would feel the heartache of her loss, as I had felt and constantly feel Emily Bloom's loss.

I telephoned Margot. Explained why I was now certain Ariel Warning was an integral part of the nightmare.

"Stop thinking so much," Margot advised. "The more you think, the less you know. You know what my feeling is? You're as inept an investigator as those four feeble words."

"What words?"

"Maybe we'll never know."

Two hours later Margot called back.

"She's a monster!"

A hit-and-run had run over Margot's dog, motoring uptown on a downtown street.

"Ariel lured Boggie into the street. There was a trail of burger meat half a block long."

"Did you see Ariel in the car?"

"I didn't see her, but I'm sure. I'm sure!"

From the St. Paul-Minneapolis airport I telephoned Ariel Warning.

"You're back. How was London?" She chirped merrily.

"I'm in an airport and I didn't go to London. I went to Milan."

"Milan?" she intoned. "I thought you were going to London. Why Italy?"

Without thinking, with thinking—better yet feeling very much as if I were making my last compulsive bet, wanting to get it over with, take the plunge, lose everything, win everything, I said, "I was in Milan, Minnesota. From there I went to Emily. I was on Lake Doubtful. And from there I went to Bemidji. Visited George Miranda."

"What were you doing in those places? Who is George Miranda?" Ariel asked, her voice filled with unrestrained surprise. A moment later her voice expressed real urgency. "Whatever your reasons, it doesn't matter. You have one more day. Twenty-four hours."

On the flight to New York I read my brother's short story, "Matchsticks," an allegory of the city. It was about a boy who decides to make a city of matchsticks. By the time the boy finishes he has thousands of matchsticks, vertical, horizontal, curved, squared, slanted, oblique, an entire city of sticks. The boy gazes at what he has created and realizes that with one trembling breath his entire city can crumble. The last image in the story is of the boy silent, fearful, too terrified to breathe.

From LaGuardia I taxied home, drop dead tired I flopped into bed. I couldn't sleep. I kept recalling the boy in "Matchsticks." I kept thinking matchsticks, count matchsticks…I thought of the touchstones of Ariel Warning's life: Amy Roberta, George and Simone Miranda, Jane and Janice, Drs. Miller and Doblin. David and me. All of us touchstones. Without all of us: What? I focused in on Ariel Warning. The most crucial matchstick.

Each one a warning. A revelation. It hit me no differently than my checklist for selecting a game at one time hit me: strong home court plus points plus sound defense plus excellent coach plus solid guard play plus REVENGE. I tossed and turned with the "warnings" from Ariel's subconscious—not the revelations force-fed and extracted from *The Tempest*, but the personal ones. The common sense ones, if you will. Warnings were there: At Jason Wyler's party Margot had worn a polka-dot tie. Ariel had freaked out. Damn, in the photograph Dr. Doblin had caressed of William Miller, he was wearing a polka-dot tie.

Not everything I thought of was menacing. I thought of the sandpail that Simone Miranda used to wash the dirty laundry. The way David described Ariel's effusive behavior with the homeless lady. I thought of George Miranda mentioning how Alice and he, as children, would only confide in each other. The only outsider—a priest at confession. Perhaps Ariel did go to confession. Maybe at church she confessed.

I kept thinking…Handicapping. I thought of the umbrella made in Taiwan. Ariel smashed it against the curb. Matchsticks were everywhere. More and more I was piecing matchsticks together. No different than when I had handicapped college basketball. At that time in my life I had created a handicapper's handbook and prayer book. All the information I gathered was jammed into the prayer book. A grapevine of matchsticks from beards, scouts, sports magazines, industry journalists, wise guys, players, hoop gurus, and coaches. Collated everything. Prepared. Prepared some more. And just before I dialed the BMs, I'd go over my power ratings and checklist one last time. Make certain everything, including my formula and psyche, was covered. And then, finally, when I was ready, I cautioned myself: "Manage every dollar as if it were your last. Maximize when you win. Minimize when you lose." You don't pick the games, the games pick you. If I'd learned anything, I'd learned that. I also had learned that it's only when you lose that you're labeled self-destructive. When you win you're everybody's best friend. Win often enough and you're tabbed a genius. From "The Donald" to a Lotto winner, a winning streak is a winning streak. And the winner takes home the biggest toys. Is it any wonder we need spiritual healers?

I kept jotting down information. Checklisting matchsticks in my brain. Preparing. Preparing for Ariel Warning. The afternoon I met Ariel Warning at the Blue Room, she stated that the two comely gay men who approached the dance floor upset her. She didn't know why. But she did admit to being upset by them. My mind traveled back to the evening Ariel had dinner with my uncle Leo. He placed his Rolex

timepiece on the table. Ariel jumped up. Ran for an exit. At that moment she was giving us a warning.

Suddenly it was obvious. All this time a large chunk of me didn't
want to believe it. Like Emily Bloom leaving. I was too soft. My uncle
Leo was hard. Since my twin and I were little boys he boasted to us how
one day in Germantown, at a Nazi Bund rally, he beat two of Indian Joe
McWilliam's henchmen with a baseball bat, kept clubbing away at them.
My uncle was hard. I was soft. Somewhere deep inside of me I was still a
Cantor's son. Denying the truth. Not heeding Ariel's warnings.

I incorporated into my handicapping as many matchsticks as I
could think of. Besides the Rolex timepiece, I asked myself, what else
was found in the waters of Lake Doubtful. Dr. Miller's ring finger. The
NCAA championship ring. My mind danced: Herb Leno was the team
manager of one of the UCLA basketball teams in the late sixties. These
were John Wooden teams. Coach Wooden teams won ten NCAA championships. Like the players on Bruin teams, team managers were also
awarded rings. What freaked Ariel Warning out in Leno's office was—
"she kept staring at my hands"—that he had on an NCAA championship ring. Matchsticks were everywhere.

I continued handicapping the trail of blood: the articles among
the property of Dr. William Miller's remains. The Rolex. The ring. The
Snickers wrapper. The silver scalpel. An enfant for an enfant. An eye
for an eye. Of course Alice Miranda/Ariel Warning had murderous
thoughts. It was only natural. The law of the jungle. The mea culpa of
American jurisprudence. Dr. William Miller's trail of blood. What else
was programmed? Think it through. Break the code. Handicap, Adam;
handicap! What could be programmed? What triggering mechanism
could be used to make Ariel Warning explode?

The sweater. The periwinkle knit sweater that I first came across
in her railroad flat. That was a trigger. I had borrowed it from Ariel.
Margot likewise thought it was magnificent. She borrowed the pullover

from me. Wore it more than once when she was with Ariel. One of those times was the evening of Jason Wyler's party. Ariel exploded. What else: Dr. Doblin. Why was Henry Doblin still alive? I telephoned Dr. Doblin.

"Mr. Remler. I was just thinking of you. This weekend I'll be in New York. Thought we might have dinner."

"What's bringing you to New York?" I asked.

"It's George Miranda. You see, Mr. Remler, George is returning some belongings of mine. Did I mention to you that he and I ended up pretty good friends in Taiwan? Strange bedfellows you might think. But Miranda's an exceptional man. Don't you agree?"

What came to mind was that day Beyoncé was gyrating on TV. The strongbox. "Memories."

"Dr. Doblin, exactly what is it that George Miranda's returning?"

"Some of Bill's things were found on Lake Doubtful. I didn't have the heart to take them home with me. It sounds peculiar, I know, but I gave George written permission to pick them up from the Coast Guard, store them for me. I'm just grateful that he's holding no grudges. I mean, I testified at the trial against him, yet, still, he doesn't hold a grudge. I did tell you George Miranda wasn't fond of sailing. That if it were anyone who had caused the crash, and I'm not intimating it was anyone's intention, but…Of course, it was never proven that Alice Miranda was there. You don't have proof of that, do you, Mr. Remler?"

"No, Doctor. I don't."

"That George. When I finally told him that I have Bill safely tucked away in my heart, he strongly suggested that it was a good time for me to gather up Bill's possessions. He insisted on returning them in person."

"Why New York?"

"The Taiwanese embassy has arranged for an awards dinner in my honor; as for George, he said for him it would be killing two birds with one stone. He's been thinking about hooking up with an old friend who resides in Manhattan. I think he meant Alice. But don't hold me to that speculation," Doblin said, cheerfully.

It was then that I began explaining to him about Ariel, David, myself. How my conclusions had evolved.

"My God, Mr. Remler. What you're putting yourself through," was his response.

For two nights I couldn't sleep. Hour after hour I continually thought of trees—trees because when I gazed out of my bedroom window, at the park, they were bunched together. To me it seemed as if they hadn't sufficient room to breathe. It was as if one was entangled with the other. Strangled it. Usurped the space that was meant for the other. But each of those sturdy trees survived. Ripe green leaves in the summer, more beautiful than emeralds; stripped of leaves in the frozen winter, as stoic as empty fortresses: they survive. Finding and fighting for their own space, they survive, nature's miracles. Twins, David and I, we're like trees. Rooted in the same soil, we bunched together, hid in the same bushes, jumped the same fences, climbed the same walls, came down with the same childhood illnesses at the same time or promptly one after the other. The same physician, Dr. Aaron Katzman from Riverside Drive, with his kindly bedside manner and his little black leather bag from which he would take his omnipresent thermometer and stethoscope, would visit and treat us both. Until we were fourteen our clothes were the same, our barbers, hairstyles and food. We'd both drink from the same pitcher. Chocolate syrup with milk was a must for the both of us as were Hershey almond bars and chocolate milkshakes. Even our teeth had cavities at the same time. Subsequently the pockets were filled by the same dentist, during the same visits. In grade school we'd have the runs at the same time, anxiety the provoker. We'd select the same crayons and draw the same or similar pictures, and the teachers (they couldn't tell us apart) would think we were both so cute. And whenever David and I argued, and we certainly had our share of boyish fights, our mother would scold us with what was her own, our own, bedtime lullaby:

"Boys! You're twins! Twins shouldn't fight. Being a twin is quietly understanding that whatever, your twin is always there. It's not fighting or leaving, it's only returning. Sharing everything and questioning none of it."

"And questioning all of it, Mom."

"Boys! It's forever! Forever!"

David and I were rooted to the same tree, sunrise and sunset. Yin and yang. As together, as far apart, as two people could possibly be.

I hailed a cab. The taxi hurried west on 59th Street, stalling on the north side of the Hampshire House. I jumped out of the vehicle, almost tripping over a panhandler who was sitting in a pothole filled with sand and rainwater. Stepping around him, I continued my journey. I trudged along with my hands in my pockets; the closer I got to my destination the slower I moved. Reaching Columbus Circle I turned uptown. I walked up Central Park West past Trump Tower. In front of the Ethical Culture School I nearly collided with a schoolteacher handing out raspberry lollipops to children leap-frogging around her. I was so preoccupied with my thoughts I didn't even see the woman. I moved past Latino doormen at the Century and the Prasada who stood in soldierly protectiveness of the well-lit doorways. For a while I lost my courage and sat down on the steps of the Lutheran Church of the Holy Trinity gazing out at the abundant park. While I sat there, a sleepy-eyed rector in a carmine robe asked me if there was anything the matter.

"I have to tell someone I love I betrayed him," I said.

Making no fuss, the pastor invited me inside the chapel as if I were one of his most welcome parishioners.

"We can talk or you can pray," he said.

"Perhaps another time, Father," I said, declining. "For now I just need to sit here for a while."

When I rose and trudged along again, I tried to fortify myself by reciting my mother's lullaby: *"Boys, being a twin is quietly understanding that whatever, your twin is there. It's not fighting or leaving, it's returning. Sharing everything and questioning none of it...Boys, it's forever! Forever!"*

I spluttered, "It's forever. Forever!" Continued chanting my mother's words as I progressed uptown. The blocks were short and few and all at once I was heading for the latticed doorway leading to David's building.

I took several gulps and two huge breaths, told myself, "Everyone is guilty of something," before knocking on my identical's door. Inside I was feeling the kind of airless aliveness, dread and terror, I experienced when I gambled.

"Who is it?" David asked.

"Me!"

He unlocked the door.

I peered at my twin. Finally ready to tell him everything. When it came down to it, I had nothing to say. What could I possibly say? When it came down to it, words were insipid, unsubstantial. Words would only banalize my culpability. Here I was with my other self, trying to muster up enough courage to tell him what words could not convey. I stood in front of my identical. Mute. Thinking to myself: I had to tell him. I had to. Choose my words. Blurt it out. Just say it. David kept waiting for me to say something.

Finally I summoned up the courage.

Did I say I'm sorry? Were there tears? Was my stomach churning? Did I feel contempt for myself? Did I express to my twin how I felt?

"You're always crying about the ache in your heart for what's missing. It isn't Emily. It's you!"

On my twin brother's aggrieved face I could see, as if in slow motion, his pain manifesting itself. First it showed in his eyes, then his entire face contorted into a Munch-like scream. No!!!

David looked directly at me. "I have to be alone," he said in a suppressed voice, before promptly racing for the door.

In our entire lifetime together, David had never said to me that he needed to be alone. Without me. This one time he did.

When you hit rock bottom, when the losing streak has nowhere to go. When you're figuring out which credit cards have some leverage. When you start calling friends for money, lying to relatives about why you need the money, when you stop answering your phones, returning calls, when you stop eating, aren't hungry, when you don't want to see a woman, or party, or watch TV, or do anything. When you can't even get yourself to get out of bed…

I had to force myself to move. I needed desperately to keep an appointment. It wasn't that I had the ability to put David out of my mind. To disconnect. It was just something I had to do. Make one more bet. I forced myself to get out of bed. Keep moving…Make one more bet!

From my rooftop I gazed out into the all-too-rare perfectly pigmented New York sky. I thought, how beautiful, how serene, and wondered why my mind wasn't as tranquil. I continued contemplating the approaching restful night. Below me, flashing lights, zigzagging yellow taxicabs, missile-shaped stretch limos and countless state-of-the-art bedazzling vehicles. Eager drivers heading for destinations or destiny. Adventure or disaster. I thought: Why did it have to turn into this cloak-and-dagger affair? Why was I so weak?

I picked up the phone and telephoned Dr. Doblin's hotel.

"Mr. Remler…It was a wonderful tribute…Come on over. We can go to dinner…"

I paced through the hotel lobby, heading straight for the elevator. The boxcar didn't have a grate but it did have an eerie clang as the door banged shut. When I reached Dr. Doblin's floor, I walked down a narrow corridor, looking for his room. The door was ajar. I walked in. George Miranda was sitting in a straight-backed cushioned chair, that thousand-yard stare in his eyes. His corded arms involuntarily jerking. He looked up at me, continued staring at me for a long while, all the time rubbing his scarred face from above his brow to the very bottom of his jawline. He mumbled something from Hamlet:

"And now I'll do't: — and so he goes to heaven. And so I am revenged."

I walked over to the windows, pushed aside heavy maroon drapes. My eyes scanned the street: a giant billboard advertising a Broadway musical, people scurrying to theatres like dots, or ants, or something in between. The honking, crawling fleet of yellow cabs reminded me of potato bugs on their backs. I checked the four corners of the room. Underneath a lime-green sofa, behind a lemon-colored dresser, whatever other hidden pockets there were. No corpse. Nothing. Slowly I approached George Miranda. When I was close enough to touch him, before shaking hands, he wiped his damp palms on his jeans.

"With all the investigating you've done, Remy, you missed a lot. There never was no chapel in Hospital Number Nine." He paused to allow that fact to sink in. "Alice didn't give her permission to Miller or Doblin while praying in any hospital chapel. Two of them, both Miller and Doblin, had a rule. More like a command. If we needed to discuss Jane and Janice, it had to be in one of their offices. On that last day, for the very first time, Miller and Doblin confessed to us they couldn't save

Jane. Alice and me, we got down on our knees. We begged them to save Jane and Janice. By that time Alice and me were of the same mind. Neither one of us could choose one twin over the other. Try and save both of them, we begged them. Jane and Janice belong together, either here or with God. Both Miller and Doblin insisted they couldn't save Jane. After all their promises, they now said they couldn't. Alice got up off her knees, marched straight out of the room. Leave her alone, I told myself. She needs to do her own figuring. Yeah, Remy, Jane didn't die on a table neat and clean. Alice ended Jane's life with her own two hands. Doblin covered it up. I was grateful for that much. After that it all went amok, and the rest of it you sort of put together, I guess."

"Where is Dr. Doblin?" I asked.

He pointed towards the bathroom.

At first I saw nothing outside the usual. Then I noticed the shower. I slid open the glass door. The silver scalpel was lying at the foot of the drain. Doblin's nude body was cleaved straight down the middle like a butchered calf. A Snickers wrapper was lying like a postage stamp on his belly. The championship ring on a severed finger. The Rolex wrapped around his flaccid penis. Doblin's topknot was also cut off. After heaving into the toilet bowl, I gargled sink water, rinsed my face, took some deep breaths and returned to George Miranda's side.

There was blood on my jacket. He took out of his pocket a red handkerchief and gingerly wiped it off. "They were both bastards, Remy. Not only Miller, Doblin, too. Whatever Miller said, Henry parroted. All that stuff he fed to you, it was just stuff. It ain't the way it went down. What they both wanted was to make the record books. Celebrity and the important money that follows was their only motivation." He wrung his hands, his knuckles turned white. "Arrogant bastards," he sighed. "Just different presentations."

Taking tight hold of my arm, Miranda raised himself up so that his eyes were level with mine. "I swore to Alice we'd get even."

For a moment Miranda remained very still. Then he lit a joint, took a drag. "In a few minutes I'm gonna be calling the police. Before I do there's one thing I want you to promise me. I want you to help Alice to disappear. There was no conspiracy. I took advantage of her subterranean state. She ain't responsible. I swear. Now get out of here," he said. "You can talk to the cops in a day or two."

I kept thinking: Alice Miranda/Ariel Warning—it's all been rehearsed. All façade and subterfuge. Her temper tantrums. Crossed messages. The anomalies. She too is a...I stopped myself from saying murderer.

Should I wait for the police? Share with them the information I had discovered? Should I leave?

"Believe me, Remy, Alice had it real rough from the very beginning. You can't imagine how rough."

"George, I know all about her twin's death."

"What do you know?" he said, his voice consumed by rage. "That Amy Roberta died of Sudden Infant Death Syndrome. You didn't buy that song and dance. Did you, Remy? It wasn't the way it was. It happened in the crib they shared. One night Alice rolled on top of Amy, they interlocked. Somehow they couldn't move independently. It was Alice that did the smothering." He slumped back down in the cushioned chair. Took a deep drag. "You know when Mrs. Frohman went to the crib in the morning and found Alice lying on top of Amy, she weren't crying or nothin'. Just gazing down at her sister. It was Simone started feeding Alice them lies about SIDS, circulating the same pathetic story to everyone else. My Alice," he said, "she sure had enough tragedies. Didn't she, Remy?"

Why do things fall into place all at once? Belatedly? What makes for a contented life? If one takes a virtuous path, does that guarantee happiness? The three things to choose carefully are school, career, and wife, my father always advised. Those are the three things that matter most. As I left the hotel, losing was on my mind like losing games in my gambler's memory. If Emily had said yes, would David be safe? I content? What is the antidote for betrayal? Guilt and remorse? There is none.

It was thirty minutes before sunrise when I telephoned Ariel Warning.

"David refuses to speak to me. We must talk. I'm coming over," she cried out.

I went through my bureau drawers, desperately searching for the periwinkle knit pullover George Miranda had given me for Ariel. Slipped it on. Stuffed several Snickers bars in my pocket. Grabbed off the top of the bureau my uncle's Rolex. David didn't vault the timepiece. I had found it when I confessed to him. It was in his bottom desk's drawer, sandwiched between his Glock automatic and a Hallmark Valentine's card that professed Ariel Warning's eternal love. I paced the terrace. The doorbell buzzed. I raced to the door.

Her hair was still a golden field of corn, yet she appeared different. She wore no lipstick, a musk perfume, there were tiny lines appearing at the corners of her eyes. Her brow was contorted, angry, quizzical, her entire face suspicious, as if she were the one investigating me. Loosely hanging over her shoulder was her woven bag. The kind professional models, theater people and dancers carry, carry so gracefully, ever so hip, their backs arched, seemingly born to carry. Ariel's woven bag was tossed over her shoulder in a similarly hip fashion, but something was missing. It wasn't hip.

Ariel nervously brushed her hair back from her forehead. "I'm glad you've returned," she said.

Suddenly, several minutes into the conversation, she shouted,

"You're wrong and David's wrong. It doesn't matter how much you love. What matters is how much you are loved. You loved Bloom with your whole being. Did it matter? I won't stop needing you, Adam, and I won't stop needing David. The two of you will always have one hundred percent of me. What more is there?"

I remained silent.

"Say something," Ariel demanded, her voice rising, once again that trilling sound, that warble at the edge. We were on my rooftop. Birds were chittering in the trees. For a second Ariel gazed at them. And then she said more softly, "Don't worry. David's an intelligent man. He'll understand. The three of us together. We can still work it out."

Ariel touched her heart. "What you never really understood is how attached I am to both you and David. The three of us attached. David, you and me."

Ariel collapsed into a beat-up Natalia chair in front of a teakwood table with a forest-green umbrella. It was jammed, could not be opened. A strong morning breeze made her skirt of India cotton billow. "The three of us are conjoined. The three of us," she repeated. She reached out, double-clutching at my arm.

With considerable effort, she raised her body from the Natalia chair. Faced me. I moved closer. Hesitated, deliberating carefully what to say. "Let it come back naturally," Dr. Porder had cautioned me.

"David and I are two separate people, Ariel. My life ended when I lost E. David's was renewed when he met you."

I waited for Ariel to respond. When she didn't speak I tried once more to get through to her.

"See David, Ariel. It's your pain that has blinded you. Let go of your pain. Seeing David will help you to give up your pain. It's time to let go of it. Just as it's time for me to let go of mine." Once I began I couldn't stop myself. "Listen to me," I said. "You don't need me. What we shared was nothing more and nothing less than ephemeral compensation for what we've lost forever. Yes, we both came alive in that moment, but that's all it was, Ariel. A moment. Your genuine feelings are for David. You love my brother. And he loves you. Please, Ariel. David's the best man I know. He's tender and compassionate. Decent. His entire life his first thought has always been to be fair. Even when we discuss a contract at our lawyer's, David asks only one question. 'Is it fair?' Not for us, but for our opponent."

Ariel smiled wryly. "Every woman needs a sinner as much as a saint. I need both of you."

I don't know for how long, but it must have been quite some time that my identical had been standing on the patio. He was stationed in back of the dandelion-colored swings, close to the area where Emily's pinewood shed had once stood. A rotted plank covered by wisteria and thick green-leafed ivy lay on its belly near the edge of the guard railing. Every time I patrolled the area I made a mental note to remove the rotted plank. It made the area unsafe. But I didn't have the heart to remove the board. The plank was the last remnant of Emily's shed. And so I ran away from discarding it, much like I had run away to Minnesota to avoid confronting David. The weathered remnant on the ground was chained to a nineteenth-century grappling iron with sharp hooks for grasping things. The block of warped wood was covered by swirling willow leaves, as well as thriving wisteria, the dense vines entwined, pushing up the coping stones, the guardrails covering maybe an eight-foot section, the verdure vines camouflaging the board. A plank for remembrance (of those faultless days when Emily and I, in winter and summer, fall and spring, made love) of Emily's pinewood house.

Suffering can age a man. In the short time that had transpired my twin had suffered. He looked spent, unkempt. Even his hair seemed aggrieved, the soft curls lank, listless. Yet I saw something else, too. I saw my brother's resolve. He was determined to get Ariel Warning back.

He gazed at Ariel. She at him. She spoke first.

"You know, David, we were like Romeo and Juliet."

"What do you mean?" he asked.

"You know. The inevitability of it all. Two star-crossed lovers. A love that is doomed from the beginning. They never had a chance."

"We do!" David exclaimed, jumping on Ariel's words.

"David!" I exclaimed.

He turned toward me. In my twin's penetrating eyes I could see him struggling to control his anger. In his taut face I saw what he was feeling. That Ariel was a victim. That I was the one blameworthy. In that brief moment I felt that he had separated from me completely. Severed our conjoining. Loathing myself more than ever, I gazed at my identical. Where was the strength of our love? Measure my frailty. my gaze pleaded, not only my cowardice. Is there more? There must be more.

David turned back to Ariel, said in a deliberate voice, "What is between Adam and me is between Adam and me. Not you."

Ariel's eyes narrowed. "If you leave me, or if Adam leaves, I'll just leave."

I remained silent. My concentration broken by David's glare. *Why did I have to have a brother like you? Why couldn't I have had a brother that makes my life easier?* that glare asked.

It is strange what things come to one in moments of crisis. What came to my mind was cream of asparagus soup. David had said that his happiest moments with Ariel were when they were at her Sullivan Street railroad warren and she made cream of asparagus. He told me it made him feel as if he had achieved some restful place in the world. I knew what he meant. In all my adult years before Emily Bloom, I could not count on one finger a time I was truly content. Whether it was a novel inside me or an ache, unrealized goals, longings of one kind or another, I was always driven. It was only with Emily Bloom that I achieved a blessing, a state of grace, a time of cream of asparagus. David believed he had found such renewal with Ariel Warning; and from such renewal follows relationship, dialogue, mutual sharing, contentment.

For a short while my twin brother had experienced such hope. What made me rob my twin brother of this hope?

"Without both of you it's no good. It just isn't," Ariel cried, peering at the two of us. "What's the use?" she stammered, as she strode toward the dangerous area where the plank, chained to the grappling iron, lay on the ground.

I trailed Ariel, stepped over the grappling iron, reached out to her. "Be careful," I cautioned.

David hurried over, pushing me violently. "Don't touch her," he shouted.

Ariel turned to face David directly. "Before Adam's trip, for weeks I warned him that he had to tell you. That I needed both of you. I was honest. Now he returns and you know everything and nothing has changed."

David bit his lower lip. No blood. He peered at Ariel. "Don't you see it? Adam can't let go of Emily's ghost and you can't let go of yours." He turned to me. "You've never seen me," he exclaimed. "To you I've always been an extension of you. Never once did you ever think of me. Only of yourself. What you wanted. You don't have a clue what's inside me. How I feel. I'm not an extension of you. I'm me!" he screamed. His whole body shook. "Don't you get it? Me!"

My identical bit his lower lip. This time blood gushed forth. I stepped closer, wiping the gore from his mouth with my fingertips. He pulled away. Wiped the remainder of the blood from his lip with the back of his hand.

"Emily you helped. What about helping me? Your whole life you never once thought of me as a separate person."

When you have pain in your arm you rub, in your leg you limp, in your heart you ache, with your twin, you die.

Suddenly David's rage left him. Drained, he showed no emotion. Just lassitude. Resignation.

He grasped Ariel's shoulders. "Ariel, if you'd rather be with Adam… if you love Adam the way he loved Emily…at least then all of this would be justifiable."

"Emily," Ariel sputtered.

"If you choose Adam I'll live with it; or you can choose me."

Ariel cried out. "You're trying to be noble. I'm being honest. I desperately wanted to tell you. I waited only because of Adam. His trip to Emily," she stammered.

Ariel peered at the dandelion swing, walked over to it, pushed it forcefully, watched it sway back and forth. Back and forth. "Emily," she continued to stammer. "I've lost both of you, haven't I?" she cried. She turned and took two giant strides to exit the terrace.

David grabbed her wrist. "Don't leave, Ariel," he said. "I love you."

"You're not hearing me," Ariel exclaimed. "I need both of you. Please, David, give it a chance. I'm not a monster. Give it a chance. I need both of you. Just as much as you two need each other."

"It's impossible. You must make a choice," David answered.

For a moment she gazed at the two of us, her eyes darting back and forth, as if she were trying to choose, then her misty eyes returned to the dandelion swing. She stared at it, watching it rock back and forth. Back and forth.

My identical looked over at me. "Adam's weak. He's always been weak. Since Emily left he's been a cripple. He needs you more. If you choose Adam, I promise I'll try and accept it. But don't just leave. Ariel," he said, grasping her arm, she pulling away. "Please don't leave."

Ariel didn't stumble over the rotted plank. She didn't impale her luring flesh on the grappling hooks. She just stood there staring at the rocking swing. "Emily," she spluttered. "Emily…" And then she touched the back of her head, as if she had a migraine. Once more Ariel repeated "Emily," then she made this crying sound, and then it happened.

✤

For a long time Ariel Warning did not move. Then she moved slightly, gazing vacantly at David. "Jane…Janice…My babies…" It was as if she were coming out of a deep celestial sleep. Possibly a dream. She kept repeating in a tremulous voice, "My babies…Jane…Janice…" And then she cried out, "I know who you two are. You're Dr. Doblin," she said, pointing a finger at me. "And you're Dr. Miller," she said to my identical.

She continued gazing at both of us, yet she was not actually looking at us. "I have good news. I can save both Jane and Janice. Isn't that what you told me?"

She was reliving her traumatic experience, until now repressed. Forgotten. Ariel paused for an instant. When she spoke again, her voice became a plaintive cry.

"Clearly we are sad that Jane will not be able to continue with her sister."

A part of me felt Ariel was acting, didn't want to believe that the ghosts of her grief had taken possession not only of her mind, but of her heart and soul as well.

She peered at David, her face shining and distant. "You promised you would save both of them."

She slowly marched, as if she were a shell-shocked soldier, to the area where the plank and the grappling iron lay.

My eyes remained riveted on her. She didn't appear possessed at all. In a way she appeared calm. As serene as she was on that difficult evening when she was with my twin and myself at Gulag. She, unperturbed. I, posing. Ariel with me? I with her? Was it possible? David stood silent, his eyes fixed on Ariel.

From the area where the plank rested I could hear Ariel sobbing:

"At first you told me that both Jane and Janice would live. Then you told me that Janice would live. That Jane had to be sacrificed, but that Janice would live."

My identical looked at me. I was about to caution her again, when David hissed, "Keep quiet!"

He strode to the area where she stood. As soon as he reached Ariel Warning/Alice Miranda, she started moving her two arms in a swaying motion as if she were rocking an infant. "My two babies," she whimpered. She looked up with glazed eyes, staring at the two of us. "I lost my Snickers bar on the lake water…" She began to whistle. Turned, faced David directly. "You were supposed to save both Jane and Janice. You were…" She stopped. Swung her frayed woven bag from her shoulder. Pressed it against her breasts, unzipped it, rummaging inside. Removed her Glock automatic. Pointed it at David. "Why didn't you?" She looked vacantly at him. "Why didn't you? When you met with me it was as if you possessed godlike powers. You promised me you could save my babies. You were their doctor. You were supposed to watch over them. Keep my babies safe. Now my two babies are gone," Alice Miranda intoned, her voice trembling and low. "Dead. Dead. Do you understand?"

She continued pointing the revolver at David.

"Alice. What time do you have?" I yelled out. I brushed my shirt sleeve. The glittering Rolex shone in the dappled light. As Ariel peered at the timepiece, I slowly moved into her path. George Miranda's periwinkle sweater, the one Alice Miranda had knitted, her target. I took out of my pocket a Snickers bar.

"Hi, Alice. It's George. I was just released from Sandstone."

I tried to think and speak like George Miranda. What would he say? I tried to effect his gestures, his body language—the tilt of his head, the sway of his shoulders, the way he pawed at the ground, the way he chewed on his cheek, the way he brushed back his thick black hair.

"Alice, honey, it's me, George. Remember the Auf Passen Bridge. Us splashing around with them squishing tadpoles and minnows. Alice, honey, here, I brought you a Snickers bar. Here. Take it."

Alice Miranda took a step back. Whistled. Aimed the gun at my chest.

"Alice, listen to me," I said, waving the Snickers bar. "Listen up. The one thing I've learned while I was at Sandstone is that it can be the most important thing in the world to you, and you're still going to be disappointed. It doesn't matter what it is, how much you want it, how much you prayed for it. You're still going to strike out, fail, not be rewarded. That's the way it is and there's absolutely nothing we can do about it. Alice, honey, do you understand what I'm saying?"

Ariel Warning continued to whistle.

"Remember Dr. Lindstrom, honey. Remember what he said? He said what we have to do is learn to live with it. Move on, push our legs and move on. That's it. That's all we can do."

With both hands, Alice Miranda gripped the Glock.

"Listen up, Alice. Whistle and think. Dr. Miller, Dr. Doblin, both of them tried their damnedest to do the best they could. Whistle, honey. Whistle." I motioned to David to start whistling. As did I.

One shot was fired.

Ariel Warning blinked. "Who are you?" she asked David. "Where am I?" she implored as if she were coming out of a coma.

The shot ended Alice Miranda/Ariel Warning's life.

David didn't move for a long time. He looked down at Ariel, over at me, his eyes traveling from one to the other. Then he slowly knelt down and lifted Ariel, her corn-colored hair draped over his arms like the yellow trimmings on my father's prayer shawl. He stared at me. Always he was there when I needed him, as a burden he'd have to carry, his conjoined cross. "Why did I have to have a brother like you?" Moments later David burst into tears, his body heaving and trembling.

There was little time taken by the investigating officers, the legal professionals involved. All of them were polite, formal, grasping from the very beginning, it seemed to me, what had actually happened. It helped a great deal that a NYPD helicopter circling the park had caught sight of much of what had transpired.

☙❧

David walked straight into the kitchen, splashed his face with brown sink water, and stood there looking at a photograph of Ariel Warning and himself that was part of a collage. The two of them were in matching candy-striped swimsuits, gathering seashells on a beach at Sanibel. On a butcher block shelf, on the left side of the sink, was a collection of world-famous shells from Sanibel and Captia Island that they had brought back. He nodded to himself, gazing at the photograph and then at the shells.

"Do you want to talk about Ariel?" I asked.

"You don't get it. Ariel Warning no longer exists. Besides," he sneered, "you're unworthy."

"David, we have to talk."

"Let it go," he said quietly. "Ariel Warning no longer exists. I don't want to hear any more about it." He bit his lip. "Ariel Warning has ceased." His expression changed. "That's not what I mean. What I mean is, at the very end Ariel was no longer mine. She no longer existed. She was Alice Miranda." He took a deep breath. Sighed. "Ariel was never mine. It's just," he said, looking at me with tender merciful eyes." The more you give, the more you love."

My twin brother walked into his one room, slumped down into a leather chair.

"I'm sorry. I don't hate you." He looked up at me. "That poor man, Miranda. He loved her, too."

He lifted himself off the chair, walked over to his writing desk. Turned to face me.

"According to you, the fugue Ariel experienced was to lift all at once.

You were correct. For her it did. For me it's more insidious. Each day it seems as if a part of me is being sliced away. As if I'm losing Ariel piecemeal." His eyes bore into mine. "With all your talking about Ariel/Alice you'll never know what I've gone through since that day. I tried to bury it, you know. I tried putting all of it out of my mind. But I can't. I keep thinking…"

He was not living. Living as I had lived during the one band of time that was a perfect memory of my life. In that band of time I embraced each perfect moment with a burst of laughter and an arrogant quiver at my own recognizable failings. One of them, the failing to remember that joy in life, as life itself, is not forever. It only seems that way in the moment.

David looked intently at me. I looked back at him. I had this weird feeling that it wasn't him. It was somebody else. A stranger. And, of course, I had always known my twin. Better than myself. The one constant in my life. He was a stranger. Perhaps the inadmissible stranger I had first become to him/myself when I started lying, betraying, diminishing.

I looked at my brother. He didn't have a wife. He knew not the love of children. Intimacy was not his privilege. All he had was his work. Yet if you mentioned to him what was missing in his life, his eyes would blaze with abnegation. He'd shout, "I have my work! That's all I need." Of course he had me.

I reminded David of our mother's lullaby.

"Boys, you're twins. Twins shouldn't fight. Being a twin is quietly understanding that whatever happens, your twin is always there. It's not fighting or leaving, it's only returning. Sharing everything and questioning none of it."

"And questioning all of it, Mom."

"Boys, it's forever. Forever!"

Our custom as children had been to attend films together. I

suggested we do that. We ended up at the Angelika theatre. The film was a bore. I reached out for David's hand. "Tic-tac-toe," I said. He jerked his hand from mine. Neither one of us giggled. We watched the remainder of the film as if we were two separate people. Divided. Separated. Alone. When the film ended David stood up. As I peered at him I felt as if an enormous band of flesh, a part of both of us, had been cut away. A forbidden fruit, a vital organ that we once had shared. Half of it ripe. The other half rotted. In his eyes I could see his ascending silent prayer. The courage to go it alone. To be alone.

"I must be alone," he said. He turned from me and walked to an exit door. I followed, taking another. I knew, as I knew with Emily Bloom, it was after forever.

EPILOGUE

"Give David time," Margot said. "Time is what he needs. So do you."

Almost three years passed before David and I both tried to talk things out. We decided to meet once a week. Talk. Really talk. Our talks do help. Now our confidences to each other are honest, as genuine as they should have been throughout our entire lifetime, nothing left out, nothing unsaid, at times as surrendering, as communicative, as filled with grace, as heartfelt as mine were to Emily Bloom.

If I judge correctly, there are still spaces between us, silent spaces, but maybe that is all to the good for we are acknowledging these spaces; it is the first real signs of both of us coming to grips with being separate and alone, both of us alone and together, like all of us. All that is human.

Yes, our talks help. There are positives: I am able to speak without lying. I am able to live without thinking. For David, too, there are positives. He is writing again, not product, a full-fledged honest novel. But, still, for David, there have been no more women. "Take another chance. Never again!" As for myself, I haven't stopped hoping. I keep looking. You see, I, too, have not found another woman to love. But I do keep looking. Yes, I have faith, I'm searching for a special someone to share whatever time is left to me. Someday all of us will be able to change not only our physical organs, but our ontology as well, I suspect; for now I'm content I do not have to be constituted the way I am. I'm confident that I can recreate myself. For example, these days I'm letting go more than ever. Only hours ago I made it my business to junk the rotted plank. Yes, I do think I can recreate myself, and even if I am not successful, there are no sure bets, I still realize that the bonding between the two of us, though not complete, is something that we can continually strive to strengthen. Each of us can work at becoming closer. I know this much is true. You see, earlier this week, David visited. In his own wordless way he emphatically told me he wants to get closer. How did he do this? He ambled over to my desk, to the Jacqueline Raphael sculpture of the twined rope. The twisted strands were frayed. Unraveling. He carefully began putting the strands back together. Binding them. He kept trying to put in the last strand, which kept loosening…For days now, every day, the two of us continue to try.

— Thank You —

Cornelius "Corky" Smith
Michael Roloff
Martha McPhee
Joe Weintraub
Susan Braudy
John Farrar
Mel Mandel
Michael Jay Feldman

and a special thanks to Elaine Gargiulo